HOLDING ON

HOLDING ON
RACHAEL BROWNELL

TATE PUBLISHING
AND ENTERPRISES, LLC

Published by Tate Publishing & Enterprises, LLC
127 E. Trade Center Terrace | Mustang, Oklahoma 73064 USA
1.888.361.9473 | www.tatepublishing.com

Tate Publishing is committed to excellence in the publishing industry. The company reflects the philosophy established by the founders, based on Psalm 68:11,
"The Lord gave the word and great was the company of those who published it."

Book design copyright © 2013 by Tate Publishing, LLC. All rights reserved.
Cover design by Allen Jomoc
Interior design by Mary Jean Archival

Published in the United States of America

ISBN: 978-1-62854-850-1
1. Juvenile Fiction / General
2. Juvenile Fiction / Love & Romance
13.09.10

DEDICATION

For my son Nicklas, the love of my life.

ACKNOWLEDGMENTS

I would like to thank my family.

My boyfriend, Jeremy, who finds a way to make me smile every day, who puts up with all my oddities and repeats himself countless times because I wasn't listening the first time.

My son, Nicklas, who is the absolute center of my universe and always will be. I love you very much.

My mom and dad, who have taught me a lot about life, how I want to live and who I want to be. Mom, you have always been my greatest supporter—thank you.

Finally, my sister who is the beauty and the brains in our family. Julie, I could not be more proud of the person you have become. Thank you all for helping me become the person that I am today and supporting me in my efforts to reach for the stars and achieve my dreams.

I would like to make a special thank you to my very first official reader, Jessy. She has been a great friend throughout the process of this book coming to life and a huge supporter of my writing. She gave me the courage to submit my work and the strength to remain positive if the outcome had been different. Thank you for your countless hours of listening to me worry and complain, bounce ideas off of you, and just plain talk about myself.

PROLOGUE

Eight months, that's not nearly long enough, I thought. There are so many things that can change your life completely in eight months, but is this one of them? As I sit there, watching him pull his shirt over his head, the muscles of his back rippling, the tattoo around his bicep teasing my eyes, I realized that eight months should not be long enough to fall in love. But was I?

I think I was trying to fight those feelings, knowing that in six short hours, it would be over. Things were changing. If things could change that much in eight months, then what would the next six hours bring? What about the next four months? The truth of the matter is that I am pretty sure I fell in love with him the first moment I saw him. Then his eyes, they remind me of my ring. It's a beautiful dark-green princess-cut emerald. It's not large, but the color is defined. In the darkness of the room you cannot see the color clearly, but I can see it perfectly in my mind. Looking down, twisting my ring as I stare at it, I realize that I will never forget this man or the things that he's made me feel.

Getting lost in my thoughts, a dip in the bed brings me back to reality. He's dressed now, but his proximity to me makes my stomach flip anyway. You would think after everything that's happened between us, I wouldn't be affected by him this way, but I think those feelings are just intensified now. I have never felt this way about anyone before. His touch charges my body in a way that nothing else does. His proximity has my pulse racing the second he steps into a room. It's almost like I can feel his presence before I can see him.

A year ago, I would have never pictured myself in this situation. There was nothing more important to me than tennis. I had no time for a boyfriend. I barely had time for my friends. I was completely focused on my recovery. I lost all sense of focus on New Years Eve, and it feels like I have yet to regain my composure. I think back on all the things that have changed over the past eight months and realize that I have changed too. My physical appearance, as average at it has always been, is about the only thing that reminds me of who I use to be and even it has changed in a way that I cannot describe.

"So what time do you have to leave in the morning?" I ask, glancing at my alarm clock over his shoulder. I've been watching it all night, even before he showed up, and it's now close to 3:00 a.m. My mom's at work, and my sister is in the other room sleeping. She probably can't hear us, but I feel the need to whisper just in case. Or maybe I was whispering because I was afraid to hear his answer. Either way, it was hard to miss the hesitance in my voice.

He reaches over and grabs my hand, stroking my knuckles lightly with his thumb. For a minute, I think that maybe he didn't hear me because he hasn't answered yet. I want to ask him again, but I can't seem to find my voice. At the moment, I can't even muster the strength to make eye contact with him. I know that he's looking at me, but I don't have the strength to look at him, so instead I just stare at our hands. His touch makes my hand feel like it's on fire, and I am enjoying the burn just a little more than I should be. I don't want this to end. I don't want to give up this feeling.

"My parents think that I should try and be on the road by nine so I can beat traffic." He had a long way to drive, I think, and I should not have kept him up so late. He should have stayed home to get some rest. We had said our good-byes yesterday afternoon, but I couldn't let him go without one last night, and when he showed up a few hours ago, I knew he felt the same way. Now he was going to be driving on very little sleep, and I felt like an ass.

"Huh." It's the best I can come up with at the moment. Like usual, I am at a loss for words around him. I hear that he is saying something to me, but my mind is beginning to wander again. I can see the barbell piercing his left nipple through his shirt, and I feel the need to reach out and touch it, to touch him.

As if reading my mind, he reaches, pulls on my hand, and puts it flat against his chest over his heart. When I finally look up he's staring at me. This feels all-too familiar, and my breath catches in my throat. I can feel the muscles in my throat constricting as I try to exhale. My pulse is racing, and the only thing I can think about is how much I want to kiss him in that moment. I want to wrap my arms around his neck and pull him to me. I want to hold on to him, to this feeling, forever.

I have to say something, but I can't find any words that I want to share with him because I sure as hell can't tell him I love him. I don't know how he'll react. I would much rather live in my little bubble, where I can pretend for the next few minutes that maybe he does love me somewhere deep down inside. I want to live in that little bubble where I feel like everything we've been through, everything we worked so hard for, the odds that we beat were all for something greater than a short-term romance.

"So is that all you have to say? I'm leaving in a few hours and you have no thoughts to share with me? Because I find that hard to believe," he says, pausing only for a brief moment like he needs to catch his breath before he continues. I can feel his heart rate starting to increase beneath my hand. His eyes are starting to dilate, and I'm finally able to release the breath I've been holding. "If those are the only words that you can manage right now, then maybe we can fill our time another way."

There it is—his million-dollar smile. I can't see his dimple winking at me, but I know that it is. He runs his hand though my long, thick dark-brown curls and starts to massage the back of my neck. As he leans towards me, I find myself playing with his pierced nipple. His lips are centimeters away from mine, my heart is pounding in my head, and I can barely remember to breath. His other hand slides up my bare thigh, and I close my eyes. I can feel the heat from his breath along my jaw. His lips graze the bottom of my ear lobe, and when I hear him whisper those three little words in my ear, I wonder if I am actually dreaming. When he brushes my bottom lip with his tongue, I know that I am wide awake.

I can feel my heart beginning to crack, knowing that this will not be able to last much longer. He begins to graze kisses along my jaw. When our lips meet, I know that I will be broken for a long time. I could kiss him forever, and I want to, but I only have minutes. I want days. I want weeks. I want forever! As he pulls away and our eyes meet, I realize that I don't get any of those things. All I get is one last swift kiss before he's gone.

I lie down on my bed, curl into a tight little ball, and begin to cry. When I hear his car start, I feel the crack in my chest getting bigger, and as the sounds of his engine start to dissipate, knowing that's he's gone, realizing that I was head over heels in love with him but didn't tell him, that's when my heart shatters completely.

CHAPTER 1

NINE MONTHS EARLIER

I t's freezing cold outside and I should have brought a jacket. The sweat still dripping between my shoulder blades was making me shiver even worse. I tossed my bag in the backseat of my car and immediately pulled out my running pants and slipped them on over my tennis skirt. Why I didn't change inside was beyond me. I was so excited to have my last "ordered" therapy that I just want to get home. Plus, it was my best friend's birthday, and I couldn't wait to celebrate.

Pulling out of the parking lot, I noticed the fresh snow that had fallen while I was inside. Michigan winters can be rough, but they are also very beautiful and very unpredictable. Last week, we had just a light dusting on the ground, and now it looked like we had close to three feet. It made me wonder how much more we'll get before Christmas. Last year, we didn't have any. We had a warm spell a couple of days before, and it all melted until after the holidays.

As I pulled into our apartment complex, I started to go through my to-do list in my head when I realized that my mom's car was home. Why was she not at work? I glanced down at the clock on my dash, and it was 7:03 p.m. She was supposed to start her shift at the hospital at seven. *This has to be bad*, I thought. Mom never misses work; we can't afford it.

I trudged inside, not really wanting to leave the warmth of my car since I was just beginning to feel my legs again. When I opened the front door, I was immediately surrounded by the smell of dinner. Not just any dinner, either, but enchiladas! That's my mom's famous "bad news dinner." *Crap!* I didn't need this right now. I had to be ready in less than forty-five minutes if we are going to make it to the movie on time.

Rounding the living room, I decided to head straight for the shower. Her news was going to have to wait. As I reached for the handle, thankful that I made it past my mom undetected, I heard my sister. The door was locked, and I could hear she was crying to someone on the phone. *Crying? Double crap!* This was worse than I thought it was going to be. My sister never cries. Broken finger, twisted ankle, softball to the eye, she is tougher than I am and has her emotions completely in check. I am the family cry baby, and it has always been that way. I wear my emotions on my sleeve—you never have to guess how I feel.

Choices? I could try to slip into my room and go to the movie without a shower. Yuck! I couldn't sit that close to someone else and fear that I smell bad. I could beat down the door, but that would not solve anything, and my mom would know that I was home. If she knew I was here, she would corner me, and then I was stuck talking about her news. The only other option was to leave and go somewhere else to shower. That would put me way over my forty-five-minute time limit though. *Crap!*

Just as I was about to tangle with option 1 and which perfume I was going to overspray on myself, the door opened, and my sister, bloodshot eyes and tear-stained face, walked out. I gave her an "Are you all right" look, and she started to cry again and bolted for her room. I heard the lock click into place and began to wonder just how bad my mom's news really was, but I needed a shower. I needed to get ready to go out. I needed to avoid my mom at all costs now, or my eyes and face were going to look twice as bad as my sisters, and that was not what I needed right then.

Shower, check. Hair, check. Makeup, check. Time, 7:35 p.m. Excellent! I had ten minutes before I had to be ready. Just enough time for me to pick out what to wear. I opened my closet and grabbed a sweater. It should work, but now to find some clean jeans, I don't think I had any. Looks like I was going to have to wear a skirt and my legs were going to freeze. I really needed to do laundry this weekend.

A knock on my door brought my thoughts back to reality. I bet it was my mom. She had left me alone this long, but I knew she would get me before I was able to get out of the house. I heard her open the door and walk in, but I kept my back to her, head still in my closet, pretending to pick out my clothes. I pulled my sweater on, but I needed to change out of my sweat pants still. I stared at myself in the mirror and continued to pretend that I hadn't noticed her.

My hair looked great. I had straightened out most of the natural curls, curled the ends, and pulled it up into a high ponytail. My friends always wonder why I straighten my hair and then curl it. I was so used to the natural curls that this made me look different, and I liked it. It's such a dark shade of brown that I really should consider doing something special with it over break. Maybe I could try blonde highlights? I gazed at my reflection in the mirror and tried to picture myself with highlights when I noticed my face. It's flawless this week, and the little bit of makeup I put on really brought out the natural rosy tint on my cheeks. My eye makeup had made my bluish-hazel eyes pop and look a little smoky. Wow! I like the way that made me look.

I had almost forgotten that my mom was in the room when she cleared her throat, and I realized that we were going to have this conversation right now. So much for being able to escape unnoticed. I glanced at my alarm clock to check the time. I only had five minutes before I had to be ready, or we were going to be late to the movie.

15

"Hey, Mom, what are you doing home? I thought you had to work tonight," I said.

Smooth—like I had no idea about my sister crying or the fact that making her special meal was a big red flag that something was wrong. I turned to continue digging in my closet, looking for my cleanest pair of jeans or cords. I needed something besides sweats to be able to leave the house.

"I took the night off, Becca. I needed to talk with you and your sister about something, and even though I wanted to do it together, your sister already got me to tell her. She seems to think that the only time I make enchiladas is when I have bad news." She sounded confused by that statement, but all I could do was smile at her. It was amazing how bright and completely clueless my mom could be at the same time.

"She has a point, Mom. Last time you made them was when you told us you sold our house and we were moving into this crappy apartment. The time before was when you told us you and Dad were getting divorced. It seems like a bit of a pattern." I had to pause at that point because I could feel myself getting emotional. "What's the bad news this time? Did you lose your job?"

She looked nervous from where I was crouched down, and today, she looked a bit older than normal. She shuffled over to the bed and patted her hand beside her, so I moved to where she was at and sat down. As she took my hand in hers, I knew this was worse than I could have imagined.

"I didn't lose my job, but I did find a new one that pays better. We'll be able to get out of this little apartment, and I've even found us a perfect house that we can afford." She was looking down now, so I knew this was not the only news and that the bad news was still coming. So far, everything sounded good. There was no reason that my sister should be crying about this.

"That sounds great, but I have a feeling I am not going to like the rest of what you have to say," I replied, standing and crossing my arms. When she didn't say anything right away, I looked at the clock and saw that my forty-five minutes was up and I had to get out of my sweats and into something more appropriate. "Mom, I have to get changed. Brad is gonna be here any minute and—"

"It's in Tucson, Becca. My new job is in Tucson. We're leaving on January 1."

She never looked up from the floor, and I never looked back as I left my room in a dead sprint. I grabbed my purse and keys off the entry table and ran to my car. I needed to focus on driving as far as I could, as fast as I could. *No time for tears*, I kept telling myself over and over again. *No time for tears.*

I pulled into the school parking lot and killed the engine. That's when I broke. I could not even contain the loud sob that came. I opened the door and started to walk toward the courts. I should have grabbed shoes and a jacket. I ran back to the car and found my rain boots in the trunk and a blanket. I quickly swapped out my slippers for the boots and grabbed the blanket. I would have to make do with these.

The closer I got to the courts, the more I realized that with all the snow, I wouldn't be able to open the gate, so I veered left and went into the baseball dugout. At least I was out of the wind. I plop down on the bench and curl up in the blanket the best I can. My body was numb, but not from the cold. It's starting on the inside and working its way to my limbs. I was still crying, and I wanted to stop, but I just didn't know how. My eyes were like a faucet that wouldn't turn off.

I wasn't prepared for this. My life was finally getting back on track. My shoulder was healed. The trainer had cleared me to practice today. I was going to be able to play with my team in the spring. My grades were good. I have finally been able to spend some quality time with my friends. I only have another year and a half until I go off to college. Why now? Why was she destroying everything now? Couldn't she wait until I finished high school?

My phone began ringing in my pocket, but I didn't even bother to look. I knew it was probably my mom wondering where I ran off to. She probably wanted to finish our very one-sided conversation. She wasn't asking us; there was no talking about this—she was telling us that we were moving. The ringing stopped and then started again right away. *Really? Can't she just let me be alone right now? Does she not understand how upset I am?*

"No," he said from about ten feet away. Had I just said all of that out loud? Probably. When I get emotional, that tends to be my MO. "You are not allowed to be alone right now."

As I turned my head, I couldn't help but smile. He was such a beautiful person, inside and out, and he was mine. He towered over me in height and could probably bench-press me as a workout. His body was always in great shape because he was always at the gym trying to strengthen his upper body for football. He was doing a great job. I could see how impressive his build was, even through the sweatshirt he was wearing.

We had been best friends since middle school, and I wouldn't trade him for anything in the world. This was not the first time I had noticed how incredibly desirable he was. I had been pushing those thought from my brain for years now. It's a dance I had been doing for a while and had perfected. I would start to lose control of the fact that we are friends, and the next time we see each other, he has a girl on his arm, usually a new girlfriend. It always helped to bring things back into perspective for me.

I was staring at him, taking in the "view," as his long legs bring him the ten feet or so in about four steps.

"What are you doing here?" I asked him as he sat down next to me on the bench and wrapped his long, muscular arm around my shoulder. I put my head in the crook of his neck and exhaled the breath that I didn't even know I was holding.

"You mom called me when you left the house. I was running about five minutes late, so I took a detour and figured you would be here if you were upset. I saw your car, but I didn't see you on the courts, so I called your phone and listened for the ring to find you." He knew me too well sometimes. As he hugged me tighter,

I began to shiver. He gave my strange appearance a quick once-over and started to laugh.

"What's so funny?" I know I sounded defensive, but I really didn't see the humor in anything at that moment. The only thing I was focused on was the pain in my stomach and the fact that my brain was refusing to process what was going on. I was starting to get a headache.

"Do you see what you're wearing? You would be laughing too," he replied while trying not to laugh too hard. He was successfully failing.

I looked down and started to laugh too. I had on my hot-pink rain boots with my favorite purple sweat pants and a very deep red-and-black sweater. To top it off, my blanket was an ugly burnt-orange—school colors. I looked like a very ugly rainbow of colors. I had to laugh, and once I started, I couldn't stop. Brad always knew how to make me laugh, and he always knew how to make me feel just a little bit better about any situation or at least make me forget about it for a moment. I actually felt the tension begin to melt from my body.

"So are you going to tell me why you ran out of the house before I got there, or are we going to the movies with you looking like that?"

Welcome back, tension.

"Calm down, birthday boy. First, I think we are missing the movie right now. You should probably call the GF and tell her you are going to be a bit late. Second, you know you're jealous of how hot I look in all these fabulous colors," I stopped to smirk at him for a minute because he knows I never refer to myself as hot. "Last, I want to tell you, but I don't really want to ruin your birthday. Lets get out of the cold, and we can talk about it tomorrow."

He pulled out his phone, typed out a quick text, and shoved it back in his pocket. "I just told Claire that we won't be making it to the movie. I told her that we would meet up with her and everyone else when the movie ends. So in the meantime, I think you need to tell me what's wrong." As if realizing that his phone was going to chime any minute with an unpleasant reply, he pulled it back out of his pocket and turned it off.

He talked about his girlfriend so dismissively that I forgot she was not a fan of our relationship. If she saw us right now, with his arm around me, she would flip out and start to throw a tantrum in front of whoever was willing to watch her. She was a very sweet girl, but very possessive and clingy. It struck me as odd that Brad would even date her, considering he was so incredibly laid back. They were complete opposites, and I had been trying to figure out their relationship since they started dating last spring.

Last week, we were celebrating my birthday. Today we were supposed to be celebrating his. Nothing about this situation constituted celebrating. We've always had a ritual for our birthdays since they are so close together, but my "situation" was messing everything up. We were supposed to be going to a movie and then to a party at Emma and Ella's in celebration of his birthday. It was the same thing we did last Friday night on my birthday. It was the same thing we did last year for our birthdays. It was our tradition. This was not on the agenda for today.

A quick poke to the ribs brought me out of my thoughts and back to reality. Ugh! I really did not want to talk about this. I did not want to cry again. I did not want to think about what's really going to happen in less than a month. This sucks! I did not want to have to tell my best friend that I was leaving him.

Another nudge and I realized that he was not going to let me stall any longer. I stood up and started to pace the length of the dugout. As I pulled the blanket tighter around myself, I realized that I couldn't feel my toes—my socks were wet and frozen to my feet. I must have gotten snow on my socks when I was wearing my slippers. My day just kept getting better and better. I quickly turned toward Brad before I realized that he was right behind me, and I ran square into the middle of his rock hard chest. He grabbed my shoulders to steady me and pulled me in for a hug. He smelled so good that I couldn't help but take a deep breath.

Deep breath in, exhale, repeat. This was my new mantra. I repeated it over and over in my head before I opened my eyes again and realize that Brad was still holding me, stroking his hand over my back and kissing my hair. I was crying, and I didn't even realize I had started to shake again. *Deep breath in, exhale, repeat.*

"Tell me, Becca," he said, breaking the silence that I was beginning to appreciate. "Tell me, or I will have to call your mom, and you know she will tell me."

Crap! He was right. She would tell him my bra size if he asked. She trusts him with me completely. She knows that he will always take care of me, that he loves me in a way that is completely hard to come by and only happens once in a lifetime. It's that special kind of love where nothing-will-ever-come-between-us-no-matter-what. It's the eternal kind of love. He's my best friend and always will be. This news would not break us—that's why she sent him to find me. Damn her!

"Fine. You are not going to like this, though, and it will probably ruin your birthday. So when I start to cry and fall apart again, you cannot blame me when we show up to your party, with me looking like a freak in hot-pink rain boots." I was trying to get him to smile, but his face stayed the same. His mouth was firm, not a trace of amusement at all. *No use is stalling. Just say it. Quick, like ripping off a band-aid. The quicker you do it, the less it hurts. Right?*

"Mom found a new job," I continued. "We have to move to Tucson at the beginning of January."

I was crying again before I finished my statement. I was able to get it out without any emotion in my voice, but the tears running down my face conveyed everything I was feeling for me. I was beyond sad, beyond angry. I was devastated. This small town was everything I needed. It was my home, and I was being torn from it without a second thought from my mom. Realization hit hard then—I only had three weeks before I was leaving.

"It's going to be just fine, and you know it." He stated it so simply. He made it sound like it wasn't life-altering news. He made it sound like he wasn't the slightest bit affected by this. Then it hit me. He already knew.

I stepped back, and his hands fell to his sides. He went to reach for me to pull me back in, but I took another step back. The look on his face was of genuine concern. We had known each other long enough to know when the other one was lying. He was definitely not lying, but omitting. He took a step toward me and tried to grab for my hand, and I pulled away. The look of anger on my face must have been apparent because he stopped mid step and pulled back.

"When," I asked him, "when did she tell you?"

The blank stare was a dead giveaway. He tried to pull me in for another hug, but I pushed him away. My blanket fell to the ground, and I left it there. I turned my back on him and walked away. I couldn't believe he knew before I told him. He made me tell him, made me say the words. He made the situation real when I was forced to say it out loud. Was he on her side? Did he really believe that everything was going to be all right? Did he want me to leave?

I was practically running by the time I reached my car and jumped in. I started it but just sat there. I was in no condition to drive. The tears were flowing freely again and dropping on my sweater from my chin. The heater started to kick in, and I could almost feel my toes again when I noticed that Brad was standing in front of my car just watching me, holding my ugly orange blanket. We made eye contact, and that was all it took. I gave in, just like always. He was no match for my willpower. One look and I would melt like butter over an open flame. Damn him!

I unlocked the doors and motioned for him to get in. Once the door was closed and the only sound was the hot air rushing from the vents, he turned toward me and ran the back of his hand over my cheek, wiping away freshly fallen tears. This is the man that I love. His friendship means everything to me, and I was going to leave him. There would be phone calls, emails, text messages, and visits, but things would never be the same as they were right this very moment.

"I'm sorry I yelled at you," I started, but he put his finger over my lips to silence me. I had seen him do this before with Claire, with his other girlfriends, but never with me. We didn't share those types of moments. The kind of moments that cause all of the air to rush out of your body had always been reserved for his girlfriends, not for me. My body immediately tensed up, and my eyes opened wide. I turned to face him better and knew what was going to happen only mere seconds before it did.

He leaned forward and kissed me. It was gentle and innocent, but my entire body felt alert and on fire. It only last a few second, and when it was over, he rested his forehead against mine and closed his eyes. *Wow!*

"I agree."

Crap! I was thinking out loud again. I really had to get that under control before I start saying things I really don't want people to hear. I opened my eyes, and he was looking at me in a way that had never happened before, and then he kissed me again. This time there was more urgency, more passion, and more emotion behind his every movement. Before I could stop myself, I was just as involved in the kiss as he was, and a small moan left my throat that I had been trying to contain.

He pulled away, and you could see the shock on his face—the "Oh crap, I just kissed a girl that's not my girlfriend" expression. Then he smirked, and I released the breath that I didn't know I had been holding and started to laugh. I couldn't control myself. It's not that the situation was funny. It wasn't, but the look on his face was priceless. I knew him better than he knew himself sometimes, and he was feeling like a complete ass at that very moment.

He was not a cheater. He would never intentionally cheat on anything or anyone. I understood this; his girlfriend did not. She did not understand our relationship and because of that, she always assumed that we had something going on behind her back. We never gave her a reason to think those things, but she just assumed, and when they would fight, that was what she would always bring up as a means of defense.

Crap! We've given her a reason not to trust us, and all I can do right now is laugh. Brad was looking at me like I was crazy, and I was laughing so hard I was crying. He reached out and grabbed my hand, and the instant he touched me, I stopped, sucked in a very large breath, and held it. He took my hand and put it over his heart and held it there.

"You live here, Becca. You will always live here."

That was all he said before getting out of my car and driving away. OMG! What was I going to do? In that moment, I wanted nothing more than for him to hold me again. I wanted him to kiss me again. I wanted him as more than just my best friend, something I had contemplated over the years but had always pushed out of my mind. I wanted more. I could feel my heart breaking inside my chest at the thought that we would never get that. There just wasn't enough time.

CHAPTER 2

I didn't see Brad the rest of the weekend. We texted a few times. Nothing about the move was mentioned and nothing about the kiss, either. I was trying to ignore what had happened. I chalked it up to an "Oops…" We were having an emotional moment. It was an accident. He didn't mean to kiss me, right? What about the second time? Was that just an "oops" too?

Ignoring what had happened between Brad and I was impossible. We both attempted to act normal and pretend that it never happened. Our friends didn't seem to notice, or at least they didn't say anything to me, but still there were moments when I felt that things were different. The slight brush of his hand when we were walking to class or when he put his hand on the small of my back sent shivers through my body and heat to my cheeks. I felt like the entire world could see right through me.

I was a fraud! For the past five years, I had been telling people that we were just friends and defending out nontraditional relationship. Now I couldn't possibly say a word to anyone without feeling like a fraud. I was trying hard to hide my feelings from everyone, myself included. If I admitted it, then it would be real. If it was real, then leaving was real. If leaving was real, then I would have to face losing him. I wasn't delusional enough to think that I wasn't going to have to leave him in the end anyway. I just wanted to avoid it until the last minute. If we started *something*, anything, it would be finished before it could really begin.

Not to mention, Claire was still upset about what had happened Friday night. Brad never showed up to his party, and neither did I. When she questioned him, he told her that we had been dealing with some personal issues of mine and that afterward he went home and passed out. I wasn't buying that he went home and passed out. I knew that he was upset when we parted, and I figured he went home. I just doubt he slept at all that night. I know I didn't. She wasn't buying it, either, until he told her I was moving. I've never seen her so happy in my life, but I couldn't even find the emotions to get angry at her reaction. I was too full of guilt for anything else to sneak its way in.

After he left the other night, I sat in my car staring out the window at where he had been parked. I don't know how much time passed before I finally drove back home, but it felt like an eternity. I ran every possible scenario through my mind on how to change my situation. I could live with the twins. I could get my own place. I could live with Brad and his family. The problem was I knew that my mom would never let any of that happen.

The only scenario that would work would be to go live with my dad, and I didn't want that. My dad is great—when he's around. He's constantly working or traveling. My parents marriage failed because my dad couldn't devote enough time to family. Back then, it was all about work, getting promoted, making money. Now after losing us, he realized that work should be a number 2 priority and his number 1 priority is traveling with his latest fling. I could not live that kind of life.

The buzz around school about me leaving swept through the halls quickly, thanks in large part to Claire's elation. By the end of the day on Monday, it was pretty much common knowledge. Walking into the yearbook room the last hour of the day was when all my emotions rose to the surface again. I had worked so hard to get where I was. I had earned my title as editor-in-chief. I was going to have to give that all up, and instead of walking into that room and telling my teacher what was going on, I walked right past the door and out to the parking lot to my car.

As soon as the bell rang for school to end, my phone started to blow up. First, there were a few messages of concern from my close friends who noticed that I had skipped last period. Then came the excited messages about throwing a party in my honor. My friends were sad but felt that since I was going, they would send me off in style with a big celebration. We were not leaving until the first of the year, so New Year's Eve was the big bash. My friends Ella and Emma, the twins, asked their parents if they could host the party, and being that I was such a "good kid" in their eyes, they agreed. It took about ten text messages and three phone calls before our very large group of friends and plenty of other people knew the plan, and the party was officially on.

Tuesday was even less exciting than Monday had been. Instead of the bright smiles I would normally get in the hallway, I saw plenty of pity on the faces of my friends. Brad was the worst. Per usual, he met me at my locker before each class and we walked together. Our normal, upbeat conversations had been replaced with deafening silence as we walked. I was always thinking about ways to bring up the kiss, but it never seemed like the right time. Would someone overhear our conversation? Did he regret what had happened? I know that I was confused, but I definitely did not regret our kiss.

Friday morning, my final day of school before break, before I moved, before I said good-bye to all of my friends, things were even weirder than normal between me and Brad. He held his head high as he grabbed my hand on our way to my first period class. I tried to pull away, knowing that Claire could be lurking anywhere, but he held tight and pulled me along. Thankfully, we didn't see her, but plenty of other people saw us.

The same thing happened on the way to all of my other classes. Finally, I quit trying to pull away because holding his hand felt right. Yearbook was my last period of the day, and the closer we got to the classroom, the slower my feet started to move. I didn't want the day to end. I didn't want to let go of his hand. I saw the looks we were getting, and I didn't care anymore. I wanted to hold on to him. He was my rock. He was the only thing that was getting me through this last day, and he knew that I would need him today before I even knew that I would need him.

As we rounded the corner to the yearbook room, I tried to pry my hand from his. Claire was my junior editor. She was bound to be around somewhere. We had managed to avoid her all day, but I knew that we would get caught if I didn't find a way to break free. I stopped walking just short of the classroom and pulled him into the girls' bathroom. He was inside before he even realized what was going on.

"Um, I'm not supposed to be in here."

"I know that. What is all this?" I was holding our intertwined hands up high for him to see. His only response was a smile and a quick squeeze of my hand. "Claire could be anywhere around here. Are you trying to cause a fight between you guys?"

"No. She's not here today. Her family left last night to go to the Bahamas for the holidays."

Oh! So he knew that we wouldn't get caught holding hands and that by the time break was over, everyone would have forgotten what they saw. Genius plan on his part, but I didn't want to be a part of it. I pulled my hand from his and shoved it in my pocket. I love this man to death, but I did not want to be the reason for a fight between him and Claire again.

"Look, I have to get to class. I'll meet you at my car after school? We can go get coffee or something, okay?"

"Fine, but how do you suggest I sneak out of here without being noticed?"

Fair point. He was standing in a girls' bathroom. Walking out into a hall full of people would not exactly be easy. He was just going to have to wait until the bell rang.

"I guess you better wait for class to start." I could feel the smile on my face growing bigger as I inched closer to the door. "I gotta go."

I darted out the door before he could grab me and make me wait with him. I crossed the threshold of the yearbook room just as the bell rang for class to start and stopped dead in my tracks. The entire room was decorated, and there was even a cake. I was going to be spending my last hour of my last day eating sugar and hanging out with my friends. Nothing could be better.

When the bell finally rang, I hugged each of my classmates before walking into my office. I took one look at my desk and started to cry. This was it. I created this book, and now it was going to be taken over by someone else, someone less qualified. I felt like I had when I found out how bad my shoulder injury was. My heart was crushed.

Walking to my car, waving as my friends sped out of the lot past me, made me realize that I made it. This was a tough week. Saying good-bye to everyone and telling the story over and over again because that's all people wanted to talk about had completely drained me. Somehow, I made it through. Even today, I made it through as hard as it was.

Now I just had to get through the holidays. Christmas use to be my favorite time of year before my parents split. The people who say that the holidays are better after your parents get divorced because you get twice the presents obviously are not from divorced parents. Being a child of divorce during the holidays just makes things more stressful, and my stress level was code red already. I didn't need anymore stress.

Two more weeks. That was all I was going to get. Two more weeks of normalcy with my friends that I had known since I moved here in middle school. Two more weeks with the best friend I have ever had, who was currently leaning against my car waiting for me.

It went by fast. Before I could really comprehend what was happening, I was walking in Ella and Emma's front door as their parents were walking out. New Year's Eve! The end of one thing and the beginning of another. How fitting to my situation. I had spent the last two weeks of break packing up my entire life, and today I spent loading it into a U-Haul truck. We were leaving bright and early in the morning, and I was expected home at a "decent hour" to make sure that I got plenty of rest for the drive.

Yes, I was driving across the country. You can only hook up one car to a U-Haul, so when I refused to sell my car, I was told that I would have to drive it out. The only highlight was that I didn't have to be stuck with my mom for the entire ride. I was still barely on speaking terms with her. The longest conversation I'd had with her since she told me we were moving was at Christmas dinner with my grandparents. I was doing my best to be social and somewhat civil. I realized about halfway through dinner that I should probably just stop talking by the looks I was receiving from my grandparents. Let's just say that they were less than enthusiastic about some of my comments. Grandpa actually poked me in the elbow with his fork twice.

As the rest of my friends started to arrive, I got restless. I knew that this was the last time I was going to see most of them, at least for quite a while. I planned on coming back for the summer and staying with my dad for a couple of weeks, but things change. People change. Friendships are hard enough when you see each other every day, let alone when you live 1,905.6 miles apart. I wasn't going to hold it against anyone if our friendship died out—anyone, except Brad, that is, who had yet to show his face at the party.

I mingled for a few hours and spent some quality time with a few friends that I knew would still be in my life after I crossed state lines. As midnight got closer, I began to get worried about Brad. He was supposed to pick up Claire and meet me at the party. She was not excited about their plans, and I wasn't excited about her being present, but he knew it meant a lot to me for him to come tonight. Normally, I wouldn't have thought twice about not celebrating the New Year with him, but this was different.

We had only spent one New Year's Eve together since becoming friends. It was eighth grade, and our parents had insisted that we stay in because of a huge snow storm that was supposed to be blowing in. Brad came to my house, and we were going to hang out and watch the ball drop with a few other friends. Their parents had decided that they needed to stay home. It ended up being just the two of us, eating junk food and acting crazy from too much sugar and caffeine. We both passed out before midnight. It's one of my favorite memories of us.

We all counted down at midnight, and shortly after, people started to leave with their designated drivers. I found my purse and pulled out my phone to send Brad a nasty text since he never showed up. To my surprise, I found a text from him waiting for me. When he didn't show up to the party, my only thought was that Claire had kept him away somehow. He should have been here. He should have at least come to say good-bye to me. I was about to explode with anger when I opened his text.

> I'M SRY. THERE WAS NO WAY I COULD SAY GDBYE WITH EVRY1 ELSE AROUND. TEXT ME B4 U LEAVE. HAPPY NEW YEAR! LV BRAD

Crap! How is it that I can forgive him in an instant? I should be mad at him for bailing on our last night to be able to hang out together, and I can't. Damn him! Now I had to see him in the morning, and I was going to cry, and then I was going to have to drive. Well, that was not going to work for me. I needed to be up and gone early, and crying was not part of the plan.

> WHERE R U RIGHT NOW?

I waited until I heard my phone ting and stood shocked to see his reply. I grabbed my purse, gave Emma and Ella a hug, along with about ten other people, and bolted out the door. I drove as fast as possible without breaking too many laws, and as I pulled into my apartment complex, my heart dropped into my stomach. He really was here.

Stepping inside the crappy apartment was like stepping into a fairy tale. Sparkly white Christmas lights hung from the ceiling (they were not there when I left earlier), soft music was playing in the background, and the TV was still on one of the countdown shows. Brad stood in the center of the room, wearing a white t-shirt that hugged his beautiful upper body in all the right places and jeans that sat just perfectly low enough on his hips that I knew the top of his boxers would be visible if he lifted up his shirt. Wow! He truly was gorgeous, and he was waiting for me.

"Hey," he said in such a low voice that I wondered for a moment why he was whispering. I knew my mom was home, but I was sure that she was not asleep since Brad was still here. Leaving or not, no matter how much she trusted us together, she would never allow this to happen. Me alone with a boy was equal to me grounded for life.

"Happy New Year!" I replied for lack of anything else to say. I think I was still in a state of shock over finding him here. My eyes were glued to his, and I couldn't tear them away.

As I stared at him, I realized that I had wasted the past five years wanting this—his arms around me tightly, his clean scent overwhelming me. His friendship was the most important thing in my life, and I never wanted to lose that, but this was even better. I had pushed the dreams that our relationship would move in this direction out of my mind over and over again, and it had to happen now. Why now? Why did he have to show me how he felt when things were so screwed up? It was completely unfair to both of us.

I was still in shock when he crossed the room and took my hand. As if reading my mind, he pulled me forward into a hug, and I let myself melt into him, inhaling all that was Brad. I was not going to be able to live without his warmth. *Do not cry! Do not cry!* I kept repeating this to myself until he released me from our hug and pulled me to the couch. I sat wrapped up in his arms, trying to find something to say. Nothing was going to make this easier, and nothing was going to change it.

As if he sensed what I was thinking, he laid us down and pulled a blanket over us. I snuggled into him and tried to get my emotions in check. After a few deep breaths, I look up to find him watching me. I couldn't help but look into his beautiful eyes, such a rich brown with just a dusting of gold around his irises. He was waiting for me to fall apart, and so was I. Without another word from either of us, we cuddled up together, and he held me until sleep encompassed me.

When I awoke, I immediately felt alone. Brad was no longer cuddled up with me but was at the end of the couch, watching me sleep. He was holding a small box and an envelope in his massive hands. He looked completely deflated. He must have slept even less than I did by the shadows under his eyes and the fact that there were two steaming cups of coffee sitting next to him. He had obviously been up for a while if he had gone out for coffee.

I sat up and stretched, never taking my eyes off of his. He moved a little close and pulled me in for a hug. As he pulled away, he set the box in my lap and pulled my hand to his chest, right over his heart. He kissed me lightly and rested his forehead against mine. We stayed like that for a minute before he broke the silence.

"Remember what I said"—he patted my hand that was over his heart—"Always here."

With that he kissed me once more, and it felt final. I felt the good-bye in his touch. By the time, I opened my eyes he was gone. I suddenly felt completely and utterly alone for the first time in my life. That's when every emotion I had been bottling up the past three weeks came crashing down, and I sobbed like a child.

The drive took less time than I thought it would, and we arrived in Tucson four days later. I was exhausted by the time we got there, and after unpacking the U-Haul, I felt every ounce of adrenaline drain from my body. I grabbed a blanket and snuggled up on my bare mattress, but the sleep I so desperately wanted and needed seemed to elude me. I couldn't turn my brain off. The only thing I could think about was Brad.

I could still feel his kiss. I could still smell his cologne mixed with his soap and all that made him smell so amazing. I could still picture the deflated look in his eyes when I woke up to find him sitting at the end of the couch. I couldn't get him out of my head. Every time I closed my eyes, he was there—I could see him clear as day. Every time I opened my eyes, I could smell him and feel his touch. Every time I tried to block it out, all I could feel was the pain. The pain was more real than anything.

Remembering that I still had yet to open his gift, I got up and began to rummage through my purse. The instruction on the top of the box told me to wait until I was here to open it. I didn't understand why at first, but Brad assured me that there was a very good reason and that once I opened his gift, I would see for myself.

We had talked a few times during the trip. It was mostly him calling to make sure that I was still alive since he never did trust me behind the wheel. He kept me company until I was sure my phone battery would die and we would end our call. Our conversations were never about anything important and most definitely never about our relationship or anything that had happened in the last few weeks. I don't think I would ever be able to talk to him about my feelings. Nothing was going to change the situation we put ourselves in. Nothing was going to bring me back home.

I found the package and went back to my bed to open it. The card was taped to the top of the box still with the instructions printed on the envelope. I brushed my finger over his handwriting and then carefully removed the envelope from the package. As I opened it, I realized that there was not a card inside but a photo of the two of us. It had been taken last spring after one of my tennis matches. I was glistening from head to toe with sweat, and of course, Brad looked deliciously well put together. I flipped it over to find a little message on the back.

This may not be the most recent picture of us but it is my favorite. This is the day that I realized I was in love with you. My best friend, my entire world. You will always be here with me in my heart. I know that my gift is a little much but when I saw it I knew you would love it and I hope that it reminds you of our special connection every time you look at it.

Love always,
Brad

Holy crap! I was too shocked to cry and was shaking so hard that I couldn't even grip the photo anymore. It floated to the bed and landed face up. As I stared at the handsome man standing next to me, the tears finally began to fall. I could see the love in his eyes. How had I missed that? Why did he have to wait until I was so far away to tell me? As I glanced over at myself in the photo, I saw something in myself that scared the crap out of me. Love. Whether I realized it at the time or not, I was in love with him back then. I knew I was fighting some feelings for him over the past few year or so, but I never really thought that I was *in love* with him. That's just wasn't the type of relationship that we had. Not to mention, he had just started dating Claire.

I pulled myself together, trying to imagine what's under the wrapping paper. I slowly pulled it back and realized that it's a black velvet box. Double crap! He bought me jewelry. Now I realized why he made me wait. I would have never let him spend money on jewelry for me. The only jewelry I wore was a watch, and that was to always make sure I was on time. The watch didn't really seem to help most of the time since I was often late.

My hands began to shake as I tossed the wrapping paper on the floor. I closed my eyes and tried to calm my nerves as I lifted the lid. When I opened them, I completely lost all restraints and began to cry again. It was the most beautiful thing I had ever laid eyes on, and it fit perfectly. As I slid the ring on my right hand, it felt like it was meant to be there. It was the darkest green emerald I have ever seen. Brad was right—I love it, but it was too much.

I jumped off the bed and began to rummage through my purse again for my phone. I realized that it was midnight here, which meant that it was 3:00 a.m. there, but I didn't really care. I had to talk to him. I had to thank him for my present. What I really wanted was to see him, to hold him, to kiss him. Damn it! I pressed Send before my nerves got the better of me. I knew I wouldn't be able to sleep until I heard his voice. As if expecting my phone call, he picks up after only two rings.

"Aren't you suppose to be asleep after all that driving?" he asked without saying hello.

"Yes, but I had a pressing matter that required my attention as soon as I got settled, remember?" I didn't say anything else. I was waiting for him to say something when I heard a voice in the background—Claire's. "It sounds like I'm interrupting, so I'll just call you in the morning," I stuttered out quickly before I hang up without so much as a good-bye.

It took about thirty second for my phone to vibrate, and he was calling me back. I was contemplating whether or not to answer when the vibrating stops. I don't know if I was relieved that he hung up or if I was sad. I wanted to talk to him, to thank him for his gift, but Claire was with him at 3:00 a.m., and that could only mean one thing. He had moved their relationship to the next level.

Really? The last three weeks we spent together, I got the impression that he was wanting to move their relationship in the opposite direction. He made me feel like he wanted to be with me. Now he was progressing with her. Was it because I left?

Was he regretting everything that happened between us? Was I a mistake to him? Did he even really love me? I gripped my phone and debated whether or not to throw it against the wall when it alerted me to a text message. I rolled my eyes and opened my phone.

NOT WHAT YOU THINK IT IS. ANSWER UR PHONE.

Just like magic, it vibrated again, and I knew that this would go on all night if I didn't answer. I really did want to talk to him. I wanted to hear the sound of his voice. Even when I was mad at him, it would soothe me in a way that I could not explain.

"Yeah," I said. I tried to keep my voice flat and free of emotion, but which emotion was I trying to hide? There are so many running through my body right now I can barely decide how I feel.

"Look, it's not what you are thinking. I know where your mind just went, and it went too far. She's gone now, so let's talk. I'm gonna guess you opened your gift." He said this all with such an exasperated tone that I knew they just had a huge fight and that was why she was at his house so late. I just wanted to wrap my arms around him and give him a big huge, but that was impossible.

"Yes, I did, and thank you. You were right"—I had to pause to keep myself from crying—"it was too much, but I love it."

"Well, I'm glad because that was the whole purpose of getting it for you. It fits, right?"

"Perfectly. How did you know my ring size? I don't even know my ring size."

"I've held your hand enough to figure it out," he said with a little bit of humor in his voice. "So will you wear it?"

"Of course. Why wouldn't I?" I realized after I ask that he knew me too well. I had never once worn anything other than my watch. This was something that most people would miss day after day, but not Brad.

He didn't answer right away, and I could hear him let out a heavy sigh. It must have been a bad fight this time. With me gone, Claire had to come up with new things to fight about, and I was sure she made their first official "non-Becca" fight interesting. Before I could ask, he interrupted and pulled me from my thoughts.

"I miss you," mumbled Brad. I could hear that he meant it. It had only been four days since I saw him last, but I missed him too. "She doesn't get it," he continued, and then it dawned on me. They were still fighting about me, and I was not even there anymore.

"What was it this time?" I asked, knowing the answer already.

"The usual. You are still a threat to her, even though you are so far away."

"Doesn't she realize that she's your girlfriend and not me?" *Even though I wish I was*, I thought to myself.

"Well, I kind of broke up with her, and she blames you."

"What?" I screamed, completely shocked.

"Well…" he started to say but never finished it.

He was holding something back. He wanted to tell me—I could feel it. Did this really have anything to do with me? I know he loves me—he always has in one way or another—and I will always love him. But we were worlds away from each other, and that made a huge difference. I wish it didn't, more than anything, but it did, and we couldn't change those facts. If we had started a relationship months ago, we could have tried to continue it. You cannot start a relationship from a distance. It just won't work.

"Why, Brad? Why did you break up with her?"

"It's hard to say, but I was just done. It hasn't felt right in a few months, and I felt like I was stringing her along. Plus, I'm not a cheater, and every time I think about you I feel like I'm cheating on her. I've felt this way for a while now, but it wasn't until you left that I realized that I didn't want to do it anymore."

Wow! It really was because of me, at least partially.

"I want to be with someone who turns me inside out with one kiss," Brad continued. You could hear the desperation in his voice. "Someone who makes me want more out of life. Who can see inside me and feels the same way. What I really want is to be with you."

"Wow!" I realized I was saying it out loud this time, and I meant to. I wanted to tell him how I felt, that I wanted to be with him as much as he wanted to be with me, but I couldn't bring myself to say the words. "I wish that things could be different, you know that, but I don't want you to put your life on hold for me. I want you to find someone that makes you happy, but that person can't be me right now. We can't hold on to something that isn't there."

Where did that come from? Those were not the words that were just swirling around in my head. The line was silent, as if we were both pondering what I just said. Before he could say anything, I began to realize why I chose those words. I couldn't share my feelings because at this moment, they didn't matter. The only relationship we could have right now was friendship, and as his best friend, that was what he needed to hear. We could hold on to that. Our friendship was solid. Damn, my subconscious!

"I know, and I understand. I almost didn't kiss you in your car that day because I knew we couldn't be together." Another heavy sigh came across the line, and I knew that if I didn't get off the phone with him, I would change my mind.

"Work it out with Claire, Brad. She's a nice girl. Even if she's not your forever, then she can at least be your right now." I had to stop and wipe the tears from my cheeks before I continued. "I will always love you no matter how far apart we are, but I will be really pissed at you if you sit around and allow yourself to be miserable."

"I love you too, Becca. I always will. Good night."

"Good night, Brad."

I fingered the ring on my right hand as I closed my phone and ended our conversation, knowing that things will never be the same. Of course, we would still talk and still be friends, but this would always linger between us. I picked up the photo that was still staring at me from its fallen place on the bed. I walked over to my desk and placed it in the center of my photo board that I had yet to hang on my wall.

The piece of ribbon holding the picture to the board was running right down the center of the picture between me and Brad. It was splitting the picture in half, Brad on one side and me on the other. How much more symbolic can you get? Not only were our hearts split between being friends and wanting more but we were also separated by miles and miles of country.

Anger began to well inside of me. Anger at my mom. Anger about the move. Anger at Brad for waking up my feeling and for acting on his. The anger was bubbling over, and I finally threw my phone like I originally wanted to, shattering it into pieces, just like my heart.

CHAPTER 3

I spent the next two days unpacking, blasting my music, and trying to do something besides think about Brad. The problem with that is that every song reminded me of him. Every photo I hung reminded me of something we had done together. The photo he had given me as part of my gift was still the only one on my board. It had somehow become the focal point of my room. I was looking at it more and more every day, thinking about the possibilities. I found myself thinking about the things that would change and how I wished that things could be different.

Then of course, there was the ring. I had yet to take it off, and I was sure that I wouldn't be able to. Ever. Sometimes it felt like that was all that I had left of him. If I took it off, I would be letting him go in a sense, and I wasn't ready to do that. He was still my best friend. I still loved him, unconditionally. I still wanted to be with him. The more I entertained those kinds of thoughts, the more I believed that it was possible. It all seemed possible until I would look out the window and remember that I was two thousand miles away from making those dreams a reality. My mind was whirling around in a circle most of the time these days.

My mom noticed my ring the morning after I put it on. I was in the shower when she came in to let me know that she was going to the grocery store. She must have spotted it on the bathroom counter because I heard her gasp over the spray of the water. I gave her the shortest version of the story, and I was pretty sure that she had started to cry. I was not sure if she was crying out of guilt for moving us or because she realized how sweet a gesture it was for Brad to make. She left the bathroom and was off to the store by the time I finished my shower. We haven't talked about it since.

On Saturday morning, I realized I had yet to leave the house since arriving and in two days, I would be starting school again. I needed to get a new phone, and I needed to find my way to school. Being a little OCD at times comes in handy, so when I realized these things, I planned a little adventure for myself. I may not be able to be on time when I need to be, but if there were no time constraints and I was in complete control, my OCD would kick into overdrive.

After showering and leaving my mom a note, I grabbed my purse, keys, and tennis bag and headed out. I had the address of the phone store in my GPS by the time I pulled out of the driveway. Our new house was nice. It was not as large as the one we use to live in, but I had my own private space, and that was really all I needed to get through the next five months before I could go back to Michigan. The yard was expertly landscaped before we moved in. It's amazing what someone can do with rocks, sand, and a few plants. It was different from what I was use to seeing, but it looked nice and blended in well with the rest of the neighborhood.

An hour later, after spending two hundred of my dad's hard-earned dollars, I had a new phone in my hand, and most of the numbers from my old phone had been transferred over. I had damaged my memory card a little bit when I "accidentally" dropped my phone down some stairs, or so I told the service representative. I was only able to get numbers that had been stored in my phone the longest. Basically, I had Brad's number, mom's, dad's, and a few family members. I knew most of my friends' numbers by heart and sent a mass text with my new phone number the second I got in my car.

I followed the navigator's directions to the school, and as I pull in, the sheer size makes me cringe. My little town, my little school, where everyone knows everything about everyone was lost to me at this point. The entire campus of my old school could probably fit in the parking lot I'm sitting in. This place was huge! I could only see about four buildings from where I was parked, but I knew that there were probably more just out of sight.

I gathered all my courage and opened the door. It's January in Tucson. January, to me, usually meant layers of clothing, a thick coat, scarf, gloves, and winter boots. There was no chance of playing tennis outside in January when you live in Michigan. Here, January means a sweatshirt, maybe a light coat and jeans. Today I was wearing my running pants over my tennis skirt and a hooded sweatshirt. I planned on warming up on the courts, so I knew that a jacket would have been too much.

As I crossed the enormous parking lot, I realized how quiet it was, how alone I was. I shuddered at the thought of someone sneaking up on me, and my senses went on high alert. I clutched my keys, knowing that I had Mace if I needed it. I walked up the stairs leading to the campus, and as I broke the top enough to see the rest of the school, my breath caught in my throat. It was beautiful. There were at least eight buildings plus what looked like the gym and maybe a theatre. None of the buildings were attached to each other. It was a completely open campus. The best part was the open quad in the middle, where I could see students probably gather before school or to have lunch.

I gave myself an unguided tour, roaming around freely. I passed the gym and rounded the corner to see the tennis courts come in to view. There were ten courts side by side, and I couldn't help but smile. We had four courts at my old school, and we were lucky to get ours resurfaced every couple of years. These courts were in pristine condition, and there were a ton of them to choose from.

I raced back to my car and grabbed my bag. Entering the courts felt surreal. I hadn't been on an outside court since before my accident at the regional competition last spring. All of my rehab had been indoors, and then the snow had started to fall, making it impossible to practice on my own once my shoulder was healed. This was going to be the first time I was able to practice on my own without the watchful eye of my coach or trainer.

I shrugged out of my running pants and pulled my sweatshirt over my head. I felt the cool breeze on my skin and immediately shivered. It was cold enough to need thick clothing, but I was going to be sweating in a minute, so I tried to ignore it. Grabbing my favorite racket, I headed for the closest court. *No time like the present to get my shoulder working again, right?* I bounced the ball a couple times and then threw it up and over my head. I pulled my shoulder up and dropped my racket. *Crap!*

I must have screamed it because I heard the echo through the silence. I rubbed my shoulder and started to run through the strengthening exercises that my trainer had been making me do, up until about a month ago, that is. I hadn't seen the gym in over five weeks with how crazy my life had become, my body, at least my shoulder, felt like it after one attempt to serve.

I stretched for about five minutes and went through the motions with my shoulder like I was going to serve for another five. Once I felt like I wasn't going to cry from the pain, I picked my racket up from where it had fallen. I did a few more minutes of practice swings to adjust to the weight of the racket, and then I couldn't hold back any longer. I bounced the ball a couple times, tossed it up high, and slammed it across the net. Out.

Well, my shoulder was working just fine, but my aim was off. I hit a few more, and slowly, my shoulder hurt less and my aim improved. By the time I couldn't feel any more pain, my aim was exactly where I wanted it to be, and I felt alive for the first time in over a month. Tennis had always been my go-to when I needed to calm down, when I needed to think, or when I needed to vent. My inner calm resurfaced today, and I was thankful that I was able to find it again.

I gathered up my balls from around the courts and started to pack my bags when I noticed movement out of the corner of my eye. Slowly grabbing my keys, I moved the can of Mace so that it was hidden in the palm of my hand. I kept pretending like I didn't know someone was behind me, letting them think they had the element of surprise. The closer they got, the more my body started to shiver, and I could feel the goose bumps on my arms and legs.

"I would prefer if you didn't spray me in the face," he said.

I still had my back to him, and I knew that he was still a good distance away from me, but I could feel the tingles run up my spine. His voice was smooth, deep, and oh so sexy.

Slowly, I stood up and turned. As I took in the view, I felt my knees go weak, and I thought I was going to pass out. I let out the breath I had been holding and tried to smile, but my lips were protesting. His eyes were hidden behind dark sunglasses, but the rest of his amazingly delicious body was visible. His voice and his body were a perfect complement to each other.

Unconsciously, my thumb ran across the palm of my hand and started to move my ring. "Why is that? Afraid I have good aim?" I tried to sound snarky, but I was sure I sounded unsure and weak, maybe even a little scared. The simple words made me breathless, and I had to inhale deeply.

"I can see that your aim is great. I'm actually more afraid you will use your racket on me than the Mace."

He was trying to lighten the mood, and it was working for some reason. I didn't feel as uneasy as I was before. After all, he looked like he was about my age, so being at the school was not that out of character, and his natural good looks and to-die-for body made me want to wrap myself around him more than it made me want to run. *Crap!*

"What's the matter?" he asked this with a twinge of concern on his face, and I realized that I was thinking out loud again.

"Nothing. I just have to get home." I tried to sound nonchalant, but I was pretty sure it didn't work. As he took a tentative step toward me, I wanted to step back, but my legs were weak again, and I was afraid any movement on my part would cause me to fall. Another step and he was within arm's reach to me, and my body was reacting to him in a way it had never reacted to anyone, except Brad recently.

"What are you doing out here all by yourself? Isn't it more fun to hit the ball back and forth than chase after them every five minutes?" As he said this, I realized that he had two tennis balls in his hand and that he was trying to give them to me. I reached out, and as my fingers brushed across his hand, I closed my eyes. Once I realized I was doing this, I opened them quickly to find him smiling at me, and I could feel his gaze deep within my soul. His sunglasses were not hiding much of anything from my body.

"Yes, but I needed the practice. Thank you for returning these, but I really have to go." I made myself step away from him, tucked both balls under my skirting, and grabbed my bag. I didn't look back as I exited the courts, but I could feel his eyes on me. My body shuddered at the though of him watching my every move, but then I realized that he had been watching me practice.

It's finally the first day of school. This sucks. I arrived early, and the parking lot was still pretty empty. I trudged up the stairs to the building marked Administration and opened the heavy double doors. I walked into the first office to find an elderly lady sitting behind the counter, with her head buried in a pile of paperwork. I cleared my throat to let her know I was there, and without looking up, she told me she'd be right with me.

I took a seat in one of the plastic chairs by the wall and waited. After about five minutes, I saw another elderly lady walk in, and she smiled at me. I took that as an invitation to speak.

"Hi! My name is Rebecca Blake, and I need to get my schedule. My mom registered me last week sometime and was told that I could stop in this morning and someone would have it for me."

"Sure, sweetheart, give me just a minute," she said with a big, sincere smile on her face.

I walked up to the counter and waited. The first lady still had her head in a pile of papers and never once glanced at me. I wondered for a moment if she'd fallen asleep since her head was resting on her hand until she glanced up at me. She didn't smile; she just pretended like I was not there and went back to whatever she was doing before.

"Okay," the second lady said, bringing me back from my thoughts. "I don't have anyone here this early to show you around, but if you want to wait, I have an office aide during first period and she can help you."

"No, thank you. I should be able to manage. I have enough time to at least find my locker and my first few classes before first period starts," I said.

"Well, that sounds like a good plan. It looks like your first class is in the farthest building, second floor. If you want to find the rest of your classes first, that should help you make it there on time. Good luck, Rebecca, and welcome to Tucson." Her smile was still sincere, and I wondered how the two old ladies got along, being that their personalities were completely opposite from one another.

I smiled and exited the office. Once outside, I decided to take her advice. I should be able to find my first four classes before the bell for first period rings. At lunch, I'd find my last three classes, and that way I would be able to avoid sitting alone. I'd never eaten lunch alone, and I couldn't imagine how awkward that would be.

As large as the campus was, I felt pretty confident in finding my way around. I remembered the building letters from my self-guided tour, and I found my locker with ease. Once I got it open, I started to unload all my crap into it. I put everything in there but my class schedule and a notebook. I slid my new phone in the front pocket of my jeans after turning it on Vibrate and head off to find my classes.

The first few classes were easy to find, and once I heard the first bell, I sprinted to my first-period class. I walked into the room and up to the teacher. I could feel everyone's eyes on me, wondering who I was. It was something I'd gotten used to since it's been happening for the past twenty minutes. As large as the school was, with as many students as it could have, you would think that one new person would be hard to miss. I was sure that I would be able to stay in the shadows for a few weeks. I wanted to blend in, not stand out.

I was given a textbook for physics and was told to grab an available seat. I chose to sit at the front of the room, hopefully away from anyone who wanted to strike up a conversation. I was not feeling especially friendly. I was nervous, and more than anything, I felt completely alone. As I took my seat, the last bell rings, and a few stragglers slid into class.

I could feel my cell phone vibrate in my pocket, and I resisted the urge to take it out and check my messages. I hadn't spoken to any of my friends since Thursday. I sent a mass email about my phone "breaking" and then a mass text with my new number when I replaced my phone Saturday morning. I was surprised that I didn't receive any calls last night, or even a text, from any of my friends.

I know that all my friends went back to class today without me, and the thought alone broke my heart a little. I wondered what they were doing right now. With the time change, they were probably at lunch. I wondered who was texting me. As the last thought crossed my mind, I was pulled from my own little world into the land of the unknown and the start of my physics class.

During lunch, I made it a point to find my last three classes. I took my time wandering around the campus. I found the library and spent a few minutes checking it out. By the time I had accomplished everything I needed to, I only had about five minutes before the end of lunch, so I decided to head to my fifth-period class.

I was the first to arrive, and thankfully, the teacher was already there. I was given a history book and found my seat, opening it up to avoid eye contact with anyone. *Blend in! Blend in!* It worked for the first few minutes until I felt someone tap me on the shoulder from behind. I turned to find an average-looking, tall and incredibly-built-looking guy in the seat behind me. He asked to borrow a pencil, and I handed him the one I had in my hand before turning back around without saying anything at all. Awkward!

I was extremely grateful that none of my teachers made us do the whole new-student tell-us-about-you introduction thing. That was until last period. I thought I was going to escape the miserable display, but as I tore off six too many pieces of toilet paper (yes, toilet paper), I was beginning to regret signing up for electives.

"Okay, you have six sheets of industrial strength TP. You have to tell us six things about yourself, and your name does not count." My teacher was a little too excited about this. Of course, this was yearbook. I got excited just walking into this class at my last school, but back there I was the editor-in-chief. I was responsible for the damn thing, and now my baby was being taken over by someone else. I didn't want to think about that because I knew who it was, and I knew that she was smiling about it. I wanted to smack that smile off her face and kick her little...

Focus! I was going to lose my mind dwelling on the past, wishing it was still the present and future. I was going to deal with this situation, like I have every other situation, and make the very best of it. I was going to love this class! Just as that last thought crossed my mind, I opened my mouth to speak—at the same moment, the door swung open, and my heart dropped into my stomach.

CHAPTER 4

As casually as possible, I averted my gaze from his. No sunglasses this time, and now I could see his beautiful eyes. I wanted to look deep inside of them, but I was supposed to be telling people about myself, and they were all staring at me, waiting. I wondered if they even noticed him come in. Was I the only one who noticed? I cleared my throat and looked back out around the room.

"Well," I began, "I'm from Michigan." I tossed one piece of "industrial strength" TP in the garbage can. "I moved here with my mom and little sister for my mom's new job." I toss another piece in the garbage can. "I was the editor of the yearbook at my old school, so hopefully I will be able to contribute here as well."

I took a small breath before I continued. What else do I want to reveal about myself? "Um, I like to play tennis." One more piece in the garbage can. Only two more pieces to go, but I was at a loss for words. "Uh…I…well, um…" I had revealed about as much as I want to, and the teacher could see that.

Ms. Phillips cleared her throat to draw the attention away from me. "Well, that's enough for today, but once you feel a little more comfortable, you can share the rest with us. We have all been working together for a while now, and we are like a big incredibly dysfunctional family." Her emphasis was on the dysfunctional part. She motions for me to take a seat, and as I'm about to sit down, he speaks up.

"Did you plan on telling us your name, or do we get to choose one for you?" he asks, his voice rich with sarcasm.

I turned to look at him, but that was a huge mistake. I could feel my throat tightening, and I needed to answer him before I lose my voice. "Oh, my name is Rebecca. Becca." With that, I took my seat and tried to drown myself in whatever the teacher was going to talk about today.

The problem was that she didn't break out in a lecture. Instead, everyone got up and headed to the computers or out of the room, and I was left sitting by myself. Yearbook wasn't about lectures; it was about the school, the people, the photos, and the layouts. They were all either gathering or inputting information to complete their book.

"Ethan, why don't you give Becca a tour of the campus while I figure out what I need for you to work on next? I will have assignments for both of you tomorrow." Ms. Phillips's words made me take notice who was left with me in the classroom, and I cringed on the inside. I don't know if being alone with him was the best idea. My body was hypersensitive to him. Even being in the same room with him was causing my heart rate to increase.

As I stood to grab my things, I felt my phone vibrate in my pocket. I forgot to check my messages earlier, so I decided to check once I get out of the classroom. He was waiting for me at the door, holding it open, before I realized that I was just standing there staring at him like an idiot. I slid my bag further up my shoulder and slowly walked toward him.

When his eyes meet mine, I realized that they were the most amazing shade of emerald, and as I went to grab for my phone, I realized that I was playing with my ring again. His eyes were the exact same color. *Crap!*

JUST WANTED TO WISH YOU LUCK ON YOUR FIRST DAY.

That was the first one I missed this morning from Brad.

SINCE YOU HAVENT TEXT ME BACK I HAVE TO ASSUME
U R NOT TALKING TO ME.

That was the one I just missed.

It wasn't that I was avoiding him. I just happened to be busy since the last time I talked to him. Who was I kidding? I was completely avoiding him. I was trying to make things easier by telling him to get back together with Claire, but it was making me miserable, and I couldn't stop thinking about it. I was trying to decide what I really wanted, and hearing his voice would make that decision harder for me. I knew the second I heard his voice I would fold and tell him the truth. The truth would only make things more complicated. Today, as busy as it really has been, was the first day that I had not even thought about the situation. Until now that is.

The thought made me smile, and I realized that Ethan was staring at me and waiting to give me a tour. I snapped my phone closed without replying to his text and shoved it in my pocket.

"So where to first?" I tried to should nonchalant, but I thought I heard my voice squeak a little.

"Well, we can take a minute if you want to return your boyfriend's text," Ethan replied, sounding hesitant.

He was staring at me, waiting for my reply. Brad's not my boyfriend, but he didn't need to know that. I could live in the fantasy that he was if I wanted to. Why? I wanted to live in reality, and maybe eventually, I would find someone here that I want to date. Then I would have to go through the trouble of breaking up with my fake boyfriend. Maybe I have already found someone I want to date?

"No boyfriend, just a friend, and I can text them when I get home." I was extra careful using the word "them" versus "him."

"Okay, then lets go for a little tour. How about we start at your locker and work our way toward the tennis courts? By the time we get there, school will be over, and we can hit for a while if you want."

Straight to the point much? Holy crap, this guy is forward.

"Um, okay," I replied with obvious shock in my voice. That was the best I could come up with. I wasn't sure if I wanted to hit around with him. How did he even know that I had my stuff with me?

He started to walk toward the stairs, and I followed him, eventually catching up to him and walking side by side. We made our way into the next building and grabbed my bag and purse out of my locker. As we walked toward the tennis courts, he gave me what was actually a pretty good tour, much better than the self-guided tour I gave myself.

Right before we got to the quad, we detoured into the last building and stopped at his locker. He grabbed a large bag and his car keys. I didn't realize that I was staring at his chest until he cleared his throat. He had shut his locker and was waiting for me to move so that we could head to the courts. I felt the blush creep into my cheeks and turned quickly around. I walked out the doors, but no matter how fast I walked, I could feel his eyes on me and his body was close.

As we rounded the corner to the tennis courts, I came to an abrupt halt, and he slammed into me from behind. He grabbed onto my shoulder to make sure that I didn't fall forward, and his touch ignited something deep in my body. I hadn't realized that he was so close. I inhaled deeply and let it out. He was still standing only inches from my back. I wanted to turn around, but I was actually afraid of what might happen, of what I might do if I was that close to his face, his lips, his chest, his anything. I tried to move forward a few steps, but he still had his hand on my shoulders and was holding me in place.

"Just give it a few minutes, and the courts will clear. The class will go inside about ten minutes before the final bell rings." As I turned to look at him, his hands slid down my arms to grip my wrists. I watched his hands as they glided down, and when I look up at him, he was smiling at me, of course.

"How is it that you can read my thoughts like that, and you don't even know me?" I asked. I was completely out of breath and almost at a loss for words. This boy, this man, had me completely unraveling at the seams. No one has ever done this to me, not even Brad.

"Your body language gives you away most of the time." Ethan smirked.

With that, I turned back around to see the class was headed inside, and so I headed down the walk to the courts.

As we were stepping inside the gate, I realized that this was the very spot we were the first time we met. It brought on some creepy feelings, and I gave a small shudder. He had been watching me practice that day, but I had never given any thought as to why he did. I didn't realize that he must have come down here to practice himself.

"How old were you when you first started to play?" I asked. I had given away enough about myself today. I needed to focus on learning something about someone else.

"I've been playing since I was about five or six I guess. What about you?"

Back to me again. Crap!

"Same," and I left it at that. It was the truth, but I didn't feel the need to elaborate on it. The special coaches, special travel leagues, and special attention my parents paid me until the divorce was not something that I wanted to rehash with someone I barely knew. I threw all my stuff in a pile and pulled out a racket. I had planned on practicing after school today, but I had also planned on changing into something other than jeans and a sweatshirt. I had nowhere to keep extra balls except my sweatshirt pocket and that was going to be annoying.

"I am probably still going to be a little rusty. Do you mind if we just hit back and forth for a while? I worked my shoulder pretty good Saturday, and I don't think I am fully recovered yet." My voice cracked as I spoke. I was afraid to make a fool of myself in front of him.

It was the truth. I had iced my shoulder most of the day on Sunday to keep the swelling and throbbing to a minimum. The sweatshirt today had more to do with hiding the swelling than the weather. It definitely didn't have much to do with style. I was trying to blend in, not stand out.

"Sure. I haven't had much time to hit lately anyway, so this will be a good workout for me too," he replied with a smile, sounding sincere.

With that said, we volleyed for a while without saying a word. Before I knew, it my shoulder was killing me, and we had been there in utter silence for almost an hour. I had sweat dripping from my forehead, and I could feel it rolling down my back between my shoulder blades. I tossed my racket on top of my bag and ripped my sweatshirt off without giving any thought as to what I was wearing underneath—an incredibly see-through white tank that barely covered my midsection.

I rummaged around in my bag for the bottle of water I had left from lunch and finished it in just a few gulps. By the time I looked up to say thank you to Ethan, he was only inches from me, and his eyes were locked on mine. I backed up to get away from him, but he followed. Eventually, my back hit the fencing, and I had nowhere to go. His breathing was labored, and mine fell in stride with his. I was at a complete loss for words, and his eyes were doing all the communicating for him.

As he leaned down toward my mouth, I found myself leaning in to him. When our lips met, it was like an electric charge. We both pulled back instantly, but just as quickly, our lips met again, hungrier this time. It only lasted a few minutes, but even after he pulled away, I could still feel his lips on mine. His hands were burning against the bare skin of my hips. I found myself wanting more, but he pulled away completely.

He stepped back, and all I could do was stare. His eyes looked different. The green that I found myself getting lost in was not there anymore. His eyes had grown dark with need. It scared me just a little to think that I may be looking at him the same way. I had only known him, really known him, for a couple of hours, but it felt like longer. Those things that seem important—the little things people know about each other after years of friendship—were not important in that moment. The only thing I wanted from him right then was another kiss.

He turned slowly, gathered his things and began to walk out the gate. When he turned around to say something, his eyes now hidden behind his dark sunglasses, he noticed that I still hadn't moved. I could feel his gaze slowly work its way first down then back up my body, and I shuddered. I could see that he wanted to say more, but all that came out was "See ya," and then he was gone.

I took a moment to compose myself. Once the feeling returned to my legs, I gathered up my stuff and headed toward the parking lot. I got in my car and cranked up the air conditioning. It was only about sixty degrees outside, but my body was still on fire from his touch. Wow! That was the most amazing first day of school ever. That's when my thoughts drifted back to my friends and to Brad and his text messages.

My heart began to ache instantly. Was I trying to jump into something that wasn't right for me because I was missing the one thing that was right for me? Was I getting lost in Ethan's eyes, in his touch, because I really wanted to be with Brad? I missed him. I tried to deny it to myself, but I knew the truth. I wanted to be with him. I had spent so many years succeeding at pushing these kinds of thoughts from my mind. Why now? Why was I able to torture myself with these thoughts now?

I pulled out my phone to see that I had missed a call from my mom and one from Brad. I called my mom first to let her know I was on my way home, and then I typed out a quick text to Brad saying I would call him later tonight. I had no sooner put my phone away, and it was ringing.

"Hey there," I said, trying to sound as normal as possible. I was dreading this call more than anything. We hadn't talked since

Friday night, and I knew that things still felt unresolved for me. I knew what I wanted, what he wanted, but I was also aware that we couldn't have it.

"Hey, did you get my texts?"

"Yeah, but I didn't want to get caught on my cell the first day of school. I'm still in the parking lot, so I was going to call you when I got home." That was the truth, mostly. I really wasn't avoiding him, was I? I was trying to avoid the thoughts I was having of him more than anything.

"Why are you still at school? Isn't it after four?" he asked, sounding somewhat concerned. I looked at my dash to see that he was right. *Crap!* "What are you doing there so late for?"

"I went to the courts after school. I didn't realize it was so late. I should probably let you go and head home. I just told my mom I was on my way." I tried to keep my voice flat, like being at school almost two extras hours was no big deal. "Can I call you when I get home?"

"Yeah, that's fine. Are you okay? You sound kind of different."

Really? I wanted to ask what he meant, but that was going to turn into a whole conversation that I was sure I was not ready to have yet. I took a few deep breaths before replying, trying to calm myself. "Just tired is all. I'll call you in about a half hour okay?"

I heard him mumble something, but I was already hitting End Call. I put my car in Drive and pulled out of the parking lot.

Once I got home, I made my way to my bedroom to drop off my stuff and then immediately went into the bathroom and turned on the shower. My skin was still on fire, and I couldn't stop thinking about Ethan or Brad. This was not normal behavior for me. I was the responsible one. I put my other priorities before relationships; that's probably why I didn't really have any.

I stepped under the spray and tried to rid myself of the random thoughts that I was having. *Will he kiss me again? Do I want him to kiss me again? What will I say to him in class tomorrow? Am I trying to replace Brad? Crap! I have to get this guy out of my head.*

After I got dressed, I settled at my desk to call Brad. I wasn't sure what I was going to say to him, but I knew that I needed to be honest with him. He didn't have a reason to ask about anything specifically involving Ethan, but he knew me well enough to know if I was hiding something. He always knew.

"Hey, so how was your first day?" he asked. It should have been an easy question to answer, but somehow it wasn't.

"It went fine, I guess." I replied trying to sound unaffected by my day. "How was your first day back? Did you find someone new to walk with to class yet?" I tried my best to tease him, and I hoped it came across the way I wanted it to.

"Nope, I still have that spot reserved for you if your skinny butt ever returns." He was teasing. Good. "So did you make any friends today?"

"Not really." That wasn't a complete lie.

"That does not sound like the Becca I know. You are the easiest person to get along with. Did you even try to make any friends today?"

Busted! He really does know me too well.

"I wanted to get a feel for the school today, ease myself into it. I'll make friends, and you know it. I just want to be invisible for a while." That was the complete truth. I want to be invisible now more than anything. I want to put myself in a bubble and make sure that no one pops it.

"I get it, I guess."

What else could he say?

"I wish you could see this place," I said, trying to change the topic and lighten the mood. "The campus is beautiful—huge but beautiful. Everything is so open. It has a beautiful view of the mountains."

"It sounds pretty. Maybe I could come out and visit you for spring break?" Brad replied. It was a statement, but the inflection at the end made it sound more like a question. He wanted to come and visit but wanted me to invite him. I wanted him to come and visit me, but I knew if that happened, then I would have to let him go again. I didn't want to let him go last week, and I don't want to let him go now. If he came to visit, I was going to keep ripping my heart in two.

"That would be fun. Do you think your parents would let you come visit? You know my mom won't care. We have a spare bedroom so you wouldn't even have to sleep on the couch." I exclaimed excitedly. I wanted to tell him the truth that I was scared of him visiting, but I told him what I knew he would want to hear instead.

"I'll ask them this weekend and see how much tickets cost. I have some money saved, so maybe they will split the cost with me." I could hear the excitement in his voice. I could see him smiling in my mind. I could see his eyes shimmering and the gold around his irises catching the light.

"Sounds like a good plan. Call me this weekend, and let me know what they say. I have to get started on my homework before I fall asleep standing up." I needed to end this call and process all this information. I was tired, but it was more a sense of mental exhaustion. My brain was working overtime. It was almost like it was volleying my thoughts around in my head like they were a tennis ball.

"Okay, get some sleep, and I'll give you a call this weekend."

After we hung up, I started to process the situation. I would have to figure out some fun places for him to go. What would Mom actually say? She loved Brad, but him flying here for a week would scream that he wants to be more than friends. Would he read into it that I wanted us to be more than friends? I knew that I wanted to be with him, but I also knew that I couldn't. I didn't want to get his hopes up, knowing that my heart would break when he goes back home. It had only been a week, and I already missed him so much.

Then it hit me. Claire? What about her?

CHAPTER 5

The rest of my week went by in a blur. I would go to class, go home, and do my homework. I had been avoiding Ethan at every turn. I was not sure why, but it seemed like he had been avoiding me as well. I knew that our kiss was not planned and probably should not have happened, but it did. I couldn't ignore the drop of my stomach every time he walks in to the only class we shared together. I couldn't ignore the fact that I always look forward to my very last class of the day, knowing that it was the only time I get to see him.

I tried to focus on other things to keep my mind occupied. I hadn't talked to Brad yet about Claire, even though I have talked to him every night this week. I wondered what's going on with them. I wondered if he took my advice and got back together with her. I wondered why I even cared if I want to see him so much. Can a relationship as strong as ours last if we were to try? Our friendship was going to last no matter how many miles we put between us, but a relationship is different. We never had the opportunity to discuss what we felt or what we wanted to do about our feelings. I never let that happen out of fear that things would become real. I was caught off guard for the first time in a long time, and instead of trying to figure things out, I tried to ignore the situation and pretended like it never happened. I was doing the same thing with Ethan.

I had to get someone else to weigh in on this. I needed an outsider's opinion. Maybe Ella? Emma and Ella were probably two of the smartest, most opinionated people I knew. Neither of them would hide their thoughts from you, but neither of them would share my secret either. They both knew how to keep a secret, even from each other, which I thought was amazing since I've heard that twins generally know what the other is thinking.

Thursday after school, I dialed their house without hesitation. I had spoken to Ella once since I left, and Emma had pretty much been unavailable. She had started dating a new guy that I didn't know and was never home anymore, according to Ella. I was surprised when she answered after the first ring.

"Becca!" Emma screamed. The excitement in her voice surprised me. I was closer to Ella, and I thought that Emma sometimes got jealous.

"Hey, Emma. How are you?"

"I'm good. How are you? How's the new school?" She was going a mile a minute.

"Everything is fine." I paused to take in a deep breath. Should I ask for Ella, or should I just talk to Emma? They seemed like the same person sometimes, so what did it really matter? "Do you have a few minutes? I'm kind of having a minor crisis, and I need some good advice."

"Sure. What's going on?"

"Well, I have to work out some things with Brad, and I don't know how to do it. I don't know what to do at all or even where to begin…" I let my voice trail off. Everyone knew that Brad and I were just friends, but the only person I had told about the kiss was Emma.

"Is this about what happened before you left? If it is, then I don't really know what to tell you."

Great! No advice available. "Just answer me this. Do you think that I should give *us* a try?"

"No." She said it quickly and without hesitation.

"Oh, okay. Do you have a reason? Is there something going on that I don't know about?"

"No. I just think that it's time for you both to move on. I see the way he is right now, sad look on his face all the time, pining away for you to be here. If you give him even the slightest glimpse of hope that there can be something, then it will be even worse for both of you if it doesn't work out. You guys can't do this from far away. If you had started something before you left, you could have continued it, but you can't start something with the distance. You don't want to ruin your friendship, do you?"

She was making sense. She basically stated all the thoughts that I was having myself. If we had started something before I left, then we could try to continue it now, but we didn't. Plus, the last thing I want was to ruin our friendship. He was my rock. He was my lifeline most days. We'd been through too much to risk losing all of that.

"No, I don't want to lose his friendship." I let out a sigh before continuing. What did I have left to say? I summed it up in one sentence, but I knew that there was more. If I didn't get it off my chest, then it wouldn't be real. "Can you do me a favor, Em?"

"Anything. What do you need?" Emma asked.

"I need for you to find him someone, anyone. Encourage him to get involved with someone. Get him back together with Claire if that's what it takes. I'm not even sure if they are officially broken up at this point. There are plenty of people who would go out with him. Help him see the light."

My light was shinning through right now. I was going to do the same thing. I was going to move on, heal my broken heart, and find someone who makes me happy and lives less than two thousand miles away.

"I can try." she stated. I heard the hesitance in her voice. "Are you sure this is what you want? Are you sure this is the right decision to make?"

"Yes."

"I wasn't trying to break up your friendship. I was just making you realize the reality of the situation."

"I know, and you did. Thank you."

As my last class approached on Friday afternoon, I decided that I was going to break free of the shell I had encased myself in my first week of school. I walked in a few minutes before the bell rang and sat in the same seat I had been all week. Instead of opening my physics textbook and staring at the pages to try and remain invisible, I turned to the pretty brunette who was sitting behind me and tried to strike up a conversation. Her name was Natalie, and she seemed friendly enough.

The last bell rang, and I turned back around in my seat just as Ethan walked in. I heard Natalie say something to the girl next to her. I think her name was Jill. Ms. Phillips took role, and people started to scatter to begin their work. I walked up to Ms. Phillips's desk to find out what she would like for me to do. I was assigned to take some photos of the campus from my "new" perspective earlier in the week, and we went through the prints yesterday, so my plate was clear.

"Why don't you partner up with Natalie? I'm sure she can use some help wrapping up the editorials for the sports pages." She never looked up from her desk as she spoke, and I could see that she probably never even noticed me talking with Natalie earlier. I was starting to reply when she motioned for me to get going by moving her hand through the air.

I went into the computer lab to find Natalie. She was tucked in the corner talking to Jill and staring at the pictures on the screen. She would move them a bit left or right before stopping to ensure they were where she wanted them and then would start to move them again. It was obvious that she was a bit of a perfectionist, maybe even a little OCD like me.

"Hey, Ms. Phillips wants me to get with you and lend a hand with the sports editorials. What would you like for me to do?" I asked trying not to sound overly excited.

"Well, I have everything printed out over there if you want to proofread it. The player stat sheets are in the pile too, and the professional sport stats we are including this year are at the very bottom somewhere." Natalie stated plainly. Her tone was warm and polite, but her smile was not, and when I realized she was not looking at me, I felt a bit of relief. She was staring over my shoulder at someone. "I will be right back if you want to get started," she said as she got up and walked out of the lab.

I sneaked a peek over my shoulder as she walked past me, but no one was there now. I grabbed the stack of papers and started editing the articles. They were really well written, and I enjoyed reading them more than I thought I would. As I got down to the bottom of the stack, I see stats about each athlete, and then the last few pages fascinated me. The information they planned on including about each sport was unique. They were including things like who won the World Series this year, how their local college teams performed, and who from the school's teams were most likely to go pro.

When I reached the stats about tennis, I knew them already, most of them anyway. I read who of my favorite players were doing well and who where not. I wondered if they were going to wait for the results of any more big tournaments before getting the book published, and as the thought crossed my mind, I saw *his* name.

Most likely to go pro: Ethan Green

I dropped the page, and it floated to the floor in slow motion. I thought back to Monday when we played after school. He kept up with me, and most people can't. He had some really strong volleys, and I would kill for the power on his backhand. He kept the ball in play, no matter how hard I tried to get it past him. He was good, really good. *Crap!*

I should have noticed it sooner. He was a great player, but his amazing looks seemed to distract me at every turn. He said that he started playing at a young age, just like me, but that didn't always mean that you turned out to be a great player. All the practice in the world won't make you a great player unless you love the sport.

I should have known that someone who just happened to have a racket with him at school would be able to keep pace with me. It's the off season, so why would anyone be bringing their equipment to school unless they had ulterior motives? He didn't just want to play tennis after school—he wanted to play me.

I picked up the piece of paper on the floor and scanned it again just to be sure I read it right. His name was there in black and white, and I still couldn't believe my eyes. The bell ringing pulled me from my thoughts, back to reality, and I tried my best to pull myself together. Everyone was shuffling out the door as I placed the stack of papers on Natalie's bag next to the computer. I accidentally hit the mouse, and the screen popped up. I saved her work for her, and closed the computer down, but not before I adjusted the picture to the exact spot it needed to be to make the page symmetrical.

I grabbed my bags and headed for the door. I may not have found my new BFF today, but I felt like I could be friends with Natalie. She was nice and friendly and seemed to be an all-around good person. I wanted to get her number before I left for the weekend, but she never came back to the room. I guess I could try to see if I could find her at lunch on Monday and maybe eat with her and her friends.

I step out into the deserted hall to find Ethan standing against the wall. Was he waiting for me, or was he surprised to see me? His eyes didn't give much away as he pushed himself off the wall and started to approach me. I heard a door slam in the distance and look toward the stairs to see Natalie approaching from the other end of the hall. I gave her a small wave, and she smiled before entering the far door to the computer lab. I turned my attention back to Ethan, but he was gone.

I stood there confused for a minute before I realized that I looked like an idiot and turned toward the stairs. I reached my locker in record time. I wanted to be able to hit some balls before I went home, and with the warming weather this week, even though it was still January, I thought I might have to fight for a spot on a court. By the time I reached the courts after changing, I realized that I was wrong. The parking lot was almost completely empty from what I could see of it, and the courts were desolate. Then I realized that no one but me would stay after school on a Friday by choice.

When my phone rang at seven o'clock Sunday morning, I knew it had to be Brad. The early hour told me that he was probably excited and his parents probably said yes. I knew how the conversation was going to go, but I picked up my phone anyway and mumble something that was suppose to sound like hello into the receiver.

"You bitch! I cannot believe you!" A female voice screamed into my ear.

I was wide awake now and was staring at the number on my phone. I didn't recognize it, but it has a Michigan area code. Someone from home?

"Excuse me? Who is this?" I tried to sound unaffected by the rude awakening I just received, but there was a hint of anger in my voice that I could not seem to hide.

"Claire, you bitch! How could you do this to me? He's leaving me for you, you home wrecker!" she shouted at the top of her lungs.

Really? She made it sound like I broke up their marriage when I'm thousands of miles away and had nothing to do with it. Well, almost nothing.

"I knew this was going to happen. All those times you two would hang out as 'just friends' when really you were seeing each other behind my back. I knew it!" Claire continued.

"Claire, it's 7:00 a.m. here, and you just woke me up." She tried to interrupt me, but I continued before she could. "I did not steal him away from you, and I do not believe he is leaving you for me. He's my best *friend*, and we were never seeing each other behind your back. Now do not call me this early ever again, and unless you want to apologize, I am hanging up."

I could hear her breathing heavy with anger on the other end of the line, but she never spoke. I gave her no more than ten seconds, and I hung up on her. I was wide awake and pissed off. Either Brad told her it was because of me—and it really is because of me—or he told her that as an easy way out. Either way, he was going to get a very large piece of my mind after I down a cup of coffee and beat the crap out of some tennis balls.

I threw on my clothes and pulled my hair up high on my head. After washing my face, brushing my teeth, and putting on some deodorant, I was in my car and on my way to grab some coffee. My phone rang, and I didn't even bother to see who it was before I sent them to voicemail. Whoever wanted to talk to me this early was going to have to wait. I needed to blow off some steam before I can even imagine being civil to anyone.

I stepped onto the court, and for the first time since waking up this morning, I felt a little more relaxed. There was a slight breeze blowing my ponytail, and I closed my eyes to enjoy the sun on my face for a minute. Before I opened them, I heard the squeak of the gate door, and my stomach dropped. I smelled him before I saw him. It was a familiar smell, something I think my dad used to wear, but somehow different in the best way possible.

"You're here early," he said.

I was not planning on seeing anyone, and I know that I looked completely disheveled. I kept facing forward, hoping to hide most of myself from him.

"Yeah, just needed to blow off some steam this morning. What are you doing here?" I did not want to talk about me. "I figured you were the kind of guy to sleep until noon on a Sunday after staying out all night."

"Nope."

That was all he gave me. A single word with not so much as a small explanation attached to it.

Fine, I won't make small talk if he was not interested in making small talk. I was willing to talk to him Friday in the hall, and he disappeared. He lost his chance. I came here to be alone anyway, and now I really felt the need to beat the crap out of some balls.

I removed my sweatshirt and started to stretch. My shoulder had been feeling pretty good, but I planned on working it hard for the next hour or so. Hopefully, a good stretch beforehand would help keep some of the pain at bay. When I glanced over at Ethan, he was two courts over, stretching as well. He was wearing a fitted white t-shirt and running pants, the kind that snap up to the side and with one quick tug I could pull off him completely. *No!* I won't go down that path with my thoughts.

I grabbed my racket and a couple of balls. I warmed up my shoulder, and then I couldn't wait any longer. I tossed the ball and struck it hard. It hit on the line, but close to where I was aiming. My shoulder was getting better every time I worked with it. A small grin formed from the satisfaction it gave me, knowing that I may be able to compete again, despite what the doctor and therapist said, even if just in high school.

I heard the slam of the ball from Ethan's court and turned to watch him. He was graceful and powerful in his every move. I could see the muscles of his back stretch and move under his shirt. It was already soaked with sweat, and I was secretly begging him to take it off so that I could see what's hidden underneath. Then before I realized what's going on, I was standing only a few feet away from him as he nailed his next serve.

"Enjoying the show?" he asked, but I was pretty sure he already knew the answer to the question.

"You're good." I stated very manner-of-factly.

It was an understatement, but it brought out his smile, and for the first time, I notice that he had a dimple in his right cheek that was just too cute for words. That smile was getting closer to me, and I could now pretty much see what was hiding under his sweat-soaked shirt. His abs were impeccable, his arms were more muscular than I noticed before, and his pecs are—pierced?

I reached out to touch his left nipple and found a barbell piercing. I quickly pulled my hand away when I realized that I just crossed a line that I didn't even want to be near in the first place. Ethan was a "bad boy." I took a step back and turned to gather my stuff, but I felt him following me. He was behind me and placed his hand on my right hip. Before I had an opportunity to process what's about to happen, he spun me around and captured my lips with his.

I wanted this. I knew I shouldn't, but I did. His mouth was warm and inviting. His tongue grazed my lower lip, and I opened to him. He tasted sweet and salty from sweating, but it took everything I had to not try and devour him. I pulled back just a little, and his hand moved to the small of my back, pressing me closer to him. I wanted to resist him, but it was pointless. The moment I returned his kiss, I stopped all rational thinking and my legs went weak.

He pulled away quickly, and we were both gasping for air. I was trying to get my legs to cooperate and hold my weight, but they wouldn't, and I slid down the fence and landed with a small thud. I couldn't take my eyes off of him. He was so beautiful, his body was amazing, and by the size of the bulge in his pants, he was completely turned on. I shifted my gaze back to his face and saw that he was still watching me.

"Wow!" That was all that I could say between gulping huge breaths. I saw the beginnings of a smile crept up on his face, and I could feel the smile on mine starting to form as well. Both of our chests were rising and falling quickly. My attention was drifting toward his piercing again when he finally found a way to speak.

"Uh…next time I won't be able to stop." He said this like it's a simple statement, but the real meaning behind it hung in the air.

Wait, next time? He wants this to happen again? If he won't be able to stop then, was I ready for that? I just met this guy, yet I was trying to devour him every time I see him. It was like my body had a mind of its own. I was drawn to him in the most animalistic way.

"Okay." I knew what he meant, and I wanted to tell him that. I wanted to tell him that stopping was hard for me too, but that was all I could say. This man had reduced me to single-word answers.

"I have to go. I guess I will see you tomorrow." Again, he made it sound like a simple statement, but what I hear is, "Can I see you before then?"

"Okay."

Stupid girl. Give him your number, and let him decide it he wants to call you. I want to give him my number, but the words just won't come out.

I reached my hand in the air, and he grabbed it and helped me to my feet. I felt empowered by the things that keep happening between us, and so I reached into his pocket and pulled out his cell phone. If I couldn't say the words, I could at least do something about how I was feeling. I typed my number in and called myself. Once I heard my phone ringing in my bag, I hung up and put his phone back in his pocket.

Last time, he walked away from me, but this time, I was taking the lead. I threw all my stuff in my bag and headed toward the gate. I heard my phone ringing again and started to rummage through my bag for it. When I saw the number on the screen, I answered it without looking back, knowing that he was watching my every move.

"Hello?" I tried to sound confused, but the excitement in my voice was overwhelming.

"Would you like to go to dinner with me tonight?" Ethan asked with a hint of laugher in his voice.

"I would love to." I replied, trying my very best to keep my excitement in check. I hung up on him before he could say anything else, and even though I could feel the concrete of the parking lot beneath my feet, I felt like I was walking on air.

I jumped in my car and typed a quick text to him with my address. His reply was simple: "7pm," and the butterflies in my stomach started to fly freely. The entire drive home was like a dream, and even as I was getting out of the shower, I felt like I was on cloud nine. I had forgotten all about the way I woke up that morning and was now focused on my "date" tonight, if you want to call it that.

I jumped when my phone started to ring. I realized that I was still going to have to face this stupid situation with Claire when I saw Brad's name on my caller ID. I was trying to decide if I want to answer it or not when my voicemail snagged the call and decided for me. I felt instantly like crap for avoiding him. Did he know that Claire called me this morning? Selfishly, I waited for my voicemail to chime and listened to it before I decide if I should call him back.

"Hey. I just wanted to chat. I talked to my parents about coming out for a visit, and they said they would think about it." There was such a long pause I was about to hang up when he continued. "I know Claire called you this morning, and I am sorry. I want to talk to you about that and a couple of other things, but I can't do it in a voicemail, so you have to call me back. I'll talk to you soon hopefully."

During the last part of his message, I could hear the difference in his voice. He sounded wounded, defeated, and empty. Emma had said that he looked sad, and now I could hear it in his voice. Was I actually responsible for this? He was my best friend, and I was avoiding him, even avoiding answering his phone calls. I missed him terribly, but I couldn't even take a few minutes to talk with him, hash out the problems that seem to keep arising? I felt like a horrible person.

Just as I was about to call him and apologize, my mom knocked on my door and opened it. I waved her in and tossed my phone on my bed. Before she said anything, she took in her surroundings. My room was destroyed. I had clothes tossed everywhere, some clean and some dirty. Most of them had been tossed there in the last twenty minutes while I had been trying to find something to wear tonight.

"So are you cleaning out your closet?" She said this with a smile because the last time she found me in my room like this, I was getting ready for my first real date.

"Nope. Just trying to find something to wear. All my clothes are less fashionable here. I really need to go shopping. The trends are way different," I said trying not to sound like I was complaining. It's all truth, but I really don't care that much about the trends. I'm not much of a girly girl. I go more for comfort.

"Well, if there's a special occasion, then you should buy a new outfit." She knew what was going on but was going to make me say it. I was seventeen years old, but I think she still wanted me to ask permission to go out. Thankfully, she didn't ask anymore probing questions because I really didn't have any really good answers for her.

"That would be great if I could. Just one outfit though. I don't need anything else right now."

"Okay. Well, let's get your sister around, and we can take a trip to the mall. I heard it's pretty big, so we should be able to find you something there."

A trip to the mall with my mom was going to lead to a lot of girl time, a lot of talking, and probably a lot more shopping that I needed today. It would also give me an excuse to not answer my phone, and that was what finally drew me in, I guess.

"Sounds good. Thanks, Mom." I meant it. I had been pretty mean to her and barely spoken to her in weeks, and now I was trying to make it up to her by spending the day with her at the mall. That was a lie. I was trying to spend a day with her at the mall to get a new outfit and avoid the part of my crazy life that was thousands of miles away.

CHAPTER 6

Shopping with my mother wasn't as bad as I thought it would be. She bought me a few outfits and didn't ask any prying questions. I knew she was waiting for me to give her details or at least tell her what was going on, but I couldn't. I wasn't sure what was really happening, and I didn't want to get myself any more excited than I already was.

Once I got home, I decided that it would be better to call Brad and get the conversation over with. If I continued to avoid it, I was going to become consumed by it, and that was the last thing I wanted to be thinking about tonight. I wanted to get a few things off my chest and be able to relax during dinner.

"Hello?" He sounded like he was confused.

"Hey, what's going on?" I wanted to sound carefree. I didn't want him to know that I got his voicemail, but why else would I be calling?

"Oh, hey! I wasn't expecting to hear from you today. What's up?"

Really? He left me a voicemail and called me twice this morning alone, and he wasn't expecting to hear from me? Did he think I forgot Claire called me? What the hell! The longer I let myself think and the longer the pause lasted, the more upset I let myself get. I took a deep relaxing breath and decided to not think too much into what he was saying.

"You called me, remember? I was just returning your call. What did you want to talk to me about?" I could hear the irritation in my voice, so I knew he could. So much for calming down.

"I just wanted to make sure you were okay. I know Claire lit into you this morning for no reason, and I figured I owed you some sort of explanation."

"That would be nice. It sure sounded like she thought she had a reason to be pissed at me."

"Well, after we broke up that night I was on the phone with you, I haven't really been returning her calls. She finally showed up here the other day and wanted a better explanation for why I broke it off. When I didn't want to talk about it, she went on a rant about you and me. She pretty much figured out that I broke up with her because of you."

"What! Why would you let her think that? I told you to get back together with her. We are too far apart right now to even consider moving ahead in our relationship." Did I just say *relationship*? I meant *friendship*. Crap! I needed to calm down and think before I speak, or else I am going to give him mixed signals, and I already have enough of those to deal with these days. I couldn't tell him how I really felt.

"I let her think that because it's true, Becca. Don't you see it? I don't want to be with her because she's not you!"

Oh my god. I know this is the part where you are suppose to tell the other person that you love them and want to be with them. I know there are things that I was supposed to say to him right now but I just couldn't find the words. The distance isn't suppose to matter when you care about someone. You are suppose to push harder to get what you want, not push the other person away. But that's what I had decided to do. Not because I don't love him and not because I don't want to be with him. I decide to do it because of the distance. The only thing going through my mind right before the words spill out is that I am going to lose my best friend.

After I hung up, I started to cry and successfully cried myself to sleep. I knew that I just lied to him. I told him that I didn't want what he wanted, that I didn't want to be with him, that it wouldn't work with the distance. I gave him all the classic reason when you break up with someone. The problem with that scenario is that we were not even dating. I really just broke up with my best friend and that sucks even worse.

I woke up and realized that I only had about an hour to get ready for dinner. I started to rush around and get ready, and before I knew it the doorbell rang, and I wasn't even dressed. I wanted to be ready and out the door so that he didn't have to come in, but that just wasn't going to happen.

I heard my mom answer the door and let him in. She hollered for me, and I stuck my head out my door and told her I would only be a few minutes. When I finally made it downstairs, getting dressed and putting on my makeup in record time, Ethan was sitting at the breakfast bar talking with my mom.

I was not really comfortable with this situation. Ethan and I hadn't even had time to sit down and have a conversation. So we said our good-byes and headed out the door. Without a word, he opened the passenger door and I got in the car. Once we were pulling out of the driveway, I felt comfortable enough to apologize.

"Sorry I wasn't ready when you got there. I wasn't planning on having you meet my mom or anything."

"Really? Why not? I put on a clean shirt just to impress her." I looked over and saw him grinning from ear to ear, his dimple winking at me, but he never took his eyes off the road.

"Well, now that we have that out of the way, where are we going?"

"There's this place I like to go. It's got a great view and the food's decent."

I still hadn't figured my way around the city yet, but I knew we were not headed toward town. The road we were on was leading us away from almost any restaurant we could want, and in just a few minutes, we would be headed up the mountain. I was pretty sure that having a "nice view" was going to be an understatement.

"So how was the rest of your day?"

I was trying to think about how I really wanted to answer that question. It wasn't suppose to be so loaded, and he probably had no idea that it was.

"It was okay. I went shopping for some new clothes with my mom and then took an unscheduled nap. That's why I was running late. Normally, I would have been ready on time, but I fell asleep."

"It really isn't a big deal, Becca."

The way he said my name made my stomach turn itself over. Wow! I was sitting there, twirling my hair around my finger and biting my lip. All would be signs to any guy that I wanted something from him, but Ethan wasn't looking at me, thankfully.

I let the conversation die as we wound our way up the mountain. Ten minutes later, he pulled into an overlook and turned the car off. We sat in silence for a few minutes before he unlocked his seatbelt and opened his door.

"Were here," he announced like it was no big deal. I looked around and saw a large parking lot and a brick half wall in front of us. Not exactly the way I pictured our night going.

He came around and opened the door for me and helped me out of the car. After closing my door, he opened the back door and pulled out a picnic basket and a blanket. This was going to be way better than I pictured.

We walked ahead to the wall, and Ethan spread the blanket out over the top of it. I was so caught up in watching him I hadn't notice the view, but when I did, I was entranced. The lights from the city were absolutely beautiful, and you could see all the way across town from where we were. Looking up, I noticed how clear the sky was. You could see almost every constellation. With the lights of the city below us, there was nothing blocking our view. It was truly beautiful up here and a little bit romantic.

He helped me up on the wall and then began to unpack the basket he was carrying. As he unpacked things, I continued to stare out at the city. I had never seen anything like it before. I was sure that the only thing more beautiful than the sight of the city at night from up here was a sunset. I wondered what it would look like. We were facing south, so the sunset would be to our right, over another set of mountains.

Ethan hopped up on the wall next to me. The food was between us, but he was still within arm's reach, and I could feel the heat radiating from his body. He handed me a bottled water and a sandwich but still hadn't said anything. We sat in silence for a while and ate before he finally broke the tension hanging in the air.

"I hope you don't mind coming up here instead of going to a restaurant," he said.

When I looked over to him, his face had such a serious look. He was actually concerned that I would have preferred to go somewhere else. I really didn't. It couldn't get much better than this for a "first date" of sorts.

"No, it's great. The view is spectacular, and the company's not so bad either," I said teasingly, trying to lighten his mood. It must have worked because a smile crept across his face, and you could see the tension he was holding in his shoulder lift.

"Good. This is my favorite place to go when I need to get away from everything. It's kind of special to me."

His words sank in, and I realized that he was trying to show me a part of who he was on the inside.

We talked for a few minutes, and I started to feel more comfortable the more I learned about him. He had just asked me about my dad. I hesitated for a moment, and as I started to reply, I heard a howling that sounded fairly close to where we were. I sat straight up and started to look around. When my eyes met his, he knew that I was scared, and he helped me down from the wall without a word.

I jumped in the car and watched him pack up our picnic. Once he put the basket in the backseat and climbed in the car, he turned to face me, instead of starting the car like I thought he would.

"It was pretty close to where we were, so I can understand why you got scared. Coyotes tend to wander up this way because people leave scraps of food behind," he explained.

His statement was simple, like he was used to being interrupted by this. If he came here often after dark, I figured it had happened before.

"I'm just glad that I didn't see it, or else I would have really freaked out," I said. It was the truth. I had remained more calm on the outside than I had been on the inside. The truth was, I was freaking out and didn't want him to see it. I was still trying to calm down a little if I was being honest with myself. I knew that I was probably safe in the car, but I also knew that if I saw the coyote that I would freak out.

"Well, do you want to head back down and grab a coffee, or do you want me to take you home?"

"Are we safe if we sit in your car and talk?" I squeaked. I knew that my voice was giving away the fact that I was scared but I didn't care. I didn't want to go home yet. I really wanted to be alone with him as long as we were safe inside his car.

"Yeah, we're safe." He took a long pause, and I knew that he wanted to say more. "What did you want to talk about because there's something that I need to get off my chest? I have been trying to figure out how to tell you all night."

That sounded bad. It actually sounded very bad. I didn't know him that well, but I knew enough about guys to know that they didn't really enjoy talking about their feelings, and if there was something he wanted or needed to tell me, I probably was not going to like to hear it.

"Okay," I said, drawing the single word out more than I had anticipated.

"Well, I know that we haven't know each other that long and that we don't know each other that well, but there are things about me that I think you need to know." The way he said it sent shivers to my core. There was no emotion behind his words. They were just words. "I want to make sure that everything is out in the open before we see what this is," he continued, motioning his hand between us.

"Okay." He had reduced me to single-word answers again and not the same way he had before. I preferred the method he had used earlier.

"Well"—he paused, not seeming overly anxious to tell me anything at that moment—"I sort of have a girlfriend right now." He said it really fast, and just as fast I felt like he had slapped me across the face. *Are you freaking kidding me right now?*

"Really? So does your girlfriend know that you kissed me? Does your girlfriend know where you are right now?" I asked through clenched teeth. I could hear the anger in my words as they came spilling out of my mouth. I could feel the tension build in the car as I turned to face out the front window, arms crossed.

"She doesn't know any of that stuff, and she doesn't need to."

Excuse me? I whipped my head back around and just stared at him. I thought that was important information, and I didn't want to be a part of his lies.

Before I could tell him any of this, he continued. "We are taking a break right now. We haven't been together for about a month."

"That does not make this right. That does not mean that you can do whatever you want just because you are on a break. That just means that you are not *kissing* each other right now." I felt like I was screaming at him and I probably was. "Take me home please. I need to go home."

With that, the conversation ended. He started the car, and we headed down the mountain in complete silence. The drive seemed to take twice as long to get home. The uncomfortable silence didn't help the situation. Once we pulled on to my street, he pulled the car over about a block away from my house and threw it in Park.

"I understand why you are upset, but please let me finish," he pleaded.

I stared at him with my arms crossed over my chest and nodded slightly for him to continue.

"I never expected any of this to happen. I never expected to meet anyone and to like them so much. You caught me completely off guard. I watched you serve that first day for what felt like forever before I even had the nerve to approach you. It was like I was drawn to you for some reason." He paused to take a deep breath before he continued. I could see the strain on his face. He wanted to tell me everything but knew that I didn't want to hear it. "I broke it off with her, and she convinced me to take a break over the holidays. She wants to get back together, and now I don't want to. She doesn't make me feel the way you do, and I just met you. I should feel happy when I'm with her when we go out. I don't, and I can't keep lying to myself to make her happy. I don't want to be with her anymore, I haven't for a while and should never have let her talk me into taking a break over the holidays. I want to be with you. I told her I didn't want to be with her anymore the other day, and she flipped out on me."

It hit me like a ton of bricks that I really liked this guy. He made me feel alive, made me want to come out of my shell. He gave me strength when I felt defeated, especially when it came to tennis. He was supportive and caring. He was amazing. He made me feel like Brad made me feel all those years.

This was the first time I actually wanted to be in a relationship, and he was taken. I had to keep reminding myself of that, or else I was afraid I would lose sight of it and do something I shouldn't. Plus, my life was a bit rocky with relationships right now, and I needed time to figure out my own dilemmas before I could move forward.

"I want you to know I've heard everything you said, and as soon as you get your shit together, you can call me, but not until then." I stated with no emotion in my voice at all.

I was so proud of myself. I stood up for what I believed in. I was not going to play second fiddle to anyone else, and I was not going to be the reason that someone got their heart broken. Apparently, I was already that person for Claire, and I didn't plan on adding another girl to that list.

I opened the door and got out. The cold air nipped at the back of my neck as I made the short trek to my house. After a few minutes, I heard Ethan start his car, but he never drove past. When I reached my driveway, I turned to see that he was still parked in the same spot watching to make sure I got home all right.

CHAPTER 7

The next few weeks went buy without any new drama. My life was finally beginning to feel normal for a change. Brad and I had talked a few times, but neither of us brought up Claire or anything about her or our *situation*. I knew that he wanted to talk about us, but I couldn't bring myself to think about it. I had said some seriously rotten things to him. I never apologized, and both of us were acting like the conversation never happened. *Fine by me.*

I talked to Emma a few times to see what the progress was with our plan. I felt like I was spying on Brad. Emma was keeping me posted on everything, from his sullen mood to the girls who were asking him out and how he was refusing all of them. She also kept me posted on Claire. The girl was not giving up on Brad or on me. She took any chance she could to bad-mouth me to her friends, some of which were also my friends. That was a big mistake on her part since they were defending me and she was creating enemies in the process.

I was also avoiding Ethan for the most part. I avoided him in the halls when I could. Since the night we went out, he seemed to be everywhere all the time. I had never noticed him outside of class before. The one place that I couldn't avoid him was in class, but I tried to surround myself with other people so that he didn't have any opportunity to corner me and try to talk about *us*. Wow! I was in two really messed up "relationships" if you could call either of them that.

I found that Natalie, Jill, and I made a great team. We worked together on the sports spreads, and by the time those were finished, it felt like we were inseparable. We had bonded over a common interest and found friendship along the way. I was proud of myself for making friends and trying to move forward in this strange new place. It was beginning to feel like home, or at least a place that could one day resemble home for me.

The Friday before Valentines Day, at lunch, the girls were giggling as I walked up to the table. As I sat down, the giggling stops and everyone was looking at me. What a way to make a girl feel welcomed. Were they talking about me? Had I done something wrong that I was unaware of?

"What?" I asked. Everyone was still staring at me.

"Well," Natalie started, "I know we haven't been able to hang out much, and we were just wondering if you wanted to come to a party with us tonight."

I could hear the hesitance in her voice. Did she think I was prude, or was she just not sure if she wanted to hang out with me? I didn't really know what to say, so I didn't say anything. I wanted to go, but I didn't really feel like she wanted me to, and the last thing I wanted was for things to get awkward between us.

After a few minutes, Jill added, "It's at Natalie's ex-boyfriend's house, so we are all going in support of her."

So that was why she was hesitant. I could support that. I knew that the next time I see Brad, ex-boyfriend or not, I was going to need a little support myself. Plus, I had been using Natalie and Jill as a support system, without them knowing, for weeks now. They have been my "buffer" with Ethan.

"Sure. My mom should be okay with it. What time?" I asked. A party really did sound great. It would be just what I needed to take my mind off all the boy drama that I had been avoiding. I needed a little girl time. I didn't even realize it, but I hadn't had girl time for so long.

"I'll pick you up at eight," Natalie said with a big smile on her face. "Make sure you wear something dressy. It's a senior party."

"Okay." I drew the word out longer than I had intended. She hadn't mentioned a boyfriend, or ex-boyfriend, the entire time I had known her. "So you were dating a senior? When did you break up?" I was trying to sound interested, but I really couldn't care less about her ex-boyfriend. I was just happy that I had friends and that I was not going to be spending yet another Friday night doing homework.

"He broke up with me a few months ago. He's a real jerk. I should have known better. A couple of girls warned me that he would string me along and then break my heart." It sounded like they were pretty serious, I guess, if she was talking about him breaking her heart. You could see that there was some serious anger growing inside of her. She was not over this guy yet, and I felt bad for him if he crossed her path tonight.

"So why are we going to his party tonight if you dislike him so much?"

"I don't know. It's a party, a senior party, and I kind of want to go and see what he's up to. I have a feeling that he's started to see someone."

"You know what you should do?" I asked with a hint of mischief in my voice. She looked at me and shook her head. I could see the tears she was holding back. "You should find a date for tonight and then show up at his party. Maybe he will realize what he's missing."

"*Oh my god.* You are a genius!" She was screaming, clapping her hands, and bouncing in her seat. I don't think she even realized it.

"Wow. That's a really great idea," Jill added. She seemed to be a bit too much of a follower sometimes. They all did. It was like Natalie was up on a pedestal, and all her friends were bowing down at her feet. I was not going to be like that. "Who are you going to ask, Natalie?"

"I don't know. I haven't thought about anyone else for the last year or so, even before he-who-shall-remain-nameless and I started dating."

I could hear the anger in her voice when she was talking about him again.

Jill and Natalie brainstormed about who she should ask for the rest of lunch. I kept out of their conversation since I wasn't sure who any of the guys were. I felt a little bad for the poor soul who was chosen since it was my idea, and I felt a little bad for her ex, even though I figured he deserved it. Revenge was not my style, but it kind of sounded like she wanted him back, and this would be the best way to make him jealous.

By the end of lunch, they had picked their "victim" and were setting off to find him. Since Natalie would be riding with Morgan if all went well, I was going to be picking Jill up instead since she didn't have a car. We were going to meet at this guy's house at eight thirty.

The rest of the day went by quickly. I was nervous about going to this party but also very excited. It really did sound like fun, and maybe I would be able to make a few more friends, not that I didn't like the ones I had. I was used to being so busy with tennis that the few close friends that I kept at home were all that I ever needed. Right now, I was anything but busy. Tennis tryouts weren't for another week, and if I didn't make the team, then I was going to be really bored here until I went home for the summer.

Just as the bell rang for school to be over, I found myself alone in the yearbook office, finishing up the advertising letters I had been working on that week. I heard the bell, then I heard the door open and close a bunch of times, and just as I was getting ready to print the final draft that needed to be approved, I heard the door one last time.

"Ms. Phillips I'm in here," I called out to her. She had been in a meeting with some of the students for most of the class, trying to finalize the layout of the book. I still needed to get her approval before I could send the letters out. "I need you to approve the final draft so that I can—" I turned around as I was talking to her and stopped midsentence, realizing that she was not the one who had come back in the room.

"Hey," he said. There was a long pause, and when I finally got the courage to look up from my shoes, I noticed that he was staring at his. Neither of us felt comfortable around each other apparently, or at least we knew we couldn't make eye contact. "I know you have been avoiding me, but can we talk for a minute?"

"Um, I really don't have time. I need to get home." I was talking fast all the sudden and shoving things in my bag. I grabbed the letter off the printer and put it in Ms. Phillips's mailbox for editing. As I moved toward him, my feet slowed on their own. I wanted to run, but apparently my legs didn't agree with me.

He put his hand on my shoulder and moved in front of me. His hands slid down my arms and ended up on my waist. At that point, I was having a hard time controlling my breathing and was still afraid to look at him. *Deep breath in, exhale, repeat.*

When I finally had the courage to look up at him, he was staring right into my eyes, into my soul. I couldn't look away. I was drawn to him in that moment. I wanted to reach out and run my fingers through his hair, tug on his barbell, pull myself into his arms, and inhale the scent that was only his. I shook the thoughts from my mind and looked away.

"Will you please take a few minutes and talk to me?" He sounded like he was begging, and I gave in with the slightest nod of my head. I don't think that I even realized that I was nodding until it was over and I had agreed.

We sat on opposite sides of the desk, but the room was small, and suddenly I felt too close to him again. I knew that we needed to have this talk. I had been avoiding this for weeks, and just when I was about to speak up, my phone vibrated in my pocket. I put up my finger to let him know I'll be a minute, and I walked out of the office to take the phone call, not really caring who it was at that moment.

"Hello?" I said, the relief apparent in the one word that I spoke.

"Hey, it's Natalie. I managed to get a date for me, but he has a friend and since I'm pretty sure you aren't seeing anyone, I told him we could double."

I glanced through the window of the office and felt a bit of relief wash over me for some reason. "Sounds fun," I replied. "What about Jill, though?"

"She'll be fine. We'll meet up like we planned. You bring Jill to the party, and I'll bring Ben, your date."

"Okay. I'll see you a little after eight then. Later."

After I hung up, I went back into the office and felt a little more confident. I didn't know who this Ben person was, but I had a date, and I could use that as a way to get out of this conversation, maybe. Did I really want to get out of having the conversation? My body was on high alert being so close to him, and I really just wanted to kiss him. I was standing in the doorway, staring at the back of his neck, watching him intently when I made my decision. I couldn't let my body dictate this decision.

"Let's make this quick," I started, trying to sound in control, pressed for time, irritated. I knew how I was trying to sound, but as the words vibrated through my ears, I sounded breathless. "I have plans, and I need to get home." I'm pretty sure that I whispered that last sentence.

"What are you doing tonight because—"

I cut him off before he could ask any other questions. "I have a double date, and I need to go get ready. Can we please talk about this some other time? I don't even really see why we are talking about it at all. You have a girlfriend, and I am dating, so there really isn't much to talk about now after all."

Wow! I can really be mean when I want to be. Since when did I grow a pair? I knew that he was no good for me, that I didn't want to be with someone who was a cheater, but still my body was defying me and reacting to him.

"I guess you're right. Enjoy your *date*," he said. He was out the door before I could reply, and for that I was thankful. I was standing behind the desk with my mouth open in shock. I was shocked by not only his reaction but also how I acted. Crap! I didn't want to hurt anyone's feeling, but I needed to protect my own first.

I pulled up to the address that Natalie had texted me earlier that night, with the radio blasting and Jill and I singing at the top of our lungs. We both sounded awful, but the music was almost loud enough that we couldn't hear our own voices. Almost.

After I turned the car off, I sent Natalie a quick text to let her know we were there and to meet us out front. There was a bit of a chill in the air that I could feel, but I only had on a sweater—a very low-cut sweater—and jeans. I had left my jacket at home, knowing that it would be incredibly hot inside the house. I wrapped my arms tightly around my chest as we walked toward the massive front doors.

As we were opening the door, I could see Natalie rushing toward us, two pretty hot guys following behind her. She almost knocked us over with a group hug when she got to us. I could smell the faint scent of something sweet mixed with alcohol on her breath. I had to roll my eyes. I knew that I wasn't going to be drinking that much tonight, but I was not going to look down on my friends for enjoying themselves. Plus, I have a feeling she would need a little "liquid courage" when she'd run into her ex.

Natalie weighted only a little over a hundred pounds but didn't look like she was sickly. She was taller than my average 5'5" by a couple inches but perfectly tan and perfectly toned. I remember her telling me that she planned to run track this spring. She had almost every inch of her well-toned body on display tonight in the not-so-modest strapless dress she was wearing. I thought that I was cold outside. She must have been freezing.

She pulled away and introduced both of us to Ben and her date, Morgan. I didn't know whether to shake their hands or give them a hug, so I just gave a smile and a small wave. I think Ben knew how uncomfortable I was because he came over and took my hand. I let him intertwine our fingers, and he gave my hand a reassuring squeeze. Out of the corner of my eye, I caught both Jill and Natalie grinning at me.

"Let's get you something to drink," he whispered in my ear, and he pulled me away from my friends.

"Sure," I replied. I had only been to a handful of parties where there had been alcohol readily available, and this one seemed like there would be more than enough alcohol for the entire high school if they were to show up. I was not going to be getting drunk since I drove, so I opted for a beer and planned to take small sips throughout the night.

As we walked back to where we left Natalie, Morgan, and Jill, I started to look around the house. It was very large and very beautiful. It was also packed to the brim with people that I didn't know. If Ben let go of my hand, I would be lost in a heartbeat, surrounded by sweaty bodies. I was completely out of my comfort zone.

We found our friends and started to move through the house as a group. Natalie led us through a hallway and then another and finally downstairs. I forgot she had probably been here before. As we rounded the corner at the bottom of the stairs, I realized that there were even more people down here. We found a small corner to talk and stayed there most of the night.

I was actually having a good time, and I was afraid to leave the circle, even though I had to go to the bathroom. Finally, after holding it longer than I thought was possible, I let go of Ben's hand and asked him to hold my beer. Natalie gave me directions to the closest bathroom; of course, there was going to be more than one in a house this size, and I dashed away.

The first bathroom was locked, and the people in it were not using it for the same reason I needed to if the moaning sounds were correct. I dashed up the stairs and started looking around for another option. There was a line for the next bathroom I found, and I knew that I wouldn't be able to hold it. There had to be one more with at least a smaller line of people. I dashed up the staircase in the main hallway and hoped that I would be able to find just one more bathroom. Thankfully, I did, and I sat down just as my bladder was about to explode.

As I washed my hands, I took in the beauty of the bathroom. Natalie's ex definitely came from money. Even the bathroom was decorated nicer than my entire house. It was almost as big as the smallest room in our house, and that room never felt so small until tonight.

I reluctantly dried my hands on the plush towels since they were the only ones available. I felt so bad about using such a nice towel to dry my hands that I spent the next several minutes trying to refold it just like the one next to it so that it didn't look disturbed. I checked my makeup, and then just as I was about to open the door to leave, it opened, and I screamed, jumped, and covered my eyes all at the same time.

"What are you doing in here?"

Crap! That voice was too familiar. Why was he here?

"I'm sorry. I just needed to use the bathroom, and all the others I found were occupied. What do you care anyway?" I was defensive. Had he followed me up here? I thought I was clear earlier. He seemed to get the message, or so I thought.

He took a step closer to me, and I could see his eyes perfectly clear in the bathroom lighting. He was in control of his body (and mine a little if I was being honest), so I knew he probably hadn't had much to drink. He took another step closer, and as I tried to take a step back, I realized that I was already flushed against the glass shower doors. I was trapped in more ways than one.

Before I knew it, his hands were on my waist and he was leaning his forehead against mine. Crap! How do I keep putting myself in these situations with him? He always seemed to have the upper hand when it comes to things like this.

"Where's your date?" It sounded like he was growling. Was he a little jealous? Maybe he was not as okay as he seemed this afternoon.

"He's downstairs in the basement with the rest of my friends. I should probably get back down there. I've been gone a while, so they might be trying to find me. I don't want to worry them since I am driving one of the cars." I was rambling on about insignificant stuff, and I knew it. I had probably only been gone for ten minutes, and no one probably even noticed. I had to distract him and myself. I pulled away and sat on the toilet. "So are you stalking me, or were you just looking for an open bathroom too?"

He cocked his head to the right and smiled. His smile reached his eyes, and I was caught in a trance for a minute. He said something, but I didn't hear him. I couldn't help but stare. His shirt was tight across his chest, and I could see his piercing. His sleeves were shorter than normal, and I could see a tattoo peaking out from underneath one. I had never noticed it before. Was it new? I reached up to touch it but pulled away quickly, realizing what I was about to do just in time.

"Becca, did you hear a word I just said?"

"No, sorry. I kind of spaced out for a minute." I knew I was blushing because I could feel the heat from my cheeks. "What did you say?"

"I said I was looking for you. I saw you come in with Natalie earlier, and then you disappeared. I saw you come in here when I was coming out of my bedroom, and I was waiting for you. What were you doing in here forever?"

His words didn't register right away, but when they did, it felt like my jaw hit the floor in shock. "You live here?" I was screaming out of shock, I think, but no matter what, I was defiantly screaming.

"You didn't know?" His eyes were wide with shock.

I got up and walked past him, and this time, he didn't try to stop me. He let me go because he was just as shocked as I was. I had kissed Natalie's ex-boyfriend while they were on a "break," and now they weren't together. Crap! I thought the drama was over.

CHAPTER 8

I sent Natalie a quick text saying that I wasn't feeling well and was leaving. I got in my car and threw it in Reverse as I noticed a tall dark figure standing on the front porch staring at me. I should have known that he would be watching me. I should have known that he would follow me, that he would come after me. I almost felt bad that he couldn't enjoy his party because of me.

As I pulled onto his street, my phone alerted me to a new text. I didn't know the number, so I ignored it and turned up the music. I knew it wasn't Ethan or Natalie, but it was a local area code. I drove toward my house with the music blasting as loud as it had been earlier, but I wasn't singing this time. I didn't even hear the music as I was so lost in thought.

I wondered if Natalie knew. Was the whole party a setup? Did she want to torture me because I had gone out with him once? If I had known then what I knew now, I would have stayed far away from him. I would have hidden my feelings from everyone, even myself. I would never try to break up anyone's relationship, and I didn't want to break up one of my only friendships. Crap!

This situation was feeling all-too familiar. Brad and Ethan seemed to be the same person only in different locations. Why was this happening again? Why was my life getting so complicated, so full of drama? All I wanted was to be a normal teenage girl, without all the excess drama.

It's all Brads fault. Damn him for putting me in the middle of his relationship. I didn't want to be the reason he broke up with Claire, even if it was the truth. I wanted to be with him, but like always, I was fighting those feelings every day to avoid hurting him even more in the end. And then there's frickin' Ethan. He knew that I was becoming friends with Natalie. Why didn't he say anything? Did he assume I would put it all together on my own? I wasn't even living here when they broke up or took a break or whatever.

I pulled myself out of my head, out of my thoughts, and focused back on the road. I only had about half a beer, but I knew that if I was caught for anything, I would be in big trouble since I was underage. My body felt nothing but rage at the moment, and the alcohol was actually the least of my concerns.

As I pulled in to my driveway and turned down the music, I realized that I was going to be home alone. It was only nine thirty, and it looked like I would be spending another Friday night at home with homework, which was fine, compared to what I had been doing thirty minutes ago. Hopefully, it would be enough to distract me from what I was feeling.

I grabbed my purse and my cell, which was lit up from another text, and headed inside. I went straight up to my room and plopped on my bed. I opened my cell to see that I had six new texts.

CALL ME WHEN U GET HOME. BEN

How did he get my number?

ARE YOU ALL RIGHT? WHAT HAPPENED?

Natalie sent me that after Ben? Did she already know what had happened? Does she know about my "relationship" with Ethan?

I'M SORRY.

I was temped to text him back, but I didn't have any words to reply to him. I understood that he was sorry, that he now realizes that I had no idea that him and Natalie had been dating but...

HEY, JUST WANTED TO SEE WHAT U WERE UP TO. CALL ME.

Okay, now I had to deal with Brad on top of everything else. This night was getting better and better. Why is it when it rains it pours? Can't I catch a break, even a small one?

ARE YOU HOME YET? BEN

It was funny that he signed his name again assuming that I wouldn't store his number in my phone. Kind of cute actually. No expectations. The last thing I needed right now was to turn this triangle I was caught in into a square.

I NEED YOU TO CALL ME NOW!

What the hell? I was not going to call him. I didn't want to speak to him. If I had wanted to continue our conversation, I would have done so in the bathroom. Who did he think he was? Demanding that I call him was not the best way to get me to call. How about asking me nicely? I was angry, and I realized it was all because of him.

I sent out a quick text to Ben to let him know I was home and that I had a nice time with him. I told him I would call him tomorrow if I was feeling better. I got a reply instantly, asking if I wanted to go to lunch on Sunday. I told him yes and that I would call him tomorrow.

I tossed my phone on the bed and stared at it for a minute, deciding whether or not I should call Ethan. I was angry enough to give him a piece of my mind but almost to the point that I was afraid I wouldn't be able to get my point across clearly. I was almost beyond angry at this point. I think it had more to do with the fact that now I knew I couldn't have him, that I wouldn't let myself have him. I was disappointed in a way.

I snagged my phone and turned it off. I would deal with it in the morning. It was close to ten, and at that point, I just wanted to go to bed. I needed to clear my head, and talking was not going to be the way to get that done. I knew I wouldn't be able to sleep, so after I changed into some pajamas, I went downstairs and popped in my favorite movie of all times, *My Best Friend's Wedding*. How ironic in a totally screwed up kind of way.

I was just about to hit Play when I heard a faint knock at the door. I wasn't expecting anyone. I walked over to the window and pulled back the shade just a bit so I could see on the front porch. Crap! Why was he here? Oh yeah, I never called him back. Crap!

I didn't want to let him in, but I knew he would just continue to knock since he knew I was home. As I turned the knob, my hands started to shake a little and my heart began to race. I was a little scared, but more than anything, I was nervous. I was angry at him. I was angry at myself. I was angry that I was in this position at all. I just wanted the drama to end.

"What are you doing here?" This was how I greeted him. You could hear the irritation and anger in my voice loud and clear.

"We need to talk, and you turned your phone off."

"It died."

"No, it didn't. I know you turned it off to try avoiding me, but it's not going to work. So are you going to invite me in, or are you going to come out here?"

"Neither. I am going to watch a movie and go to bed. You need to go back to your party—wait, what about your party? Aren't you suppose to be hosting? Who's watching your house?" All of the anger left my voice, and my concern snuck in. Crap! Why did I have to care so much about him?

"You say that a lot you know, and I don't think you even realize it."

When I looked up, he was smiling at me. I was thinking out loud again, and I really needed to stop doing that if I ever wanted to have a private thought again.

"Look, you need to get back to your party, and I am getting cold, so I will see you later." I attempted to close the door, but he stopped it with his foot. I opened it back up and put my hand on my hip, trying my best to scream at him with just one look.

"I closed the party down, and I am not leaving here until we talk. I have all night to wait, but I would much rather do it inside where it's warmer since I didn't bring a jacket in my mad rush to get here."

Mad rush? He closed down his party so he could come talk to me?

I glanced over at the clock to see that it wasn't even ten thirty yet, and I knew that his actions would be the talk of the school Monday morning. Great! Now there was even more drama that I was partially the cause of. I felt bad for causing him so much trouble, and it was chilly outside. I stepped aside and motioned him in. After I closed the door, I walked over and plopped on the couch without even looking at him.

A few minutes later, he was sitting next to me in a comfortable silence, watching the movie. I yawned a couple of times about partway through, and before I knew it, I was cuddled against his chest and failing at not falling asleep.

I woke up the next morning still on the couch, still cuddled in Ethan's arms. We were lying side by side, and our legs were intertwined. I could feel his even breathing and his heartbeat, my hand resting on his chest. I tried to lie still, but my bladder was full, and I needed to get up.

Slowly I began to untangle myself and crawl off the couch without waking him. I wondered where my mom was when I heard her humming in the kitchen. She was making breakfast. She must have seen us on the couch last night, but she didn't wake me up or kick him out. It was probably because we were both completely dressed.

When I walked out of the bathroom, I heard Ethan and my mom talking. So much for not waking him up. When I entered the kitchen, his back was to me, and he was blowing on his coffee. I walked past him and helped myself to a cup without saying a word to him. I think my mom felt the uncomfortable silence and excused herself, asking me to flip the pancakes when they were ready.

"So… sorry I passed out on you last night." I was trying to make light conversation.

"It's fine. I fell asleep a little after you did. It was easy with you wrapped in my arms."

I looked up to see him smiling from ear to ear, dimple winking at me, and I could feel the blush creeping up my neck and heating my cheeks. It was incredibly hard to stay mad at him when he was so damn cute. I had to turn around to keep myself from smiling like an idiot at his comment. I flipped the pancakes and pretended to stir the batter.

"Did you want to stay for breakfast?

"Your mom already invited me."

I could hear that his voice was closer than before. The hair on the back of my neck stood up, and I felt him standing behind me just as he slipped his arms around my waist.

"Plus, I am not leaving until we talk," he said, kissing my neck. Crap!

"Okay. Breakfast first." I was trying to sound mature about the whole situation, but I knew that in the end I was going to be a flipping mess.

I tried to wiggle out of his embrace, but he only held me tighter, and I gave up without much of a fight. I removed the pancakes from the griddle and rotate myself in his arms. His eyes were sparkling, and his look was intense. I could feel my legs begin to go weak, and I braced the counter behind me just as his lips met mine. He was gentle, and it only lasted a few seconds, but my entire body responded to him, and all I wanted was more.

We sat in silence while we ate pancakes with my mom and sister. Amy kept looking at him, then at me, then at him, like she was trying to figure out what was going on. She was incredibly smart for her age, and I knew that if she saw me look at him, she would figure it out. She had seen us asleep on the couch when she came home from the movies with my mom last night. She might only be twelve, but she was incredibly insightful. If she was just a few years older, I would be asking her for advice.

After breakfast, I took a quick shower and changed into some clean clothes. Once I was presentable, we decided to go for a walk. I grabbed my jacket, and we went out the back door. Our backyard wasn't anything special, but we did live on the edge of the desert and there was plenty of privacy and plenty of open space to explore. Walking in to the wide, open land behind the house was like walking into the unknown for me.

"So," he finally said, breaking the silence after we were about a football field away from the house, "are you gonna hear me out?"

"Sure. I just can't make any promises as to where this is going to go." I was motioning between us with my hand, and he caught it midair and intertwined our fingers. I was so caught off guard that I stopped walking abruptly.

"Look, I know that this is a messy situation. It never occurred to me that you had no idea who I was dating when we first met, and it never occurred to me that you two were becoming so close. I broke up with her after our 'date.'" He was using air quotes. "She didn't take the news as hard as I thought she would, and I think it's because we had been on such a long break from each other already. If I had thought about it at all, I would have made sure that you knew that we had been seeing each other. I kind of figured she told you. You were with her at my house, after all. What was I suppose to think?"

"She never said anything about a boyfriend or that she was seeing anyone. When she invited me to the party, she referred to you as 'he-who-shall-remain-nameless,' so I still had no clue that

I was going to end up at your house." I paused, not sure of how I wanted to say what was really on my mind, but I knew I needed to get it off my chest. "Look, it's pretty obvious that I like you, but I just can't do this. Natalie is my friend. Maybe if we hadn't become friends, then this could end differently, but I cannot turn my back on her, and I don't plan to sneak around, either."

We turned around and started to walk back toward the house. As it came in to view again, I realized that we were still holding hands, and I tried to pull away. He held on tighter, and we stopped walking again. I felt him pull me close to him, but I didn't have the strength to look up.

"You and I will be together." It was a statement, not a question, and he intended it that way. "I know that I won't be able to stay away from you. You have drawn me in, and I only want to get closer to you. So we will find a way to deal with the Natalie thing. It may take awhile, but we will deal with this if you're willing to try."

I looked up at him this time, and he was staring straight into my eyes. I couldn't help but want to believe him that it could really work, even if it was for just a few minutes. Then he kissed me, and I wanted it to work. I wanted him more than anything I had ever wanted before. I put every emotion that I had behind that kiss, wanting to tell him with without words how I felt. I wanted to show him what I wanted from him. I wanted to show him that I was willing to try. I could have kissed him for the rest of my life, but my phone rang, and the moment was lost. I pulled it out of my pocket and knew that we would never be, no matter how much either of us wanted it.

Natalie was calling.

CHAPTER 9

My hands shook as I hit the Ignore button on my cell. I wanted to talk to Natalie, but I wasn't sure that I knew what to say. Our relationship felt awkward to me with the knowledge I had gained in the last twenty-four hours. Was she even aware of what was going on? Did she know about Ethan and me? There were a million things going through my mind as we finished walking back to my house in silence. I wasn't sure what to say to him. I knew that I wanted to be with him, but I also knew that I was not willing to risk my friendship with Natalie.

As we approached the back porch, he kissed my hand and then let go and pulled his keys out of his pocket. I knew that there was still so much to say, so much to talk about, but I wasn't ready to open myself up to the destruction that was inevitable. Instead, I watched him walk around the side of the house and heard his car start before I went inside, up to my room, and let myself cry.

I was pulling myself back together when my phone began to ring again. I looked at the caller ID and saw that it was Brad. I could deal with this. Right? My heart couldn't break any more today if I didn't let it.

"Hey," I said, trying to sound as upbeat as possible.

"What's up?" Brad replied.

"Not much. How's the snow?"

"Cold. How's the weather there? Is it still chilly at night?"

"Yeah, but it's getting warmer during the days so it kind of makes up for it." I could talk about the weather, but I knew we were just talking around the bigger things. "So what else is new?"

"Not much. I finally got Claire to leave me alone after ignoring her for the last month."

I knew what he had been doing, but still hearing it shocked me a little. She deserved a better ending. I had finally come to terms with the fact that he broke up with her because of me, because she wasn't me, but it still didn't make me feel any better about the situation.

"If that's really what you want, then I'm happy for you."

He didn't respond right away because he knew that I still wouldn't talk to him about *us*. The last time we broached the subject a few weeks ago, I had shut him down by telling him that I wouldn't discuss it. I would love to be able to tell him the truth about how I felt about him, but things couldn't change between us, so why put that strain on our relationship? It already felt like it was about to break apart at any given moment.

"So anything exciting happening there?"

I really wanted to tell him about all the drama that was going on. I knew he would understand the stupid situation that I had been pulled into, but I also didn't want to talk to him about my relationship with Ethan, or the lack thereof. He was my best friend—he was supposed to be the one I ran to with problems like this. I just couldn't bring myself to say the words. My situation with him was too much like my situation with Ethan.

"Nope. Same stuff, different day." I was at a complete loss for words. I felt like I was lying to him by keeping things from him. "I was thinking about playing tennis this spring. Tryouts are in about a week."

"That's great, Becca. I told you that you would get your game back. Have you been practicing a lot lately?"

I had been practicing almost every day and sometimes on the weekends for a while, but as of recently, I had been avoiding the courts. In truth, I had been avoiding Ethan. I knew that there were other places that I could practice, but I never put the effort into finding them.

"Not as much as I want to, and definitely not as much as I should be. I still have some time to get my game back together." *Like a whole week. Crap!*

"Well, you should go out and practice today. Do any of your friends play well enough to volley with you?"

Only one.

"No, but they have boards up at the school that I can hit against, and I am still focusing on my serve for the most part. I have about twenty balls in my bag, so I can go for a while, but then I have to chase them all down so I can go again."

"Well, when I come out, I will hit with you."

Brad was horrible at tennis. He could barely return a soft volley, let alone one of my serves. It took a moment for his words to sink in, and when they did, I was shocked speechless. He was going to come and visit me? His parents said yes? Crap! I was excited and scared.

"Really?" You could hear the excitement in my voice. I couldn't contain the joy that I was feeling over just the thought of being able to put my arms around him and breathe his clean, masculine scent. It wasn't until after we ended our call that the ensuing dread kicked in, and I could feel the bile rise in my throat. I wouldn't be able to avoid anything if he was here. I was going to have to figure out what I was going to do, and then when he got here, we were going to have to deal with it.

I made the tennis team with ease. I was nervous during tryouts for the first time in my life, though. There were more girls there than I thought there would be, and the simple fact that it seemed like all of them had played before scared me to death. After I ran my drills and started to watch some of the other girls doing theirs, I mentally thanked my parents for the private lessons and the doctor for insisting I go to physical therapy for my shoulder. I had an edge to my game that I didn't see any of the other girls had. My training over the past week had paid off, and my shoulder was sore, but I still managed to ace all ten serves to the assistant coach. I was pretty sure he was impressed.

There were a few girls who were sitting off to the side of the tryouts. They looked to be my age, so I figured they were just watching. When I arrived at my first practice a few days later, I learned that they were the team captains, and by the looks that they gave me, they were not impressed. It made we wonder whose spot I had taken on the team to deserve the evil glares.

I let it go and worked my butt off the first few weeks. Our first match was coming up, and the coach still had not posted where he wanted us to play. I was hoping for singles since the other girls didn't really want to have anything to do with me. I had always played the top singles spot back home, but with the smaller size of the school, there was not a lot of competition on the team. I never had to try out after my first year, I was captain the last season, and I had held the same spot since I started playing. Competition within the team was new to me, but I was up for it as long as they understood that I was not going to be backing down.

Our first match was exactly two weeks before Brad was set to arrive. My mind was wandering from him to Ethan and back again throughout the day. I had yet to talk to Natalie about what had happened at the party a few weeks back. Ben had been calling me every so often to ask me out, but I had been using tennis as an excuse to avoid him. It was all too much to handle at once. I wanted to figure things out for myself before I opened up to anyone else.

Ethan and I had been texting but not talking. He would ask how I was and vice versa, but we never talked about anything deeper than that. He had been the first person I texted when I found out I made the tennis team, and he was who I was texting right now to tell him I was playing in the two singles spot.

CONGRATS!

THX. THE GRL AT 1 IS RLY GOOD I GUESS

NOT REALLY. YOU COULD TAKE HER I BET

I GUESS WE SHALL SEE. R U COMING TO WATCH 2DAY

I WOULDNT MISS U IN THAT HOT LITTLE SKIRT AND
TIGHT TOP FOR ANYTHING. YOU SHOULD USE UR OTHER
RACKET THOUGH

I glanced down at my outfit; it was pretty form fitting. My gaze shifted then to my right hand. I didn't even realize that I had grabbed my older racket until I read his text. Huh? My phone tinged again to alert me to a new text message.

TWO OCLOCK

I looked slightly to my right where I thought two o'clock would be, and I saw him. He was standing just outside the fence by a tree. I waved and then shot him a text, thanking him for coming to watch me play. When my phone started to ding before I could send his text, I almost dropped it.

GOOD LUCK! DO I GET 2 SEE U PLAY WHILE IM THERE

Leave it to Brad to make sure he wished me good luck. He would only get to see me play once, but I knew he really wanted to be there to support me making my "comeback," as he liked to call it. I wanted to prove to him that I really was back to being 100 percent next week.

I sent the original text to Ethan and then dropped a quick text to Brad before swapping out for my better racket and heading onto the courts to stretch. I was one of the first matches that would be played today, so I only had about ten minutes before we were to get started. Let my comeback begin!

The girl I played was extremely talented. She had a kick-ass forehand but not much of a serve, and she had a really hard time returning a few of my serves. I ended up winning, by quite a bit, but I found it hard to be excited in that moment. I wanted to play against their best player, not their second best. I was used to being at the top, playing the best available, and winning. I couldn't even begin to describe what it felt like to not be the top contender.

Brit, the girl who was playing one singles that day, ended up losing to her opponent. I was one of only three people who ended up winning. Our team was strong, but obviously not strong enough. It wasn't until I met up with Ethan after the matches were over that I learned that most of the other team had gone on to play at state last year, including the girl I had beaten. I felt a little better after learning that little tidbit of knowledge and went home with my head held a little bit higher.

The weeks went by faster than I thought they would in anticipation of Brad's arrival. I spent most of the afternoon Thursday cleaning out the guest room and getting it ready for him. Natalie had insisted that she got to meet my best friend— she could not get over that it was a guy after she saw the picture of us that Brad had given me with my ring. I think it had more to do with how Brad looked and less to do with him being my best friend. He was intoxicatingly good-looking after all.

She had been dating Morgan for a little over a month now officially. It seemed like they were truly happy, and it made me wonder if I even wanted to bring up the whole Ethan thing with her. She never mentioned him anymore, and I thought that maybe that was my all clear of sorts to go ahead and pursue something with him if I wanted to. Did I want to?

She had caught me staring at him a few weeks ago during class. I lied to her and told her that I was just lost in thought, and she bought it the first time. After she caught me again, I confessed that I thought he was cute. She never mentioned that she used to date him, so neither did I. She told me that he was a player and that I was better suited for someone like Ben if I was looking for a boyfriend. She didn't forbid me to date him. It kind of came across as a warning to be careful, more than anything else. I should have taken that moment to tell her, but I chickened out and knew that I would never be able to.

So as the final hour approached to leave for the airport to pick up Brad, I started to panic. Natalie was having a "thing" at her house tonight to welcome Brad to Tucson. I thought it was unnecessary, but she insisted, especially since her parents had taken off for some sort of third honeymoon. I didn't know who was invited, but I saw her talking to a bunch of people in class, and I knew that Jill would be there. I assumed Morgan and Ben would be in attendance, but other than that, I wasn't in the loop. She could invite anyone she wanted; it was her house after all. I was just a guest at this party.

I found Ethan waiting for me by my locker as I approached. He was smiling at me—that full-megawatt dimple-showing smile that I loved so much. His eyes were sparkling, like they had been that morning we had breakfast together. I was caught up in a trance again as I walked toward him. I wanted to put my hands in his hair, tug him toward me, and kiss him with every bit of passion I had in my body. I didn't, of course. We were in the middle of the hallway, at school, and Natalie could be lurking anywhere.

"Hey," I said as I finally reached my locker.

"Hey. Are you headed straight to the airport, or do you have time to grab a coffee before you have to pick *him* up?" The way he said *him* made me straighten my back a little and take notice of his tone. He was jealous.

"I have time for coffee, but only if you are going to behave yourself." I was teasing him, and I know that he could hear that in my voice. "I'll meet you at the Bean in about twenty?"

"Sound good."

I shut my locker, but before I could walk away, he had me pinned against it and was kissing me deeply. I forgot all about being in a public place. I forgot all about Natalie being around somewhere. I completely let my mind shut down.

He pulled away, just as quickly as he had attacked me, breathless. "Now I can promise to behave." He said this with a smile as he turned and walked away, leaving me stunned and staring at his fabulous behind.

I pulled myself together and headed to my car. There was no time to swing home now if I was going to have coffee with Ethan before picking up Brad. I could still feel his lips on mine as I drove out of the parking lot. My phone chimed with an incoming text, but I ignored it. I would check my phone once my head was screwed back on straight.

I pull into the Bean and noticed that Ethan was already here. He must have come straight from school as well. I grabbed my purse and my phone. I checked to see who sent me a text, and it was Ben. I don't really want to deal with him right now, but I open it anyway to see what he wants.

I dropped my phone on the seat as my jaw dropped open. He sent me a picture. Not just any picture either. It was a picture of Ethan kissing me. No note attached, just the picture. I wondered who else he sent it to? Did he sent it to Natalie? Was this going to be how she would find out? *Crap! Crap! Crap!* I should have just talked to her.

I got out of my car and walked inside to find Ethan at a table by the window, staring at me. He already had our drinks and stood to pull out my chair as I approached the table. He was always a gentleman when it came to the little things like that. I knew that he could see something was wrong. The concern in his eyes was evident, but he didn't ask. He knew that I would tell him if I wanted to. I didn't, but I needed to.

"So that little display of affection we shared in the hallway has gone public..." I trailed off, not knowing how else to put it. He looked confused, but I couldn't say any more than that.

"Do I need to talk to Natalie?"

"I don't know if she knows yet, but I was sent a picture of us kissing, and I'm gonna guess that she will see it sooner rather than later. It was inevitable, I guess." I sighed because there really was nothing else to say. She would have found out eventually. We were already starting to have a hard time staying away from each other as it was.

"Oh. I don't really know what to say. I don't really care what she thinks, but I know you do. I want to be with you, and if she has a problem with that, I really don't care." He laid it out there like it was normal for this to be happening. He stated it like it's normal to have to hide your feelings for your friend's ex-boyfriend because it happens every day. This was not normal in my world. What do I even say to that?

"Oh. Look, I should really get to the airport." I stood, but he grabbed my hand and tugged me back into my chair. I let him because I didn't want to lose his touch. I loved how our hands felt wrapped in each others. I loved the way a simple thing like holding hands warmed me on the inside.

"Before you go, I have to ask you something." He paused, and I know that whatever he wants to ask was hard for him. He cleared his throat and opened his mouth to continue before shutting it again. I realized that he was looking over my shoulder and not at me anymore. When I glanced back, I saw Natalie staring at us, mouth agape. I pulled my hand from his and stand, but she was already out the door and gone.

I plopped back in my seat and put my head in my hands. *This day could not get any worse.* That's what I was thinking until he spoke, and although I heard the words, I asked him to repeat himself.

"Do you love Brad? Is that why he's coming out here? I need to know because I need to know where I stand. I want to believe he's just a friend, but the way you talk about him speaks volumes about how much you care about him. Is he really just your friend?"

I was taken back, and I didn't know how to answer him. I couldn't answer these questions when I was asking myself, let alone answer them for him. This was why I was scared that Brad was coming. I thought I was going to have this conversation with him, not with Ethan.

"I don't know. We are best friends, and I do love him, but I don't know what kind of love that is. It's all a little confusing for me, for him. I just don't know." I paused as I stood up. "I do know that no matter how I feel about him, it doesn't change how I feel about you." I walked away. It was the only thing I could do at that moment. I couldn't explain my feelings for him. I didn't understand my feelings for him.

I made my way to the baggage claim with my homemade sign in hand. Instead of putting his name on it, I wrote "Michigan," knowing he would be looking for me and not a sign anyway. I was looking through the crowd for him—his plane had landed about twenty minutes ago—when I felt a large pair of hands grab me by my hips and swing me in the air. He had gotten the jump on me. Damn him!

I swung around into his arms and held on tight, wrapping my legs around his waist. I knew he wouldn't drop me, but it felt so good to hold him that I didn't want to let go, not any time soon anyway. He smelled just like I remembered, he felt just like the last time I had hugged him, and there were tears just like last time as well. The only difference was that this time they were tears of joy.

I pulled back to get a good look at him, and I saw for the first time in what felt like forever a real look of joy on his face. I smiled up at him, happy to be able to see those luscious brown eyes of his, the gold around his irises sparking with joy. He wiped away the few tears that had crept from my eyes with the back of his hand. Then he leaned down, and his mouth was on mine. *Crap!*

CHAPTER 10

I pulled away breathless. Brad was grinning at me from ear to ear, and I couldn't help but smile. I knew that the kiss meant more to him that it meant to me, and I think he knew it to. God, I missed him. I missed his smile, and the way just looking into his eyes allowed my entire body to relax. I missed my best friend. It was then that the internal struggle that I had been having with myself died.

He grabbed the bag he had dropped on the ground next to us with one hand, pulled it up on his shoulder, and swung his other arm around me as we walked out of the airport like nothing had happened. It was amazing that after not seeing him for over three months, this felt completely normal to me.

We talked like nothing had changed. As we headed to my house, I tried to give him little bits and pieces of knowledge I had picked up about the city over the past few months. I showed him some of my favorite spots, and then we took a detour so that I could drive past the high school. He was shocked at how massive it was, just like I had been the first time I had seen it.

As we pulled into the driveway, I saw my mom rush out of the house to greet us. She gave Brad a big hug and a kiss on the cheek. I knew she would be glad to see him; convincing her to let him come and stay with us had been easier than I had originally thought that it would be. She had always had a soft spot for him. I always thought that she was secretly routing for us to get together, but she never said anything.

I gave him the royal tour of the house and showed him his room. He threw his bag down on the bed and swept me up in another hug. I held on for as long as I could before he pulled back and flopped down on his back on the bed, resting his head in his hands, causing his chiseled abdomen to become exposed. *Yum! Crap!*

"I can't believe I'm here right now, able to wrap my arms around you again."

"I know. It all seems a little surreal. I'm so glad you could come. I thought your parents would be more hesitant to let you fly so far alone."

"They were, but I told them that I would find a way without their help if that was what it took. Plus, I threatened to go to Panama City with Emma and Ella for spring break if they wouldn't let me come here. I guess they figured I would get in less trouble with you." He was giving me a cocky smirk as he said that last part. He was far from being a troublemaker, and his parents knew that.

"So we have about two hours before we need to head over to my friend Natalie's for your 'Welcome to Tucson' party she is throwing you." *Was she still having the party*, I thought to myself. I should probably send her a text. What about Ethan? Crap! I needed to text him too. "What do you want to do in the meantime?"

The look on his face said that he had a few ideas that I wanted to stay away from. I looked away and started to fidget with my nails, knowing this was a clear sign to him that I was ignoring what I just saw. He stood back up, started to walk toward me, but stopped short and started to look around the room.

"Why don't we grab some dinner at that little Italian place we passed on the way here, and then we can head to her house from there?" I suggested to break the silence. I knew that Brad was a sucker for Italian food and thought that maybe we could get past the tension in the room if we were able to get out in public for a while.

"Sure, sounds good." The tone of his voice said that he really liked my idea but, looking up at him, told me that we would not be getting past the tension any time soon.

"I'm gonna change and then we can go." I backed out of the guest room and ran down the hall. I immediately sent Natalie a text and patiently waited for her reply.

YES, PARTYS STILL ON. TALK LATER

OKAY. SEE U SOON THEN

I sent Ethan a text saying that I would call him later. I was waiting for his response when my phone rang and he was calling.

"Hey," I started but was interrupted by my door opening. Brad was walking in my room, looking sexy as hell, and I think my mouth happened to drop open a bit.

"Hey. I was wondering if you would make time to call me." Ethan said sarcastically.

"I didn't," I teased him. "I sent you a text saying that I would call you later. I am headed out to dinner right now. Can I give you a call when we get back tonight?"

"Yeah. I'll talk to you later then?" It was once again a question and not a statement. He wanted to make sure that I was going to call him.

"Yep. Talk to you later. Bye."

I didn't wait for him to say good-bye before I hung up. Brad was staring at me, and I knew that he was going to start asking questions.

"Boyfriend?" He asked, raising his eyebrow a little.

Wow! He nailed that on the first try, sort of.

"Nope, just a friend." I replied trying to sound nonchalant. I was not lying to him. We really weren't technically dating.

"It was a guy though, and I could see the look on your face. You like him."

He knew me a little too well.

"Yes, but it's complicated." That was the complete truth without getting into the nasty details. *Complicated* pretty much summed up my entire relationship status with everyone right now. "We need to head out to dinner if we are going to make it to Natalie's on time."

As we drove to Natalie's after dinner, we were both so silent you could have cut the air with a knife. I knew we needed to talk about what we were feeling. We needed to talk about the fact that he knew about another guy in my life. We needed to talk about a lot of things that we had avoided at dinner, but I was afraid that I would lose him again like I did the first time. I didn't want to feel like that again. We had just gotten to a point in our relationship where we seemed to accept that we were just friends, at least until he got off the plane today. His presence was all consuming of my heart. I wanted to be with him again now that he was within arm's reach. Would I always feel like this? Would I always feel like I was being pulled in two directions?

I pulled to the curb in front of Natalie's and cut the engine. I turned to Brad, and as soon as I did, he kissed me. I tried to fight what I was feeling, but my heart took control of the situation, and I stopped fighting. I wanted to kiss him. I wanted to be with him. All the hurtful things I had said to him, all the lies I had told him and told myself about not wanting to be with him disappeared, and it was just the two of us, kissing in my car like teenagers without a care in the world.

A knock on my window made me pull away with a little jump. I turned to see Ethan staring at me through a somewhat fogged window with his mouth agape. Could this have gotten any worse? I was a poster child for bad timing today—first, Natalie catching me with Ethan and now Ethan catching me with Brad. Was I really a bad person?

I was sitting in shock, staring out the front windshield. I had two sets of eyes on me, and I couldn't look at either one of them. I felt betrayed by my heart at that very moment. I wanted to kiss Brad, to feel his love for me pour into my body. I also knew that there was something powerful between me and Ethan that I couldn't explain to anyone, not even myself. He was the only other person who got me, besides Brad, and I was literally in between the two of them, both probably waiting for me to say something.

I knew my reaction when I saw Ethan spoke volumes to Brad about who he was, but I couldn't make myself say the words. Thankfully, he didn't ask. I hadn't told him anything about Ethan. I had actually avoided the topic at all costs, and even though he knew that I was hiding someone from him, he always dropped the subject, just like he did when I changed the subject this afternoon. I wanted to be with both of them for very different reasons, and it took that moment to realize it.

I slowly opened my door, got out, and walked past Ethan, up Natalie's driveway, leaving both of them behind. I was not going to cry tonight. I kept telling myself that all the way up the driveway, through the front door, and into the bathroom. Then I broke down and let it all out. I was so confused, and I knew that if I was confused, then I had two very confused guys outside waiting for me. They would be waiting for answers that I didn't have.

After about ten minutes, I finally pulled myself together and joined the party. Brad was already introducing himself to my friends when I came out of the bathroom, and Ethan was mingling on the other side of the room. I joined Brad, and his fingers locked with mine. If felt different than I remembered. I was nervous to be holding his hand in front of other people, in front of Ethan.

The night was pretty uneventful. Natalie had managed to get a couple of cases of beer, so the drinking was pretty toned down from most of the parties that she went to, thankfully. I didn't drink, and neither did Brad. We made our way around the room, talking to people that I knew pretty well. No one asked if we were dating, even though we caught a couple of odd looks when people realize that we were holding hands.

Natalie never mentioned the coffee house to me that night. I saw her talking with Ethan a few times, but it looked civil from where I was standing. I would catch him glancing in my direction every so often, and our eyes would meet. I couldn't tell what his mood was like because of the distance, but I knew that his eyes weren't sparkling like they normally do when he looks at me.

I tried to steer us to the opposite side of the room, away from Ethan most of the night. If he was able to get me alone, he would want to talk about what had happened in the car. Brad would want to talk about it too, so I tried to keep us socially on the move. It seemed to work, and by the time we were saying good-bye to my friends, I was hopeful that all was forgotten.

Brad and I never ended up talking about the moment in the car. I was afraid that he would ask questions and that I wouldn't have any answers for him. I was pretty sure, after the way that he looked at me at the party, that Brad knew more than he was letting on. Our chemistry changed, and instead of feeling the need to be close to him, to hold his hand and cuddle with him, I felt more relaxed. I had my best friend back, somehow.

The rest of his visit was spent seeing the sights of the city, and of course, he wanted to watch me play in my tournament. We didn't kiss again after that first day. He held my hand wherever we went, and I was pretty sure we looked like a couple. The tension that had been there the first day intensified as his departure became closer. Had I pushed him away? Would I still have my best friend when I went home to visit in a few months?

The day I took him back to the airport was the worst. Once we were on the road, he grabbed my hand and started running his thumb over my knuckles. It was such an intimate thing to do that I feared we were right back where we started when he arrived. The car was filled with tension, and the fact that both of us were silent made it even thicker.

Is this really what I wanted? Did I want to let him go? The internal battles were raging in my head and my heart. I loved this man for more reasons than I could even try to count. We had been through hell and back on too many occasions. I was struggling to let him go when I really wanted to hold onto him, but in what way? Did I want him as my best friend or my boyfriend?

I had managed to avoid Ethan the entire time that Brad was here after that first night. I was expecting him to call and want to "discuss" what he saw in my car. He had asked me before I left for the airport if I was in love with Brad, and I wasn't able to answer him. Now I needed to answer that question for myself. If I was in love with Brad, love love, I needed to tell him, and we would make this work. If I wasn't, then what? Could we still be best friends? Were we strong enough to survive this realization?

Once we were at the security checkpoint, we had to say our good-byes. He knew that this was it, our final moments together before I was able to come home for a few weeks over the summer. We sat on a nearby bench, but I couldn't look at him as the tears started to fill my eyes, finally running over and down my cheeks. I found myself playing with my ring and wondering if he still wanted me to have it.

"I was surprised that you were wearing it. I figured once you met someone you would take it off," Brad said with a hint of surprise and relief in his voice.

The shock must have been apparent on my face when I looked up at him because he took that moment to kiss me. It was soft and sweet, but there was a whole lot of meaning behind it. It was the opposite of the kiss he gave me when he had first arrived. He was kissing me good-bye in more ways than one.

He was making the decision for me. I knew that I would always love Brad, but he was taking control of this situation and not making me choose.

"I will always wear it. You are the one person in this world that means more to me than anything else. You will always be my best friend." I didn't know how else to tell him that I knew what his kiss meant. My voice didn't waiver as I spoke. I was trying to make sure that he knew how much he meant to me.

He grabbed my hand and placed it over his heart. He didn't have to say anything. I knew what he was trying to say; he had said it the last time we had said good-bye. I knew he meant it with all his heart, and to show him that I felt the same, I mimicked his gesture. Our foreheads met in the middle, and we just sat there for what felt like forever, saying good-bye, without any words.

With a final wave after he got through security, he turned and headed to his gate. He was on his way back home with part of my heart in tow. I wanted to run to him. I wanted one last hug, one last kiss. I wanted to go home with him. I wanted him to hold me forever and tell me that we would never be apart again. He was my solace, my comfort. I was completely torn between wanting more and wanting what we have. I questioned his decision as I watched him disappear into the thick crowd of travelers. Was this really what was best for us?

I drove home through the tears. I knew that what I was feeling was a new kind of loss. When I finally pulled in my driveway, I noticed Ethan's car parked on the curb, and I wondered why he was there. I didn't want to deal with "us" right now. I didn't want to deal with us at all, to tell you the truth. I hadn't heard from him, not even a single text, since he caught me and Brad kissing in the car. I figured that I had ruined any chance I had with him in that very moment, but here he was.

My door suddenly opened, and I was pulled out and into his arms. He held me while I cried. He kissed my hair and stroked my back to try and calm me, but it only made things worse. I wanted to be in Brad's arms at that moment. I missed him and felt like I had lost him forever. Why couldn't my heart make up its mind already?

"You know, he's a great friend." I heard him whisper in my ear but wasn't able to comprehend what he was saying in that moment as another loud sob escaped my throat.

"I know." I sobbed.

"Do you really?"

Was he really questioning me about this? Brad was my best friend. I knew how great he was. Why did he think I was crying? My best friend just left me. We had been torn apart again. I was getting angry just thinking about it.

My tears subsided, and I whipped my head up to look at him. I pushed out of his grasp and crossed my arms over my chest. "Of course, I know how great he is. I'm the one who's had the *privilege* of being friends with him for most of my life. You only met him once! You have no right to even talk about our friendship!"

I knew I was screaming. I knew I was probably causing a small scene. My neighbors would be able to hear if their windows were open. I just didn't care. I was pissed off.

"He loves you. Did you know that?" Ethan asked.

Hearing someone else say it was surreal. I knew he loved me, but how did Ethan know?

"He told me how important you are to him. He also tried to kick my ass because he thought I hurt you. We had a nice talk after he calmed down."

Brad had tried to do what? When had this happened? Crap! I left them alone when I ran into the bathroom at the party. How long had I been in there for all of this to happen?

The surprise in my voice was obvious. "Really? It must have been a pretty short conversation. I wasn't gone all that long, and you were both inside when I came out of the bathroom. Plus, he never mentioned anything to me about talking to you. He would have told me."

"Well, we did talk. I'm sorry he didn't tell you, but our conversation was pretty short. Basically, he told me he loved you and that you would need me right now. He told me that once he was gone, I was responsible for you, to take care of you."

"God, you guys make it sound like I'm incapable of handling anything myself."

"No, that's not what he meant. He knew that you would need me here when you got back from the airport. He knew that you would need someone to hold you, to let you cry, and to comfort you. I'd say he knows you better than you know yourself."

The grin that was creeping across his face was starting to piss me off. Was it the grin or the fact that everything he was saying was right? Damn Brad! He knew I would be a hot mess when he left, and he made sure that there was someone here to pick up the pieces.

"Well, you're not doing a very good job since you've only managed to make me angry. I will have to report back to him that you suck." I was teasing him, of course. I could feel a smile tugging at my lips, and I was trying to hide it.

"Actually, I must be doing quite well if you are trying that hard to hide your beautiful smile. Not to mention you have stopped crying." You could hear the pride in his voice as he spoke.

I let my smile free, and when he reached out, I let him pull me back into his arms and hold me.

"So since I now have Natalie's approval and Brad's approval, will you please go out with me?" He was still holding me tightly, and I must have tensed up when he asked because he pulled me away slightly and lifted my head so that I was looking right into his eyes. "I told you we would get past this and we would be together."

"I don't understand. You talked to Natalie? You talked to Brad? When did you have time to accomplish all of this? Why?"

"Technically, they talked to me. Natalie caught me staring at you at her party and came over to me. I was nervous at first because she hadn't talk to me in so long, and after seeing her reaction to us at the coffee shop, I thought she was going to ask me to leave, even though she had made a point of inviting me. Brad told me to take care of you. He knew by the look on your face who I was before you even bolted into the house. I'm sure he will have some questions, but he knows that I won't hurt you."

Wow! I was pretty sure I said that aloud but before I could say anything else his lips were on mine, and I melted into him.

CHAPTER 11

The first few weeks we were "together," we kept to ourselves mostly. I still wasn't comfortable flaunting our relationship in front of anyone, especially Natalie. She never asked about *us*, and I never offered any information. I think the lack of knowledge was what held our friendship together. I wanted to talk to her about what she saw at the coffee shop, but I didn't want to push my luck. So far, our friendship was still intact.

Brad, on the other hand, wanted to know everything. The first time we talked after his trip was unbelievable. He interrogated me for almost an hour about Ethan. He sounded normal, but I could tell that he was fighting some inner battles.

"So Ethan was there when you got home." Brad stated.

"How did you know that?" I asked. I knew that he told Ethan to be there, but I was still stunned. He didn't even say hello when he answered. Instead, he started right with the questions about another guy. I just put him on a plane five hours ago.

"He promised he would be."

Simple as that. Somehow Brad had managed to make sure I was taken care of even without being in the same city. He trusted Ethan at his word, and Ethan had followed through, thankfully.

"He was. I'm not sure what you two talked about, but he was here so thank you."

"I promised you I would always take care of you. You don't have to thank me for caring about you. That comes naturally, and it's free of charge." I could hear the smile on his face growing bigger as he spoke. He sounded happy. Happy for me, I think.

"How was your flight?" I was trying to change the subject, and I knew he would catch on, but I wasn't sure I was ready to talk to him about Ethan yet. It still felt a little weird. Eight days ago, I was kissing Brad in my car, and a few hours ago, I was kissing Ethan in my driveway.

"It was fine. I took a nap and got caught up on some reading for school." He paused, and I knew he wanted to say more, to ask the questions that I didn't want to answer. He needed answers. So, I let him ask his questions, answering the ones that I could for a while until I was burnt out. My mind was reeling with questions of my own.

"Well, it's kind of late there. Why don't you get some rest and call me tomorrow. I have a tournament in the morning, but I should be home about six or so, my time."

"Sure. You do realize that you are doing a horrible job of avoiding things right?"

Damn him! "I know, but I just don't know if I can talk about him with you anymore right now. It just doesn't feel right for some reason." *The truth will set you free, right? He's going to drop the subject now, right?*

"I get it, but I want you to think about something for me. If I didn't think that you would be taken care of, if I didn't think that he really cared for you, if I didn't think that you cared about him…would I really have made sure that he was there when you got home?" His tone was serious. He wanted to make sure that I really understood why he had asked Ethan to be there for me.

My silence must have been a huge green light for him to continue.

"I know you are confused right now, and I know that our *relationship* is changing, again, but I want you to know that I am still here for you, and when you come home in a few months, I will be here then as well, no matter what has happened or does happen."

Home? I was fingering my ring again. As I stared at it, I remembered the words that Brad had said to me in my car the night I told him I was moving. *You live here, Becca. You will always live here.*

I would be in his heart forever. I could still be his friend, or I could choose to be more. He was giving me that choice, and from the way he made it sound, I had until I went home for the summer to decide. No matter what happens between now and then, I was free to choose him when I went home.

"I know." It was all I could come up with. I understood exactly what he was saying, and I knew I had a choice to make. "I'll talk to you tomorrow, okay?"

"I'll call you tomorrow night. Good luck at you tournament, Becca."

"Thanks. Good night."

It was getting close to the end of the school year, and things were starting to get busier and busier for me. I was planning the yearbook-release party that was two weeks before the end of school. My classes were getting more intense, and homework was beginning to become a bit overwhelming with my tennis schedule. Not to mention trying to find time to spend with Ethan was almost impossible these days.

I was chosen to play a few extra tournaments to represent the school's tennis team. I knew that there were scouts watching me, but since I was only a junior this year, I also knew that it didn't matter. Injuries don't take but a second to snap your dreams in half. That, I knew firsthand.

On top of all that, Ethan still hadn't asked me to prom, and I only had a few weeks left to find a dress if we were going to go. Our relationship was still going strong, but I was only able to see him a few nights a week. My weekends were spent catching up on homework, and I almost always had a tournament on Saturdays.

When my phone rang Sunday afternoon, I was surprised to see that Ethan was calling me instead of texting first. He never wanted to interrupt me and pretty much insisted that he would text me and that I could call him when I had time. That was not the case today apparently. I had just finished Skyping with my dad, and I was almost finished with my homework anyway, so I snatched my phone and picked up his call.

"Hello, handsome."

"Well, hello to you too, gorgeous. What are you doing on this fine Sunday afternoon?"

He started calling me gorgeous a few weeks after we started dating, and I couldn't really understand it. I was average height, only five feet five inches, and average build. My hair was great, one of my favorite features, along with my bluish-hazel eyes and long eye lashes. I didn't understand what he thought was so beautiful about me, but it didn't matter, and I never asked. Instead, I would go silent, just like right now, and blush uncontrollably. I think that was part of why he kept doing it.

I cleared my throat and whispered out my answer, "Nothing".

"I see that you are blushing again. Do you have any idea how adorable that is? I love that I can make you blush like that."

"Well, I don't mind it when no one else can see it, but it's a little embarrassing when people turn to stare at me in the halls." Wait, did he just say that he could see my blush? "Where are you?"

"So did you want to get together this afternoon? We can either go volley if you want, or maybe go to lunch, grab a coffee? We can do whatever you want to do."

"Sure," I said hesitantly. "Let me just get changed."

"You look fine in what you're wearing. Why are you so nervous? You keep playing with your ring." he asked. Trying to keep his laughter to a minimum.

Okay, this is creepy. How in the hell can he see me?

"You left your webcam on."

Crap! I had said that out loud. "Okay, mister," I said, turning to my laptop and turning off my screensaver. There he was—shirtless and all mine. I turned up the volume on my laptop, ended the call on my phone, and tossed it on my bed.

I was completely distracted by his body. I could barely see his piercing at the bottom of the screen, but I did get a pretty good shot of his tattoo. The first time he took his shirt off in front of me after we started dating, I jumped at the opportunity to touch it. The intricate design was beautiful, six infinity symbols all linked together. It wrapped around his upper arm completely. He said it had a meaning but had never told me what it was. That first night, I traced every inch of it with my fingertips for a long time before he stopped me. Looking up at him, I could see the lust in his eyes.

"This little stunt pretty much makes you a peeping tom. What if I had been changing?"

"Then I definitely wouldn't have told you I was watching." I could hear his voice had just a little bit of naughty behind it, but his face remained deadly serious.

"Perv! I need to change, so I am going to turn my webcam off now. How long before you're here?"

"Give me fifteen minutes, and then I'll be on my way. I need to grab a shower first." His bathroom was in his room. I could see it over his shoulder. I wondered if he was going to keep his webcam on. *Naughty!*

"Okay. I'll see you in a bit then. Later."

I signed off and let out a big sigh. Things were going so great right now that I didn't want them to change, and in just a few short weeks, everything was going to be different. He was graduating, and I was leaving for three weeks to visit my dad. Then when I get back, we will only have two months before he had to leave for college. Where was he going again? Had he told me? I should ask him today.

I needed to stop worrying about the things I could not change and get a grip on the present. I got up, changing into a cute pair of capri pants and a tank. I found my favorite wedge sandals and pulled my hair back in a messy ponytail. After a few swipes of mascara and some blush, I gazed at myself in the mirror and realized that I had achieved the perfect look. I looked relaxed. It didn't look like I was trying to hard to impress him, even though I always wanted to.

An hour later, we were pulling into our favorite coffee shop, the Bean. I waited for him to open my door for me, always the gentleman, and climbed out. As we headed inside hand in hand, I heard my phone ringing in my purse. I paused to answer it and motioned for him to keep going.

Without looking at the screen, I picked up and said hello.

"Hey girly! Whatcha up to?" Natalie's voice echoed through the phone, and I forgot to breathe. I had managed not to talk about Ethan with her up until this point, and now I had no choice. "I was gonna see if you wanted to get together with me and Jill tonight for dinner. We haven't hung out in a while, and we miss you."

"Sure. Sounds great. What time did you want to meet up?" I asked trying not to sound caught off guard. That was easy. I could grab coffee with Ethan and then meet up with them, no need to discuss anything.

"Well, how about seven? Morgan gets off work at six, and I know he will want to come."

Great. I thought it was gonna be just the girls. Morgan and I get along just fine, but his friend Ben started to creep me out after he sent me that picture of Ethan and I kissing in the hallway. After Ethan and I started dating, being around Morgan reminded me of Ben and his creepy tendencies. Plus, Ben was like Morgan's shadow. They pretty much went everywhere together.

"That's fine. Send me a text of where everyone wants to go, and I'll catch up with you guys there." I replied quickly, wanting to get off the phone with her so that I could get inside.

"Sounds good. Did you want to invite Ethan to come along?" Her voice was sincere as she said his name. There was no hint of anger.

What? Did she really just ask me that? "Um, sure. I'll see if he's interested and get back to you."

"All right. See you tonight. Later, girly."

She was so bubbly and overly eager to see me and Ethan. It felt like something was going on, and that made me a little uneasy. No time to think about it right now. Ethan was waiting for me. I walked in the coffee shop to see him at a table in the corner with our drinks.

"Who was that? You look a little confused." Ethan asked sounding concerned.

"That was Natalie. She invited *us* out to dinner tonight with a bunch of friends." I said, the confusion in my voice blatantly obvious. I waited to see his reaction, but he gave none so I continued. "I told her I would ask if you wanted to come but that I would meet up with them. Do you want to go with us?" I knew my question was asked with hesitance. I wasn't sure what he would say or how he would feel about going out with a girl he used to date.

"Sure. So we need to talk about prom." He changed the subject so quickly I almost tried to stop him until I heard *prom*, and then I was all ears. "I bought our tickets Friday at lunch. I plan on getting a limo and was wondering if you wanted to go with a group of my friends or a group of yours?"

I was staring at him in shock, but my excitement was building and about to spill over. "You know," I start teasingly, "you are suppose to ask a girl to the prom and not assume you have a date."

"Well, since you are *my* girlfriend, then I would have to take out any other guys who ask you so you are available to go with me?"

"I didn't say that I would go with anyone else. I said you needed to ask me to go with you."

At this point, we both started leaning across the table toward each other. Our words were getting softer, and I know where this was headed. When our foreheads finally met and I closed my eyes, he started to speak.

"Becca, will you go to the prom with me?"

I leaned over and gave him a kiss right before I nodded my head yes and kissed him again, this time with a bit more passion. As I pulled away, I saw that his eyes were filled with lust again, and it amazed me that it only took one kiss for him to want me completely. The feeling was mutual.

Dinner with my friends was amazing. Ethan decided to not join us, and once I got there, I was glad that he hadn't. Ben and Morgan were there along with Jill, Lainey, and Natalie. It would have made things a little awkward to have him by my side, especially since Ben kept staring at me like he was going to eat me alive. That would have caused a huge problem if Ethan had seen him.

All things aside, I stayed away from Ben completely and immersed myself in an intense conversation with Jill about next year's yearbook staff and who was going to be responsible for what. Jill had been chosen as the editor-in-chief for next year. I was happy for her, but a little jealous if I was being honest. I was chosen as an assistant editor, as well as Natalie, so the three of us were going to be running the show next year.

After dinner, I went home and shopped for a prom dress online. I found a few I wanted to try on and decided that I was going to do that Tuesday after practice. I had a big match tomorrow, one of the last for the year, and I needed to get some sleep so that I was at my best. With the season ending in a few weeks, I wanted to make sure that I gave my best performance, ensuring a spot on the team for next year. Every match counts.

Right before I turned my lights off, I got a text from Brad saying, "Good luck." I knew he was talking about my match. I quickly replied with "Thanks," and then I was dreaming peacefully for the next seven hours.

CHAPTER 12

I had my last tennis match yesterday, winning 90 percent this year. I was still celebrating when I woke up this morning until I realized what day it was. Prom is tonight. What most people think of as the biggest event of the year was finally here for me. I think I was more nervous than excited. There are so many stereotypical expectations for tonight that I just feel a little confused as to how *I* wanted things to go.

I went with my mom this morning to get my hair and nails done. I was waiting to put on my dress until I'd hear Ethan ring the bell. It was emerald green satin, floor length, and form fitting. It dipped low enough in the back that I couldn't wear a bra, which was not a huge deal, considering my size, but it also dipped low in the front. I've got my ring on, as usual, and I bought a pair of stud earrings to match. They were small and fake, of course, but they matched my ring and the dress. It all matched Ethan's eyes. I was twisting my ring around my finger when I heard the door bell and jumped out of my skin.

I slipped into my dress and shoes. I double-check my hair and makeup before I slipped my phone in my clutch and walked down the stairs, pausing before I went into the living room. As I turned the corner, I could see my mom, camera ready, waiting for me. The huge smile on her face told me that Ethan looked fabulous even before I saw him. When I did, the only thing I could think was that *fabulous* couldn't even begin to describe him.

He's wearing a black tux with a vest that perfectly matched my dress. I never told him what I bought, so I could only assume my mom did. He was holding my corsage box in his hand and was staring at it nervously. I realized that I was smiling like a fool, and that all my nerves have dissipated. Just seeing him had calmed me.

"Hey," I said. When he looked up, I could see that he was stumbling for something to say, so I continued, "You look great!"

"Wow! You look…" Ethan stuttered as he looked me up and down. I did a little twirl and that threw him off completely. "Wow!"

After all the times I had been limited to one-word answers around him, I had finally been able to turn the tables. Just to push the point home, I twirled around one more time before I made my way over to him.

"Thanks." I said trying to hide my mischievous smile.

He just nodded his head and opened the box of my corsage. As he slipped it on my wrist, I realize that it too matched my dress perfectly. Did they have to dye the leaves to make it match or something?

We posed for about a hundred pictures, inside and outside, for my mom before we headed out front. In true Ethan form, he had actually rented a limo. We had decided to ride with his friends to the prom and hang out with mine afterward. I was still a little leery about being in the same room with Ethan and Natalie, but I figured she would be a bit nicer with alcohol in her.

The first thing I noticed when we stepped inside was exactly how beautiful the ballroom was. It really made me feel like we were "Under the Stars," which was this year's theme apparently. It was decorated like an outside park, and the entire ceiling was glowing with stars laid out in the form of constellations. It reminded me a little of how the sky looked the first time I went out with Ethan. It felt romantic.

We danced for hours, not an inch of space between us. I could feel every muscle in his back as we moved, and for a minute, as I slid my hand up to the back of his neck and pulled him in for a kiss, I forgot we weren't the only two people in the room.

He pulled away and grabbed my hand. We had been dancing for a while, and I was hoping that we were going get a drink, but we were not. He pulled me past our table, only pausing a brief step to grab my clutch. We kept right on going until we were outside and stepping into our limo. I slid over the seat to make room for him, but as soon as the door closed, he was pulling me back to him. As his hands moved up my bare back, I closed my eyes, and he rested his forehead on mine. He asked the driver to take us to his house, and we were off. When I opened my eyes again, he leaned in and kissed me.

Ethan's house was only ten minutes away, but by the time we were there, I was straddling him, and we were in a full on make-out session with the driver in clear view. Ethan had forgotten to close the privacy window. This was our stop. When we got out, Ethan tipped the driver since we wouldn't be needing him for the rest of the night and asked him to head back to pick up his friends.

He slipped his fingers in between mine and pulled me to him. He only kissed me once before he helped me into his car, and we were driving to my house. The drive felt like it took forever. I wasn't sure why I was nervous or what I thought was about to happen, but my stomach had butterflies attacking it.

My mom was gone for work, and my sister was staying at a friend's tonight, so it was dark when we arrived. I turned on every light as I made my way to my bedroom to change. Ethan got us a couple bottles of water and was only a few steps behind me. I could feel his eyes on me from the doorway as I stepped out of my dress. I didn't turn around, but I knew he was there. Before I knew what was happening Ethan was wrapping his arms around my waist.

Oh my god! I was pretty much completely naked in Ethan's arms. What do I do now? I'd never been in this position before, and he knew it. My reluctance to go beyond kissing screamed *virgin.* He said he didn't care, but right now, his body was telling me a different story. I could feel the bulge in his pants pressing into the small of my back.

"It's okay. I know you are freaking out inside your head, but I want you to know that we don't have to. I don't plan on doing anything tonight that you don't want me to. Prom doesn't change anything. You know I'm willing to wait until you're ready."

I could feel my body relax as I allowed his words to sink in. He was so good to me. He wanted to wait until I was ready, but what if I would never really feel ready? Isn't tonight just as good as any? No! I would not be a stereotypical girl who loses her virginity on prom night.

I leaned back into him, and he hugged me closer. I could feel my desire for him building. I wanted this, whatever this was, to continue. I turned in his arms, and my mouth was on his. We walked backward to my bed, and I fell on top of him. I didn't have the slightest clue what I was doing, but I knew that I didn't want to take my hand off of him right now

As we arrive at the after-party, I realized that my hair was a bit messy and my makeup should have been touched up. All of Ethan's tux was wrinkled from me molesting him for the last hour. He wanted more but understood when I said no. Instead, he teased and tortured me until I couldn't take it anymore and allowed him to touch me. I will never regret that moment for the rest of my life.

I spotted Natalie and Jill in the kitchen and walked over to say hi, with Ethan just a few steps behind me. The look on Natalie's face as we approach was shocking. She was looking between the two of us. I could not tell if the look was of disgust or pure hatred. I tried to say hello to her, but she quickly turned and stormed off, leaving the three of us standing there with our mouths agape in surprise.

"Hey, Jill, what the hell was that all about?"

"Not really sure. We were having a great time, and then her mood flipped, and she was gone. You know as much as I do."

I realized at that point that our disheveled looks may have given her the wrong impression. She probably thought the worst. I was not really sure at that point why that would upset her, but knowing Natalie, when she'd talk to me again, I was sure to find out the whole story in one long breath. Should I go now, or should I let her calm down first?

"I'm going to go and find her. I'll be back in a minute." Ethan said. I could hear the uncertainty in his voice.

I had forgot for a moment that Ethan was standing behind me until he kissed me before setting off to find Natalie.

Jill and I grabbed a red cup and headed to the basement to get a beer. I spotted a couple of girls from the tennis team and waved, but I still had yet to be completely accepted enough to go over and strike up an unnecessary conversation. The fact that they looked like they had been drinking for a while already explained why their return waves were a little more enthusiastic than normal.

As we slowly made our way back up to the kitchen, we got stopped every couple of feet to talk to someone new. This would be the very first party that I had gone to and felt comfortable since moving here. The people tonight seem to be very accepting of me. It was almost like I could now be a part of their "club" because of who I was dating and who my friends were.

At the top of the stairs, I saw Morgan sitting at the bar in the kitchen with Ben. Jill headed that way before I could stop her, so I followed and made sure that I was not within arm's reach of Ben. I stood next to Jill, farthest from Ben, and tried not to make eye contact with him.

"Hey, guys, have you seen Natalie anywhere?" I asked.

"I thought she was with you." Morgan said, his concern obvious. Morgan had the most confused look on his face. Obviously, they had come to the party together, but now his date was missing.

"She got mad at me earlier and stormed off." I said. I pulled out my phone to send Ethan a text when he reappeared. "Hey, is she okay?"

"Yeah, she's fine." He stated, unable to make eye contact with me which caused a few alarms to go off in my head.

That's it? No explanation?

He must have seen the look I gave him because he leaned down, kissed me on the cheek, and whispered in my ear, "I'll explain later."

With that, he lightly tugged on my hand. I spun toward him, and he led us to the living room where everyone was slow-dancing to an upbeat, fast song. I went along with it and snuggled up to his chest, wanting to be as close to him as humanly possible. After a few beats, the song changed, and it was actually a slow one. The living room started to become crammed with people, and our space was becoming minimal, so I motioned for us to head back to the kitchen.

As we approached, I could see that Natalie was in there. Ethan stopped me and pulled me to the side, backing me up against a wall with his body. He kissed me on the forehead before resting his head against mine. It looked like he was going to explain right now.

"She was upset because she thought we had sex." He paused, trying to gauge my reaction to what he was saying, but I had none. I had already figured that part out. What I need to know was the *why*. When my pleading look and silence urged him to continue, he did. "When we were together we never...I mean, we almost but...well, she wanted to, but I couldn't bring myself to because she was a virgin and I..."

He couldn't even finish his sentence. Natalie knew I was a virgin, and she must have thought that I had given up my V card to him and that he had taken it after he wouldn't take hers. That would upset me to. Maybe I should talk to her? I didn't get a chance to say anything before he continued though.

"Look, I couldn't have sex with her, but it had nothing to do with her virginity. Our relationship was...unstable, for lack of a better word. One minute we were great, and the next we were fighting. It was like riding a rollercoaster, and the only time that she wanted to go all the way was when we were making up from a major fight. I was trying to be a stand-up guy and not take advantage of her in a weak moment. She doesn't exactly see it that way."

I could see the defeat in his eyes. I could tell that he felt bad for upsetting her, but I knew that it wasn't his fault.

It's prom night, damn it! We should all be getting along, having fun, and drinking. There should be no fighting, no drama, and no crying. I had just gotten rid of all the drama in my life and wanted to relax and have fun for once.

I wrapped my arms around him and pulled myself tight up against his body. I wanted him to know that I was happy to be here with him. I wanted him to feel the positive energy my body was giving off. *Holy crap!* I could feel him...wow!

"Sorry, my body has a mind of its own." Ethan said, not sounding the least bit sorry for his body's reaction.

I looked up and I could actually see the faintest amount of blush in his cheeks. How cute. "He may want to get a better grip on his 'thoughts' before everyone can read his mind. We have people to go mingle with. Do you need a minute?"

His smile told me he did, but there was also a hint of lust in his eyes that told me he won't be able to control himself for much longer. "Why don't we say our good-byes and head back to your place?" Ethan suggested. When he saw that my eyes got a little bigger at his suggestion, he kissed my cheek. "I wasn't meaning that. I was thinking we could watch a movie and cuddle on the couch."

"Oh!" It came out a little more exasperated than I had planned. I was relieved that he wasn't trying to push me and I couldn't hide that fact. "That sounds fine. It's getting late anyway."

As we made our way into the kitchen to say good-bye to our friends, I noticed that Natalie won't make eye contact with either one of us. As I was about to approach her to give her a hug and say good-bye, she whispered something in Morgan's ear, and they took off. She looked back at me over her shoulder and gave me a shit-eating grin. That could not be good.

CHAPTER 13

The wrap party for yearbook was the Saturday before the end of the year. Our book was finished, and the time to relax was upon us. Natalie and I seemed to be back to normal. We never talked about prom or the after party or the weird vibes that she had been giving off. I thought about bringing up the subject at lunch a few days after prom, but when Natalie got up to get a soda, Jill told me to not say anything about prom. She said she would explain to me why later, and I decided that it was best to drop the subject.

That afternoon in yearbook, Jill pulled me aside and into her new office. We started to talk about next year's book for a few minutes but when I heard the click of the outside door, I glanced over my shoulder to see that Natalie had just walked out. Jill let out a heavy sigh and told me what was going on.

"She was upset that night because she thought you and Ethan had slept together."

"I know, Ethan told me. What's up with that anyway? She knows we're dating."

"I think she may still have a small thing for him, even if she won't admit it. Don't get me wrong. She really likes Morgan, but Ethan was her first 'love', and I think she's having a hard time letting go of those feelings."

"I really don't know what to say to that. Why does that make her mad at me? It's not like I stole him away from her." But I kind of did. If I hadn't shown up, would they have gotten back together?

"She knows that. Plus, it's not like she doesn't want to be with Morgan. I think she needed to prove that to herself the other night, and she may be regretting that a little bit right now." She paused and waited for me to catch on. The look of shock on my face must have given it away. "Yep, she gave him her V card."

"Holy crap! Is she okay?"

"She says she's fine, but I'm not really sure. She doesn't want to talk about it. It's not like it was very romantic or anything from what she has told me. I think she wanted it to be more special and was upset because it wasn't."

I understood that. I want my first time to be special too. It has to be in the right place. It has to be with the right person. It has to be the right everything. That was why I was scared to let things go to far. I didn't want to regret my first time. I didn't want to look back and wonder, *Why him?* Why then? I wanted fond memories of my first time, even if I wasn't still with that person. I wanted to make sure I was in love, or as close to it as possible.

After that conversation with Jill, I decided to not speak another word about prom unless Natalie brought it up. We resumed our friendship as if nothing had ever happen. We had coffee after school most days now that I was finished with tennis for the year. We went to a few parties after prom with Ethan and Morgan in tow. Never once did it seem like she was regretting her decision, but I also caught her staring at me and Ethan every once in a while with a bewildering look in her eyes. She was jealous, but not of me. She was jealous of our relationship. She wanted to feel like we felt about each other. That's when I realized how much I was truly involved in this relationship. I wasn't ready to admit it to myself, but I was on the brink of falling madly in love with him, and it took everything that I had to fight those feelings.

The party was being hosted by Ethan's parents as a way to celebrate the final chapter of his participation in yearbook. They also mentioned that they would like to celebrate the fact that I was replacing him as an assistant editor, something I didn't even know at the time. I thought that it would cause a fuss, so I politely declined. I didn't want to upset Natalie again, and since she was going to be there, along with the rest of the staff, I figured it wasn't the place or the time.

As everyone started to arrive and the house became full of friends and acquaintances, I started to feel a little claustrophobic. I knew most of these people well, had worked with them side by side for the past five months and would work with some of them again next year. For some reason, I was feeling very out of place, and I was quickly in need of fresh air.

Standing on the back deck of Ethan's house, sweating from the ninety-five degree evening, I started to wonder what my future really held. I wondered if Natalie and I would ever truly get past this bump in our friendship. I wondered if Ethan and I would still be together after the summer when he went off to college. I wondered what things were going to be like back home when I got there. My mind was full of a variety of unanswerable questions when I felt the presence of someone behind me.

I was shocked when I turned to find Natalie standing behind me, hands stuck deep into the pockets of her shorts, looking nervous. She wasn't looking up at me, but I could tell just by her body language that she wanted to talk. I figured that this would happen eventually, but I was hoping that it wouldn't be tonight. We both had been avoiding this, and with my departure looming next week, I knew that it was better to do this now than wait until I returned. The silence that was surrounding us was almost too much to bear.

"Hey." I said. I was suddenly feeling unsure of myself. You could hear the tension in my voice, how hesitant I was to even speak.

"Hey." Natalie replied sounding sad.

It was an echo of what I just said, but I could hear more in her voice than I think she even knew. I could hear the apologetic tone and braced for what was coming next.

"I know that you must be a little confused. I was pretty awful to you and then tried to act like everything was normal." Natalie continued. That was an understatement if you ask me. "I just want to apologize for acting the way I did on prom night. You didn't deserve to be treated that way."

There were two ways I could see that conversation was going. Either I could graciously accept her apology and move on or I could graciously accept her apology and give her a piece of my mind. I wanted to keep her friendship, I knew that for sure, but I also needed answers. She was the one who told Ethan that she was okay with us dating. She needed to accept us, or else she was going to be the one to lose a friend today.

"I understand completely why you were upset, I really do, but I need answers. I know that you use to date Ethan, even though you have never volunteered that information. I know that you wanted to 'go farther' than you two did. I also know that you told him you had no problem with us dating. If all this is true, I need to know why you freaked out on us after prom. Why do you care so much about our relationship if you are supposedly okay with it? Not to mention you have Morgan. This is all really unfair to him."

I took a deep breath and waited for her to answer me. I needed to get all of that off my chest. I felt better, but I knew that I might not like her answers. Her answers would decide whether or not we remained friends. I needed her to be honest with me, no matter what. Her answers could change everything.

"I can't explain why I got jealous, but that's what happened. I thought you two had sex, and for some reason, I freaked out, got jealous, and then went and did something that I thought would make Ethan jealous." She hesitated before continuing. I knew what she was going to tell me, but I needed to hear it from her. "I slept with Morgan that night out of spite. I really thought that you two had gone all the way, even though Ethan told me you hadn't."

"Even if we had, it shouldn't have mattered to you."

"I know that now, and to be honest with you, I think I was just jealous that he was willing to do that with you and not with me. I guess I felt like I wasn't good enough, and that hurt."

Hearing her say it made it all real. I tried to put myself in her shoes for a minute, and once I was there, I saw everything clearly. I saw how disheveled we looked, Ethan especially, since I had changed out of my dress. How insecure that must have made her feel. Combine that with a little alcohol, and there went her V card. I felt bad for her at that moment. I knew how important it was to me to make that first time special. She will never be able to get that back.

"I can only imagine what went though your mind, and I'm sorry. We never meant to make you feel like that. I didn't even know about any of that until Ethan told me after you ran off." I had to take a deep breath before continuing. "I need to make one thing clear though. If we are going to be friends, I need for you to fully accept my relationship with Ethan. I am done walking the line while we're around you, never knowing what's okay and what's not."

"I get it, and I accept it, but I can't promise that it won't be hard. I really thought that I was in love with him at one point. After spending the last few months with Morgan, I know that I wasn't, but it doesn't make things easier for some reason. I'm in love with Morgan. I don't want anything from Ethan. I just need time to digest it all I think."

I can give her that. I was going to be in Michigan for three weeks. She could take all the time she needed while I was gone to get over it. "Deal. I can give you time as long as you give the effort."

"Deal." We both stood there in awkward silence. I knew we needed to hug it out, but I couldn't be the one to initiate. She finally stepped forward and wrapped her arms around me, and I returned her embrace wholeheartedly. I felt like I had my friend back.

"Back to the party?" I asked.

With a nod from her, we headed inside to find our men and grab a cold drink. I had sweat through my tank top, but it was worth it. I knew things between us were going to be okay.

The last day of school approached quickly. On one hand, this was fantastic news, and on the other, it kind of sucked. I was happy that school was out and that next year I will be a senior, but at the same time this meant that Ethan was graduating and at the end of summer, he would be off to college somewhere. Plus, I had to leave a few days after graduation to go visit my dad for three weeks, and as much as I missed my friends, that's three weeks less that I have to spend with Ethan.

He was yet to tell me where he's going to college. I couldn't understand why he wanted to keep it this big secret. It was college—you were supposed to be bragging about where you got in and where you're going. He was having the opposite approach to the situation. He was completely silent about his decision or, as I was about to find out, his lack there of.

The day before graduation, we were standing in his kitchen and I was asking him the easy questions that anyone should be able to answer, should want to answer, and should be proud to answer. That's when he told me that he hadn't made a decision yet.

"What do you mean you don't know where you're going yet?"

"I haven't decided. I have three school that have all offered me a scholarship to play tennis, but I can't decide where I want to go."

"Well, since tomorrow is graduation, don't you think it's time to make that decision?"

"I told them that I would let them know as soon as I decided."

"Didn't they give you some kind of deadline to respond? Like, two months ago, when everyone else was making their final decisions?"

"Well, technically I am enrolled as a freshman at all three right now until I make up my mind. The coaches told me to do that so that I could secure my spot."

"Wow! You truly are a wanted man. Question is, who am I going to lose you to?"

"Well, I am leaning toward one more than the other two, but I really want to go take another look at all the camps over the summer. With you being gone for three weeks, I plan to check them out so that I'm not sitting here bored all the time."

"You won't be bored while I'm gone. You get to go hang out with your friends and enjoy your last summer of freedom. The last summer you can have fun and not have to act like an adult."

"Well, I have a big decision to make, and I have to at least think like an adult for a while."

"I guess so. Can you at least tell me which three colleges are after you?" I asked, giving him a pleading look with my eyes.

"Let's talk about something else." Ethan said, trying his best to divert my attention. He's really good at changing the subject when he doesn't want to give away any information. "When do you leave again?"

"You know this. My flight is Tuesday at ten o'clock in the morning."

"I guess you'll need my help packing on Monday night then." He pulled me to him and secured his arms around my waist. When he kisses me lightly on the nose, I know what's coming next. "Are you sure I can't come with you?"

"You know my dad would have a fit. It's only three weeks. If you can't handle three weeks without me, then how do you think we are going to be able to make it when you go away to college?"

This was a topic that we have talked in circles around since prom. We both knew that long distance relationships are hard. We both knew that temptations grow when the heart is weakened. We both knew that at the end of summer, we would probably part ways. We were living in the here and now and trying not to think about the future. For me, that was a little impossible. I was not sure if I could bear to lose him after loosing Brad twice. My heart could only take so much.

As my plane landed back in Michigan, I had the sudden urge to call Ethan. He rode with us to the airport that morning, only about five hours ago to be exact, but the separation I was feeling was overwhelming. My chest felt like it was being sat on by an elephant, and I was dreaming of his face. That was until my sister poked me in the back to go. As I opened my eyes, I realized that the people in the aisle ahead of me had moved and it was our turn to get off the plane. Finally!

I couldn't see my dad as we approach the baggage terminal. The airport was crowded, and it felt like someone was watching me. My sister darted from behind me and started to run. I followed behind her at a steady pace until I saw where she was headed. I picked up speed and didn't stop until I was safely planted in his arms. My feet were airborne, and he was spinning me in circles.

Brad put be back on the ground as my dad reached over and gave me a big one-armed hug and a kiss on the head. I grabbed a hold of Brad's hand and pulled him toward the carousel that should contain our bags. I was still holding Brad's hand, Dad had one arm over my shoulder, and Amy was still attached to Dad's other arm as we collected our bags and headed for the car. We look like one big happy family.

As soon as I dropped my purse in my room at my dad's house, I send my mom and Ethan a quick text, letting them know we arrived safely and that I will call them both later tonight. Brad lugged my suitcases up the stairs to my room and plopped them next to the bed.

Looking around, I realized that nothing had changed since the last time I was here. I stood in the doorway taking in the sight of my past when I felt Brad's hands come around me from behind and he pulled me back to rest on his chest. I know the compromising position we were in, but at that moment, I was needing a little comfort.

Every picture frame on the wall was just where I left it. My flat iron was sitting on the top of my dresser with my tray of perfumes behind it. There was an empty spot on my desk where my laptop would go, and I could see all the cables underneath just waiting to be plugged in. My trash can was overflowing with crumpled-up papers that I believe were my English paper from last fall—I would have to check that out before I empty it.

Then there was my bed. I could tell that the sheets had been washed because the bed was made, something I never did because I hated to do it. It looked plush, and the pillows looked perfectly fluffy. Just staring at it, made me want to jump on it so I did.

The heat from Brad's body left me feeling chilly as I landed on my bed, but it didn't last long as he landed next to me, and we curled up together. I glanced up to make sure the door was still open and I see that it is. My dad had strict rules about open doors with boys in our rooms, no matter how much he might like that boy.

It didn't take long before sleep enveloped me. I faintly remember Brad kissing my head and saying good-bye, my shoes hitting the floor as Brad took them off, the rustle of sheets as he moved me under the covers, and the click of the door as he left. It felt like I was only asleep for mere moments, and then my phone rang.

"Hey." I grumbled trying to wake up.

"Are you sleeping? Didn't you just get there like a few hours ago?" Natalie practically yelled into the phone.

"It's a three-hour time difference and a very long four-hour flight, Natalie. I was exhausted and basically passed out." I sat up and rubbed my eyes. As I opened them, I realized that it was still daylight, so I couldn't have been out for too long. "What's up?"

"Nothing much. I just wanted to see if you made it okay."

"Yep. Safe and sound. Miss me already?"

"Not really." You could hear the laughter in her voice as she tried to hide it. "I was just bored and figured I would give you a call."

"Oh yeah? Who did you call before I came along?" She knew I was teasing her, but I forget this might still be a sore subject.

"No one important."

Yep, still a sore subject.

"Anyway, when do you get back?" She asked sounding sad.

I had to laugh. "I just got here, and you want me to come back already? I have three weeks with my dad, but he wants to stretch it to four or five and drive us back instead. 'Family road trip' is what he was thinking. We have to talk to my mom, but I'm pretty sure she's going to want us to just fly home."

"Wow. Your dad sounds like a lot of fun."

"He can be when he's not working. He was pretty lacking in the 'fun' department when my parents were still married, according to my mom." I stretched above my head and saw that my suitcases were stacked by the door. I felt like I needed a shower, but I really just wanted to change and go to bed. My alarm clock, still in the same place I left it, showed it was only 7:26. I had only been asleep for about thirty minutes at best. That was probably a good thing, considering the time difference.

I smiled a little that some things hadn't changed before I let Natalie go and told her that I would give her a call in a few days. I opened both my suitcases and quickly tried to shove clothes in my drawers and closet so that I could grab a shower. With the clothes that I already had here taking up so my space, I was having a hard time finding room for everything when my phone rang again. It was under a pile somewhere, so I decided to ignore it until I could find it. It started to ring again as I got to the bottom of the last pile. I lifted up the last of my clothes and grabbed my phone before it could send whoever to voicemail.

"Hello." I answered, almost unable to get the word out. I was pretty much out of breath at this point from all the shoving and tossing of clothes over the last twenty minutes or so minutes.

"Hey, gorgeous. Everything all right?" Ethan asked sounding excited to hear my voice.

I could feel my heart swell and ache at the same time. I missed him already, and we had at least another twenty days or so before we could see each other. I closed my eyes, and I could see his face clearly. He was smiling at me, and those eyes were saying...

"Becca? Are you there?"

"Yeah, sorry. I was just excited to hear your voice and I kind of—well anyway. What are you doing right now?"

"Just sitting here, wishing you were with me. The couch feels so empty without you here. Are you sure that you can't come home any sooner?"

"Yep. I promised my dad three weeks." I was going to leave out the part about my dad's brilliant new plan of taking a road trip. At least I would leave it out for now. "It's not like you are going to be home anyway. You have three colleges to visit, and that will at least get you out of the city."

"I guess. I leave tomorrow morning to visit the first camp. I promised all three coaches that I would have an answer for them by the end of June."

"So where is this first camp again?"

He still had not told me anything about which colleges he's going to visit, where he was leaning toward going, how far away they are, or anything. It was getting a little tense between us every time I brought it up. We had already committed to trying the long-distance relationship, so I didn't understand why he wouldn't at least tell me what his options were.

"You know I can't give you that information. It's *classified*." He was teasing, but I really just wished he would tell me.

"I need you to give me something. I feel like I'm dying here. I could help you make your decision..."

"That's exactly why I can't tell you. I want to make sure I make this decision for the right reasons."

I could hear the strain in his voice. Was he going to give in and tell me something?

He let out a long breath before he continued, "Look, I have always thought that I wanted to plan tennis for one particular college team, one particular coach. They are one of my three options. I want to make sure that I am not turning down a better opportunity for myself just because of something that I always *thought* I wanted."

"Okay, I get it, but how do you think that I will hinder this decision? I should be able to help you make the decision because I am a nonbiased party."

"Yes, but the three places are three completely different distances away, so you will be biased. I can drive to all three if that makes you feel better."

"A little," I moaned. That was a lie. I would feel a *lot* better knowing that he would only be driving distance away no matter where he chose to go.

"All right. So what are your plans for the rest of the day?'

A glance at the clock told me that my day was almost over. "It's getting late here, so a shower and some sleep sound like the best-laid plans to me."

"I have to pack still. I'm staying two nights at the first camp, and I'm going to work out with a few of the players so they can test my skills. I should probably start since I'm leaving early."

"All right. Well, I'm glad you called. I miss you already."

"I miss you too, gorgeous. These next few weeks will fly right by, I promise."

I made a kissing sound and hung up. I grabbed a pair of running shorts and a tank before heading to the bathroom. A nice hot shower was what I really needed and then some uninterrupted sleep for the next eight to ten hours. That sounded perfect.

CHAPTER 14

The first week of my vacation was spent catching up with all my friends, and by the time Sunday rolled about, I was completely exhausted. Brad had not left my side in almost two days straight, and as much as I loved spending time with him, I just wanted a break. I used to have so much going on with tennis and school that I was never able to spend so much time with my friends, and I used to think I was missing out. I knew now that keeping myself busy was the only way that I was able to survive back then.

With a restful night's sleep, I woke up knowing exactly what I wanted to do that day. I wanted to go to the beach with my dad and my sister. Dad thought the idea was wonderful so he ran to the store to get some stuff to pack in the cooler while Amy and I dug out beach towels and the other necessities. I didn't think to pack a swimsuit for some reason, so I dug out an old one from last summer and hoped it would still fit. My body hadn't changed much in the last few years, so thankfully, it still looked good on me. The lavender purple of the suit still went well with my skin tone, even though I had a little bit of a tan already from the constant sun in Tucson.

I got a text from Ella as we were setting up on the beach. There was going to be another party to celebrate me returning home tonight. That would be the third time this week they had *celebrated* my return, and eventually, I knew the excitement would die down, but it felt great to know that my friends really missed me. I confirmed that I would be in attendance since the party was for me and plopped down on the sand.

The long week must had really gotten to me. Before I knew it, my sister was nudging me awake. I rolled over onto my back and put my sunglasses on. I blindly reach for the sunscreen to apply a little bit but fell back asleep before I could find it.

I could feel the heat radiating from my skin as we drove back to my dad's house. The lack of sunscreen on my chest had left me with a red glow that would take a few days to turn to golden brown. My face absorbed most of the color. There would be no way to cover up my burn with makeup tonight or even tomorrow.

When the spray of the shower hit my skin, it stung a bit. I turned the cold water on higher and waited for the temperature to adjust. I only had about thirty minutes before I had to be ready to leave. Brad was picking me up, and I still had to call Ethan before I go. I pushed my overheated body under the spray and quickly finished my shower. As soon as I was out, I headed to my room and dialed Ethan's number.

We talked about his first visit for the second time that week and how excited he was about possibly playing for that school. He still won't give anything away as to what school it was. He had another visit scheduled in a few days and would be heading there tomorrow afternoon. He didn't sound as excited to check out this school, but I was wondering if he was still on a high from the first school he visited. If so, he'd be changing his tune come Thursday when I talk to him.

As I was changing, I could hear footsteps coming down the hall toward my room. I was standing only in my bra and underwear when I heard someone turn the knob, and before I could yell for them to stop, Brad was standing in the doorway, staring at me. His expression was full of emotion as he took in my almost-naked body, and I could feel his eyes graze up my body and back down again.

I put my finger over my lips to hush him, grabbed a towel to cover myself, and quickly said good-bye to Ethan. As soon as I clicked End on my phone, I turned to him with a "What the hell" look on my face. He was still staring and just shrugged his shoulder before coming in and closing the door behind him. He knew that my door had to stay open with him in the room. Did he forget the rules since yesterday?

"So can I finish getting dressed, please?" I asked with a hint of annoyance in my voice.

"Don't let me stop you," Brad smirked. He moved a few steps away from the door and sat on the edge of my desk, but he never took his eyes off of me. I knew that I was wearing the equivalent of the bikini I had on earlier, but it felt different. It felt wrong. I felt naked.

"Really? Get out of here. I need to finish getting ready, and you're early. Plus, you know that you can't be in here with my door closed. Are you trying to get me grounded for the rest of my vacation?"

"Actually, your dad and Amy let me in on their way out to dinner, so there is no one to get you in trouble with. Would you feel better if I opened the door?"

"No! I would feel better if you would hang out in the living room while I finished getting ready. You busted in here while I was practically naked and on the phone. You didn't even knock!"

I was getting angry. He knew that I was with Ethan, yet over the last week, he seemed to be ignoring that fact more and more each time he saw me. He had not tried anything, aside from the first night I was home when I let him hold me, but I still felt like he was headed down that road again. It was more the looks and smiles. They were too expressive of the emotions that he was suppose to be keeping hidden.

"Fine. If you won't leave then I will just go get dressed in the bathroom." I stated firmly, lowering my voice a few octaves to where it almost sounded like I was growling at him.

I grabbed my clothes and headed toward the door. As I went to open it, I could feel him behind me even before he put his hand on my arm. I could feel him getting closer to me. His right arm wrapped around my chest, and he pulled me back to him and held me there. I let out a sigh and turned to face him, which ended up being a big mistake. His lips landed on mine for the briefest of seconds before I jumped back and smacked him in the chest.

My clothes had fallen to the floor at this point. I continued hitting him in his chest until my hand hurt. When I looked up and saw him staring at me was when I realized that my towel had fallen along with my clothes. It was pooled around my feet, and when I reached down to grab it, he pulled me to his chest again and wrapped me in a hug.

"I'm sorry," Brad replied sincerely.

I could hear that he meant it. His voice was soft and caring like it always was when he was trying to make me feel better about something.

"I didn't mean to put you in a compromising situation. I know that you and Ethan are dating, and he's a good guy. I want you to be happy."

Even if it's not with me. He didn't say it, but I could hear his voice in my head.

He pulled back and opened the door. As soon as he was out, I grabbed my clothes and quickly dressed for the party. My hair was barely damp now, and I decided that pulling it up would be the most manageable for tonight. My chest and face were glowing, and the little bit of makeup that I put on barely concealed the fact that I got more sun than I should have.

I found Brad waiting in the living room for me when I came downstairs. I wondered if he would still even be here. I knew that he cared about me, but I still couldn't get past what just happened. He broke more than just my father's rule about keeping the door open. He broke at least three rules of friendship back in my room.

I was angry with him for the first time in a very long time. He was pushing the boundaries of our friendship. He would have never done this a year ago. The more I think about what happened, the angrier I got and the more I tried to analyze it. Brad had always had a girlfriend—until he broke up with Claire, that is. Maybe it was only safe for us to be close when there was a person in the way of what he wanted. With Claire or someone else as a roadblock, Brad seemed to keep his hands to himself and respect the boundaries of our relationship. Why was he not treating my relationship with Ethan in the same respect?

We headed to the party in silence. I didn't really know what I want to say to him or how to say it. He seemed calm and relaxed, like nothing even happened. That infuriated me even more. It's not like he would lose anything if Ethan and I broke up. He wouldn't gain anything either, though, and I don't think he realized that. I still lived across the country.

As we pulled in the driveway, he finally spoke. I could barely hear what he was saying, and I was not sure that I even wanted to, but I reached over and turned the radio off anyway. He was not looking at me; he was staring straight ahead.

"What?" I half screamed at him not taking into account the silence that now encompassed the car. I still sounded angry, probably because I was.

"I know that you're mad at me, and I can't blame you." He paused and continued to stare out the front window. "I have to ask you something. You don't have to answer. I have to get this off my chest though."

"What?" The anger had subsided a little, but it was still there and ever present in my tone.

"Well, I was wondering, you know, if things between you and Ethan…well, if they didn't end up working, if…well…"

Was he asking me to consider him if things didn't work out with Ethan? Was this a joke? I didn't want to consider that. I was happy with my relationship at the moment, and I didn't want to think about the what-ifs.

"I don't know what you want me to say. I don't even really know what you're asking." I stuttered a little as the words came out of my mouth.

"Do you love me?" Brad whispered.

Just like that. He spat it out, and there it was, floating around in the car, creating some serious tension.

"I...I...I don't know how to answer that." I needed to take a deep breath. Did I love him? Of course, I did, but in what way? "I do, in a lot of ways, but not in others. Do you get what I'm saying? Am I making any sense?"

We sat in silence for what felt like forever. All I could think about was saying the wrong thing to kill the quiet in the car. The tension was building by the second, and all I wanted was for it to go away. I wanted things to go back to normal. I wanted my best friend back, right? Is that all I wanted?

I had to get out of my own head. I was starting to confuse myself. I was happy with Ethan. I was enjoying our relationship. We fought to be able to have one, even though we shouldn't have had to. We were making it work. It was worth the fight.

"I love you, you know that? More than I can describe and in so many different ways. I love the way you laugh. I love the way my heart rate picks up when I get a text from you or see your name on my phone when you call. I love that you know me better than anyone else. I love that you believe in me and trust me."

There was a long pause before he continued. "What I don't love is knowing that I wasted so much time trying to fight the feelings I had for you so that I could save our friendship. I don't love knowing that there is someone else who gets to hold you, to kiss you, to be there for you because I can't be. I don't love that I am going crazy and doing things that make you angry. I don't love crossing the line with you because it makes me not trust myself with you."

Holy crap! He's just declared his undying love to me, and all I can do is stare at him. His profile was beautiful with the moonlight shining in the window next to him. When he turned to face me and our eyes met, I don't know why but I reached out and cupped his cheek in my hand. He slowly leaned into it and closed his eyes. What the hell was I going to do now?

Brad seemed to realize how confused I was with him and kept his distance at the party. My girlfriends and I were dancing and singing at the top of our lungs. A new song came on, and I started singing until I realized that my friends were silent. I followed their gaze across the room and saw who had caused them to clam up. It was Claire, of course. I should have guessed that we would cross paths over the summer, but I never even gave it much thought.

The fact that she was at *my* party *uninvited* didn't bother me. She was friends with a lot of my friends, and I was surprised that she wasn't at any of the other parties. I went back to dancing and pulled Emma and Ella with me. I could see Claire out of the corner of my eye. She was watching me. She had a look in her eye that made me a little uneasy, but I tried to ignore her and have some fun with my friends before I had to head home.

After about twenty minutes of dancing and singing, I was parched and sweating. My body felt like it was on fire, only partially from the sunburn. Ella and I headed to the kitchen, grabbed a bottle of water, and walked out the slider to the backyard. The grass was so incredibly green and beautiful. I forgot how much I loved to walk with my bare feet on the grass until I was staring at yards full of sand and rock.

I slipped out of my flip-flops and enjoyed the feeling of the blades between my toes. The cool air, mixed with the cold grass, sent a little chill up my body, which felt absolutely fantastic and immediately cooled the fire within my body. I lay down in the grass, and after a small chuckle from Ella, she followed suit. We didn't say anything to each other for the longest time. I was caught up with looking at the stars and wondering if Ethan had a clear sky tonight. The last time I took a moment to stop and look at the stars was with him, and I started to miss him. The feeling only lasted a few minutes before Ella, as if reading my mind, asked about him.

"So tell me about this guy you're seeing. Ethan, right?" Ella eagerly asked.

Ella and I texted a bit after I left, but that was about it. She was just as busy as I was. The thought that we wouldn't be friends when I came home never entered my mind. I would be friends with her ten years from now, even if I didn't talk to her again until then. I didn't want that to happen. I wanted her to be a part of my life, but being far away didn't allow us to keep our friendship close, like it did with me and Brad.

"Yep. Ethan's great. He's funny and a lot of fun to hang around with. A *fabulous* kisser, of course."

That got a giggle out of her. It felt like old times, lying in the grass with my friend and talking about boys.

"What do you want to know?" I hesitantly asked. I wasn't sure how much I really wanted to share knowing that anyone could be lurking around the corner listening to our conversation.

"I don't know. What's he look like? What's he in to? Sports? Just the normal stuff," she replied.

"He's your average tall dark and handsome guy. Strikingly gorgeous. His eyes are the most beautiful emerald green. He's a tennis player like me."

Another giggle escaped her lips. I was playing with my ring, wishing that I could see it right now, knowing that it matched Ethan's eyes perfectly. Thinking about my ring made me think of Brad too. I was still utterly confused and pushed him from my mind before continuing.

"He's actually got a full-ride scholarship to play tennis in college. He's checking out three colleges while I'm here to decide which one he wants to go to." I was whispering by the time I finished my sentence. The thought of him going away to college made me sad.

"Wow! He must be good." Ella replied sounding impressed.

"I think he takes it easy on me when we play, but I hold my own."

"So you're happy then?"

"Yeah. Why?"

"I don't know. I just figured that when Brad left to go to visit you that things would change."

I thought about it for a second from her point of view. He flew all the way to see me, and when he got there, it was obvious that he wanted more from me. When he left, though, he left me with Ethan to take care of me. He gave me up for the right reasons. Did he give me up? He wasn't acting like it lately, and it made me wonder if he was *allowing* Ethan to take care of me in his place until I was able to come home again.

Just the thought of all the drama that had occurred, was still occurring, made me inhale sharply and exhale slowly. "Not really. We've talked about it a bit, but you have to understand that being friends with someone for so long doesn't mean that they should be in a relationship together. I love him to death, and I always will, but I live so far away now. There is no way that it could work, and I'm not sure if it would even if I was still living here."

Saying those things out loud eased the confusion in me a little. I had to pause before I asked her what I really wanted to know. There was no easy way to do this, but I had to know the answer.

I sat up and took a deep breath before I found the words spilling past my lips. "Do you know how long he's had feelings for me?"

Ella's voice was just a whisper as she began to speak. "Well, I know it's been awhile now. I think the first time he told me he was feeling something *more* toward you was right before he started dating Claire. It was weird because he told me that, and then like a week later, they were together."

"Really? That was over a year ago."

"I know. When did you realize that you had feelings for him?"

Her question took me off guard, and I couldn't bring myself to look at her. I started to think back to when I first started to have feelings for Brad. I had been suppressing those feelings for so long that I couldn't remember the last time I didn't have feelings for him. That couldn't be right.

"I don't know." My voice was crackling as I spoke, and I knew that I sounded weak in that moment. "I can't remember a time when I didn't have feelings for him, I guess. He's been my best friend since middle school. I guess I always had some sort of crush on him."

Just saying those words out loud scared the crap out of me. Had I always been in love with Brad? I hadn't dated anyone serious until Ethan. I never "crushed" on anyone. I was always focused on school and tennis. I didn't have time to date anyone with my crazy schedule. The only thing I made time for was hanging out with my friends on the weekends, hanging out with Brad. Maybe I had been in love with him all this time.

A small smile appeared on my lips as I looked over and saw Brad talking to some friends through the window, all the anger I had been holding in evaporating from my body. He was a beautiful person and a great friend—he always had been. Why didn't I see this sooner?

"If you love him, doesn't that mean you should at least give it a chance?"

She's right. I should have given us a chance. Now the opportunity had passed us by, and we both needed to accept that. I had moved on, but he still needed to. If he wasn't interested in Claire anymore, then he needed to find someone else. I wanted him to be happy, and there was no way that he was going to be able to find the happiness he wanted with me, at least not right now.

"I think our opportunity has passed us by. He needs to find someone who understands him as well as I do and find happiness with them." I stated, taking note of the sadness in my voice.

Saying it out loud made it so real that I think my heart skipped a beat. Would there ever be anyone else who would be able to understand him like I do?

I glanced at Ella to find her twisting her hands in her lap and staring intently at them. She had a crush on Brad. Her body language made it apparent to me, even though I knew she would never admit it to anyone, probably not even Brad.

CHAPTER 15

I woke up Monday morning with a small smile on my face. I realized that I must have had an exceptional dream to wake up this happy. My smile faded when I had a quick flashback to my dream and realized that I was dreaming about Brad.

I was supposed to be dreaming about Ethan. He was my boyfriend, not Brad. Thoughts of him were supposed to be the ones that should awake me with a smile. Thoughts of him were supposed to be what brings sunshine to my day. Why was I dreaming about Brad?

I could only think to blame Ella. She made me start thinking about him in a new light. It didn't help that Brad had declared his feelings to me that same night, but it was her questioning me that was making me question myself and my feelings for him. I didn't want to question our friendship. I wanted things to go back to the way they were before I told him that I was moving. I wanted my best friend back.

It hit me like a brick wall at that very moment. Our relationship had changed the moment he kissed me in my car. He told me how he felt about me, and I chalked it up to him being scared that I was leaving. I never put real thought into the fact that he loved me. I had been so used to pushing my feelings for him aside that I never stopped to consider what it all really meant.

Everything Ella said last night made perfect sense now. He had developed feelings for me way before I found out I was moving. He knew that he would lose me when I left, but he tried hard to fight for me before I went—he was still trying now. It felt like he had shattered my heart in that moment because I knew that I would lose him, his friendship, and his love. How had I not seen this before?

I could feel a tear slide down my cheek, and I wiped it away with the back of my hand. Another tear fell, and I didn't even bother to catch it before it rolled all the way down my cheek. More tears were flowing before I could reel my emotions in, and after a few minutes, my face was soaked along with my pillow.

He tried to fight for us, and I tried to push him away. After so many years of friendship, I was afraid to lose him in that respect. I pushed him away, thinking I would always be able to keep our relationship in that bubble I created, and now I know that when I leave this time, I will probably lose him forever unless I could fix *us*.

Damn it! There was an "us" again. I wanted there to be a relationship between me and Brad, but just not the kind that he wanted. I *needed* him to be my best friend. I wanted that. Even if there was no Ethan, I would only want friendship from Brad, right? I guess that would be the question of the hour.

I pulled myself out of bed, showered, and got dressed. I knew that I needed to talk to Brad and get this figured out, but at the moment I wanted nothing more than to be alone with my pending thoughts. I needed to figure out what I wanted, who I wanted. I needed to decide what was best for me, not anyone else. I grabbed my racket and headed to the high school.

As I get out of my car, deja vu took over, and I was remembering the last time I was in that very spot. My eyes found the baseball dugout, and the memories came flooding back. I closed my eyes and pulled myself back to the here and now. I began to feel the inner calm I was looking for, so I opened my eyes and focused on my walk to the courts.

Once I was inside the gate, I was in the zone. My focus was solely on pounding the crap out of the ball and nothing else. I grabbed my favorite racket and headed over to the practice wall. I was pretty sure the coach had this put up just for me. It was just a large piece of plywood attached to the fencing, pretty much all our small school could afford, but it was perfect for hitting against yourself.

After only about five minutes, I was sweating profusely and thirsty. I ripped one more backhand and let the ball fly past me. I headed toward my bag where I could hear my cell phone ringing. I reached inside and pull out a bottle of water, but let my phone continue to ring.

An hour later, I was exhausted, and my body was a little sore. My sunburn had faded since yesterday, but the heat was still rising from it and was making me even hotter than I normally would be after an hour of practice. I decided to call it a day just as my phone rings again.

This was the fourth or fifth time I heard my phone ring since I got here, and I had been ignoring it. I found it just as the caller was sent to voicemail. I scanned my missed calls. I had seven missed calls—two from Brad, four from Ethan, and the most-recent one from my mom. She was getting a call back first.

"Hey, girly," my Mom said just as she picked up the phone. You could hear the excitement in her voice.

"Hey, Mom. What's going on?" I asked a little out of breath still.

"Nothing. Just checking up on you. You sound tired."

"Just got done practicing at the high school, so I'm a little worn out."

"You're supposed to be on vacation, *relaxing*. I didn't even realize that you took your rackets with you."

"Playing relaxes me. It helps me think and clear my head."

"What do you need to think about that requires you to *work* in the middle of your vacation? Is everything okay?"

"Everything is fine, Mom. I just needed to be alone for a while, time to think about everything that's changed in the last year."

"I know you miss home, and I'm sorry I took you from there, but you like it here, right?"

I didn't even have to take a moment to think about my answer. "Yeah I like it there, but being here makes me want to be here, you know? When I'm there, I want to be there, and when I'm here, I want to be here. Does that make any sense?"

"It does, completely. You know, you're going to be eighteen in less than six month and then off to college after that. You can go to school anywhere you want and do anything you want. You don't have to stay here or there."

I knew she was trying to make me feel better, but it was not really helping. I had a lot of decisions to make right now; thinking about more decisions to make in the future would make my brain go into overload.

"I know, Mom. I'm gonna get packed up and head home for a shower. I'll call you later this week, okay?"

"Sounds good. Relax a little, honey. You're supposed to be on vacation, remember?"

"I know. Love you, Mom."

"Love you too. Bye."

As I drove home, I realized that not only had I not made a single decision about my current problems, but now I knew that I had a big decision to make coming up soon. I understood why Ethan was taking his time with the college choice now. It was a really big decision to make.

With thoughts of Ethan in my head, I decided to return his call. I figured that after talking to him, I would feel better about everything. He had a way of calming me when he doesn't even know that I need him to. The sound of his voice alone would help me to relax a little—I used to get that feeling with Brad too. Crap!

"Hey, gorgeous!" Ethan exclaimed. I could hear the excitement in his voice as he answered the phone. "I've been trying to get ahold of you."

"Sorry. I was practicing, and I didn't hear my phone." Lie number 1. "What's going on?"

"Nothing. I was just finishing packing and wanted to hear your voice. What else are you going to do today?"

"I'm not sure. All I can think about right now is a hot shower." Lie number 2. I was thinking about Brad two seconds before he picked up the phone.

"Well, maybe you should relax a bit. You sound stressed out."

How did he know that? "Not really. I'm just a little tired. I didn't sleep well last night." Lie's number 3 (yes, I was stressed out) and 4 (I slept great last night dreaming about someone else). I had to get off the phone before I set a record for the number of lies in one conversation.

"Well, just relax today then. How about you take a nap, and I'll call you when I check into my hotel and we can talk then?"

"That sounds great." Truth number 1! Yeah!

"Okay, talk to you later then."

"Okay, bye."

I didn't feel better after talking to Ethan for the first time ever. I felt worse. I lied to him without even thinking about it. The words just flew right out of my mouth, no hesitation, kind of like "word vomit." I was quickly becoming a horrible girlfriend.

I should have told him about what happened last night. I should have told him about Brad walking in on me. I should have told him about our conversation in the car, about Brad's confession. I didn't want to keep things from him. I didn't *want* to lie to him. I needed to tell him those things. Tonight. I would tell him tonight... or maybe after he was done with his visit so that I wouldn't upset him. Soon, anyway.

After I rinsed the sweat and lies from my body, I decided that I need to call Brad back. He has called twice since I left the tennis courts, and he probably won't stop calling until he could talk to me. I hoped everything was all right. He doesn't normally call me so many times, and I never normally dodge his calls. After being such a horrible girlfriend, I was quickly adding being a horrible friend to my list of accomplishments today.

I was sitting on my bed, and my hands were shaking. I was staring at my phone that was on my lap. I was trying to give myself a mental pep talk, but I shouldn't have to do that. He was my best friend. I should be able to talk to him about anything without being nervous.

I chickened out on calling him and sent him a quick text instead.

NOT FEELING GREAT TAKING A NAP CALL U LATER

That was not exactly a total lie, but not exactly the truth either. I was not feeling all that great. My stomach was in knots, and I was starting to get a mini stress-induced headache. I probably should rest for a while. Maybe when I wake up, all my problems would be solved for me—probably not.

After taking two aspirins, I turned my phone off and crawled under the covers. The chill in the air from the air conditioning was just enough to make me want to curl up in the covers. I closed my eyes and wondered what I would dream about this time. *Who I would dream about?* As my body began to relax, I could feel myself being pulled under and then blackness.

I woke up with a start. My room was dark, and I could see that I'd slept all day. Great! Now I won't be able to sleep tonight. I should have set my alarm clock, but I didn't realize how exhausted my body was. I hadn't worked that hard at the courts, but I guess physical exhaustion and mental exhaustion combined drained me completely.

I grabbed my cell phone and turned it back on. I waited until it was on my home screen and dialed up my voicemail before it even told me I had any. I knew I'd missed Ethan's calls and Brad had probably called too.

> Hey gorgeous! You must be sleeping. I got here a bit early and just thought I would give you a call. I'll try you again later. Miss you.

He was so sweet. A smile began to creep across my face until I remembered that I had lied to him a bunch of times earlier.

> Becca, where are you? I've been trying to reach you all day. Call me back.

Brad sounded freaked out a bit. I wondered what was going on. He was always so laid back.

> Becca. Call me back ASAP. I can't seem to find you and I'm freaking out. I just found your water bottle at the courts but there's no sign of you. Are you all right?

Crap! He would jump to the worst possible conclusion. Only one more message and then I'd call him to reassure him I was safe and sound.

> Hey gorgeous. I hope your not still sleeping. Call me when you get this. I'm a little worried that I haven't been able to get ahold of you for hours now.

Crap! Now I've got both of them worried. Who should I call first? I dialed and hit Send right away, knowing the answer to my own question.

"Hey, gorgeous! Where have you been?" Ethan asked quickly. His voice sounded a little panicked, and I immediately felt bad for causing him stress. He needed to be relaxed and focused for his visit tomorrow.

"Sorry. I turned my phone off and fell asleep. I didn't realize how tired I was, I guess." I replied trying to sound upbeat but nonchalant at the same time.

"Next time, don't shut your phone off. Brad and I have been freaking out. Have you called him yet?"

What? He'd been talking to Brad? How was this possible? Why? The last thing I want was for the two of them to be "friends."

That would be uncomfortable, to say the least. Plus, Brad hasn't been acting like a very good *friend* to Ethan since I've been home.

"Seriously? You've been talking to Brad? Why?" I could hear the anger building in my voice, and I knew that I needed to dial it back a little. He was worried about me, and the least I could do was be grateful that he cared.

"He was worried and called me to see if I had spoken with you today. I told him I talked to you while you were at the courts, and that was it. He sounded worried. He said he had been trying to get ahold of you all day and that you hadn't called him back."

I let out the breath that I was holding. That wasn't so bad. They were discussing me, both worried about me. There was no talk about anything else. Good.

"He thinks you're avoiding him for some reason. What's going on, Becca?" Ethan asked sounding more annoyed than concerned all of the sudden.

The way he said my name was a little unnerving. Normally it rolled off his tongue in the most seductive way, but not this time. This time, it was very clearly two syllables. It sounded more like the way my mom says my name when she is being firm. Was I in trouble?

"Nothing is going on. I'm not sure why he thinks I'm avoiding him. I just saw him last night. We went to a party together." Not bad. I only lied twice.

"Well, you need to call him. He's freaking out thinking someone kidnapped you. If I didn't know better, I would think—never mind. I need to go grab a bite to eat and turn in early. Can I call you tomorrow after I get done for the day?"

"Sure." I replied, drawing the word out, showing my confusion. *Are we all right?* That was what I really wanted to ask. I could feel the tension over the phone, and all I wanted to do right now was pull him close and hold him to me. "I miss you." That was the best I could do.

"I miss you too. Talk to you tomorrow."

"Okay, bye."

I hung up feeling mentally exhausted again. I knew I needed to call Brad, and that, in itself, was going to drain the rest of my energy. Maybe I would be able to sleep tonight. As I dialed his number, I knew that this conversation might last a while, so I crawled back under the covers.

It started to ring, but I could hear it echoing in my other ear and it was getting louder. Why was he not answering? Another ring and the echoing sounded like it was coming from the hallway. I tossed the covers back and moved to open my door when it shot open.

I jumped back, not expecting anyone to be there, and dropped my phone as Brad wrapped his arms around me and pulled me in tight. I could feel him shaking a little and realized that he really was scared that he lost me.

I knew that he needed to be held more than I did, so I wrapped my arms around him the best I could and squeezed. He squeezed me back, and I let out a little chuckle. Everything was going to be just fine.

I felt him pull away, and as I got a look at his face, I could see that he'd been worried. He was frowning at me, and his eyes were filled with concern. I gave him a tentative smile, and I could feel his body relax a little against mine. His face went from concerned to serious, with a hint of anger lurking under the surface. The change in his demeanor made me want to take a step back, but I was holding my ground.

"I'm sorry if I worried you. I fell asleep." I said hoping that an apology would help to turn this situation around.

"*Worried* doesn't even begin to cover how I was feeling. I called your mom. I called your dad. I even called Ethan. I was freaking out. Then I found your water bottle at the tennis courts, and I really started to think that something had happened." Brad hollered. He was talking so fast that when he stopped, I didn't realize that I was staring at him still.

His eyes were full of anger, lust, and passion. That's when I knew that I needed to break free of his hold immediately, but I was unable to move. My legs wouldn't cooperate with my brain. My body was leaning forward before my brain could pull it back. The moment our lips met, I knew that I was in trouble. It was an innocent kiss until Brad took control of the situation, and then it was anything but innocent. Crap!

CHAPTER 16

When I started to wake up, I couldn't help but snuggle closer to the warmth. I scooted backward and found myself encased by it. The body heat he was giving off was enough to keep us both warm, and last night it had.

After our innocent kiss turned more *passionate*, I was able to calm myself down and get the situation under control. After we both took a moment to get our hormones in check, we lay down and talked for most of the night. About the time Brad was breaking curfew, I fell asleep in his arms, and that was where I ended up staying. We were on top of the sheets, and the door was open. I realize that the situation looked bad, but it was very innocent in nature.

I was going to tell Brad everything as soon as he woke up. I needed to get my feelings and concerns off my chest. I needed to be honest with him about how I felt. I didn't want to hurt him, but I was also hurting right now because I really wasn't sure what I wanted anymore. When I'm with Brad it feels right but when I'm with Ethan it feels right too. I want both of them in my life in one way or another and I was afraid that if I didn't make a decision soon that I would lose both of them.

"What are you thinking about that you look so serious this early in the morning?" Brad asked.

The sound of his voice brought me back to reality. I was just thinking about how incredibly crazy this situation was. Did I really want to tell him that? "Nothing really. I was just thinking." I said. You could hear the uncertainty I was feeling as I spoke.

"I don't buy it. I know you a little better than that, and by the look on your face, you were deep in thought."

"I was, but it's nothing to be concerned about." Now I was lying to Brad. If I was being truthful all around, I would admit I was lying to myself. There were plenty of things to be concerned about.

"Well, whenever you're ready to confess, I will be here to listen." He shifted his body so that he was propped up on one elbow. I knew that he could see my face, so lying was no longer an option. "By the look in your eyes you need to get something off your chest. Care to share?"

He knew me too well. I definitely needed to get something off my chest, but I had no idea where to start. How could I tell him how I felt until I could really decide how I felt? I needed time to figure it out. I needed time alone, without Brad hovering over me the way he was right now. I needed time without his arm wrapped protectively around my waist. I needed time without his close proximity making my head foggy with the wonderful smell of him.

I moved to sit up and swung my legs over the side of the bed. "I need to think about some things before I share them with anyone else. I have to know what *I* want first."

His silence told me that he was reading into what I was saying and that he knew exactly what I needed to figure out. I expected no less from him. He understood me better than I understand myself some days, and knowing that he'd give me as much space as I needed only confirmed how well he knew me.

I knew that our kiss last night allowed some of his currently expressed feelings to fly freely. I had a choice to make. I could tell him to reel his feelings back in, and we could move on like before. Or I could tell him the exact opposite…

I needed to figure this out quickly. My vacation was halfway over; I was leaving in ten days, and by the time I leave, I need know what I want, who I want. That was not a lot of time to figure out much of anything. With Brad here and Ethan far away, the choice could be swayed in his favor, but soon I would be back home, and the choice could be swayed the other way. What I really needed was a vacation from my vacation so that I had time to think.

I covered my face with my hands and spoke softly. "I think I am going to go to my grandparents' cabin this weekend." I wanted him to know where I was at because I didn't want him to worry. The hesitation in my voice told him that I was feeling out the situation.

"Do you want company, or is this a trip you want to take alone?" Brad asked with sincerity.

Good. He got the message loud and clear.

"I think I'm gonna head up there alone. I'll bring a couple of books and my Wi-Fi card so that I can have some contact with the outside world. I just need a few days to myself to sort through everything that's swimming in my brain."

"I get it, I really do, but can you at least take your sister so that you're not out there alone in the middle of nowhere?"

The last time I went to my grandparents' cabin was with Brad. We had decided to camp on their land deep in the woods to make it seem more real. I had only lasted about an hour in the darkness before I begged Brad to take me back to the safety of the cabin. Every noise had been accentuated by the eerie silence, and I had freaked out.

"I'll ask her but I don't know if she'll want to go. She's been attached at the hip to Kel since we got back, and I don't know if I'll be able to separate them."

"Then take them both. There's a lake up there, right? Take your suit and go swimming, relax a little, and then come back here to me for the last few days." He was pleading with me, and I didn't need to look at his face to know that he was disappointed that I wouldn't be around for the last weekend of my vacation.

"Maybe I will. I need to hop in the shower. Will you still be here when I get out?"

"Do you want me to be?"

I was expecting that to sound playful coming from him, but he was serious. I needed to get us back to playful and away from all the serious stuff until I made a decision this weekend.

"Either way." I was trying my best to sound indifferent to his decision. "I have a few errands to run today, and I promised Natalie that I would give her a call this afternoon, but if you wanna get together tonight after dinner and go to a movie or something, that's fine."

He moved to sit next to me on the bed and grabbed my hand. As he laced our fingers together, I knew that taking time away from him would be the best way to make an unbiased decision. His thumb was stroking my ring, and I could see that he wanted to say something.

"I'll pick you up at seven, and we'll go see something at the new theatre down town." Brad said, his words sounding forced.

I don't think that was what he had wanted to say. "Sounds like a plan." I replied, trying to keep my voice upbeat and light as if I hadn't noticed the change in his demeanor.

With that, I let his fingers fall from mine, stood, and I made my way to the bathroom. I could feel the loss of his warmth, but I didn't look back. Instead, I grabbed a towel from the hall closet and closed the bathroom door behind me before I slid to the floor and propped my head in my hands. I felt like I wanted to cry, but I didn't allow the tears to come.

As we pulled up to my grandparents' cabin, I could feel my inner calm descend upon me. This place had always been my saving grace. When my grandparents built it ten years ago, I thought they were crazy for wanting to spend their vacations in the woods. Now I understand that the silence can bring an inner calm that cannot even be described—as long as I stay inside the cabin after dark.

As that inner calm filled my body, I opened my door and dug the cabin keys out of my pocket. I used to think that the one-bedroom cabin was huge. Staring at it now, I could see how small and cozy it was. The wraparound porch was welcoming, but the vast amount of trees that surrounded the place still gave me the creeps. I was glad my sister and Kel had decided to come with me. I probably wouldn't have been able to get much sleep, if any.

We each grabbed our bags and headed to the front door. As I slid the key in the lock, the only thing running through my mind was which book to read first. I stopped by the bookstore before we left town. The thought process was to pick up nothing involving romance. Unfortunately, that's what I ended up picking out in the end. I was a sucker for a good love story. Maybe one of the books would lead me to my answer.

I dropped my bag on the floor just inside the door and breathe in. The cabin still smelled of grandma's cooking. How that's possible when I know they haven't been up here in weeks was beyond me, but it was comforting. Amy and Kel shuffled in behind me and dropped their bags before heading back out to the car to get the groceries we picked up.

I started loading soda and water into the fridge as Amy made some sandwiches for lunch. I was waiting patiently for one of them to ask the question that had been lingering all week: *Why?* I didn't really even know what I was going to say when they asked about the impromptu trip. I really just needed to get away for the weekend. I needed a vacation from my vacation. Hopefully, they would accept that answer.

Knowing my sister, it would not be the end of the conversation. She was too insightful to not see that there was more to the story than that, especially since Brad isn't with us. Today marked the first day of my vacation that I hadn't seen him. I talked to him before we left town—Ethan too—but I have not seen him since yesterday.

After lunch, Amy and Kel decided that they were going to take a walk in the woods. They asked if I want to come, but I declined. I pulled out one of the books I bought and stretched out on the couch, knowing that in the complete silence that will soon encompass the cabin, I won't be able to read even one sentence.

As soon as they were out the door, I traded in my book for a notebook. As I drew the line down the middle of the first page, I couldn't help but think about how juvenile this felt—comparing the two of them like I was listing ingredients for a recipe. It was the only thing I could think of to do at the moment that would allow me to put my feelings on paper.

I started listing all of Brad's positive traits on the left side of the paper. Things like his smile, his sense of humor and the way he protects me. The list went on and on. When I couldn't think of anything else to add, I started writing the things that I loved about Ethan on the right side of the paper. After just listing a few, I already knew what the answer was, and I closed the notebook. I smiled at the thought of wrapping my arms around him, the thought of him holding me close and kissing me until my knees are weak and I'm completely breathless.

With my mind clearly made up, I pulled my book back out and started to read. It was not long before I was sound asleep and dreaming of the one that I had just chosen. My dream was peaceful and light until I awoke with a start and realized that someone was going to be hurt by my decision.

When the girls return from their walk, we had a small snack since we ate lunch so late, and we all turned in for the night. I had given them the bedroom, so I was back on the couch. My thoughts were keeping me tossing and turning, afraid to fall asleep and dream. It wasn't until dawn was breaking that my exhaustion finally took over and I fell asleep.

Two very unrelaxing days later, on our way back home, Amy waited for Kel to fall asleep before asking me about the real reason for our trip. I didn't want to lie to her. I'd been doing enough of that as it was, but I also knew that she might not understand completely.

"I just needed to get away and think some things out. Thanks for coming with me." I replied not taking my eyes off the road ahead.

"No problem." Amy said. "Did you figure it all out?"

"I think so." I was pretty sure I knew what I wanted at that point, but I was afraid I would change my mind once I immersed myself back into the real world.

"Want my advice?"

Did I want the advice of a twelve-year-old girl? It couldn't hurt to hear what she had to say, I guess. How much insight could she really give me on my situation anyway?

"Sure," I said tentatively, waiting to see if she wanted me to continue. As I was about to, she spoke up.

"I think you should finally let go of Brad and move on with Ethan. They're both great, but you don't live here anymore, and if you try to make things work with Brad, you're just going to end up ruining your friendship." Spoken like an adult, Amy's words could not have been truer.

She paused for a moment, and I wanted to say something in response, but I was at a loss for words. I think my mouth had even dropped open a few inches. She took this as her cue to continue.

"No offense, but I do not want to be around when you are mourning the loss of Brad. Plus, as best friends go, he's pretty great, and *when* you choose Ethan, he will know you are in good hands. It's the only way to have a win-win situation out of the mess you've created for yourself. Plus, this way no one gets hurt."

I was still speechless, but it also appeared that she was done. We were silent the rest of the way home while I pondered what my little sister just dropped on me. She not only hit the nail on the head, but I had a feeling that this entire trip could have been avoided if I had just asked for her opinion. She obviously knew what was going on. She confirmed everything for me in just a few sentences. I was making the right decision, for the right reason.

CHAPTER 17

My last full day in Michigan was spent with my friends at the beach. We arrived early enough to get a great spot and still be able to enjoy the sun for most of the day. We were planning on building a bonfire and camping out overnight. The thought of sleeping next to Brad one last time had my stomach in knots most of the afternoon. I was trying to let go of him, of the thought of us, and letting go was hard enough without putting myself in those types of situations.

I had talked to Ethan earlier that morning before Brad picked me up. He knew that I was on the late-afternoon flight and that my mom was working, so he would be picking us up at the airport. I told him everything that had been going on over the last few weeks with Brad. I wanted to be honest with him. I wanted him to know I chose him.

He didn't want to talk about Brad or anything that had happened after I explained to him that I was coming back to him. He knew about all the compromising situations, the stolen kisses, and my constant mental debate. He knew that I was trying to make it all make sense for him, but instead of talking it out, he changed the subject. I think that he knew he would never be able to understand my relationship with Brad, so he was letting it go. All of it.

He said that his last college visit was his favorite. He hadn't spoken much about it until this morning, saying that he had pretty much made up his mind. He was on a deadline to call

all three coaches by lunch time tomorrow, so when he picked me up at the airport, his decision would be sealed. Hopefully, he would share with me where he was going when he picked me up. I close my eyes and drift off with the image of Ethan's face in the forefront of my mind.

I awoke from my daydreams as Brad plopped down in the sand next to me. We'd been inseparable since I got back from the cabin. I hadn't shared my revelation with him, but I was pretty sure that he knew. I had been keeping my physical distance from him as much as possible. Sure, we had been hanging out, having coffee, and he even stayed at Ella and Emma's with me earlier this week. Emotionally, I was pretty sure that he knew my decision and understood it mostly. Mentally, I wasn't sure if he was grasping it all that well.

It was the little things. Some of the things that he would say, comments that he would make, that threw me off balance once in a while. It had never been like that before. Nothing was as it was before he kissed me that first time in my car. Things had definitely changed and not for the better. I still wanted my best friend back. His unconditional love was about all that remained from last fall.

"So, ready to get back home?" Brad asked, the sadness he felt evident as he spoke each word.

"This is home," I said with a smile, knowing that no matter where I live, Michigan would always be my home. "I am ready to get back to my mom though—and Ethan."

That was the first time I had mentioned him to Brad in over a week. Just hearing his name made Brad cringe a little. I could see the expression he was trying to hide behind his sunglasses. I could see his body tense and then how he had to make himself relax. All these things made me feel like crap, but I couldn't help but be excited to see Ethan. As my one and only best friend, I should be able to share these things with him.

"Well, I was getting sick of hanging out with you so much, so I'm ready for you to head back." His voice was dripping with sarcasm, but he was unable to hide the hint of sadness that was lurking behind it. "Now I have time to hang out with my many other friends."

"You can always come back with me." The words were out of my mouth before I could stop them. I wasn't even sure I heard myself right until he jerked his head toward me and raised his eyebrow in question. I definitely said that. Crap!

"I don't think your boyfriend would approve of me coming home with you. I have a feeling he wants you all to himself for a while before he heads off to college."

"You're probably right."

The tone of his voice stung a little, and the fact that he's hurting made something in my chest crack. I thought my heart shattered long ago when I was forced to leave him. Now I realized that the sting of leaving him the first time didn't even compare to the thought of leaving him again.

I needed to lighten to mood. "You know, we are going to be off to college before you know it. Any idea where you want to go yet? Any colleges looking to pick up a freshman starting QB?"

"That depends on where you're going. I always thought we would go to college together, didn't you?" Brad asked.

"Yeah, but where? I have no idea where I want to go. I have no idea if I will get an offer to play tennis. What if you get an offer to play football? We may end up even farther away from each other than we are now."

We sat in silence for a few minutes, letting the reality of the situation sink in. We had planned on going to college together since freshman year when the counselor started lecturing us on getting the right grades and being involved in the right activities. We never gave much thought to the fact that we may not end up in the same place. Moving across the country had thrown that plan completely out the window, and it wasn't until that moment that I realized how far apart our lives had drifted.

"We still have time to figure it out," I said, breaking the silence that was compounding our problem by the second. "We can apply to the same schools and figure it out from there."

As if knowing that there was nothing left to say about the topic at the moment, Brad nodded his head and stood up. I watched him walk over to where the rest of our friends were starting to build the bonfire. Our friendship was struggling. I had less than twenty-four hours to fix *us*, and I didn't have the slightest clue how to do that. There were too many things that were hanging on by a thread in our relationship that if just one of those threads broke, I was afraid that it would start a chain reaction.

I watched the sunset over Lake Michigan for my final time this summer. I knew that I would see it again and that I would probably have the company of most of my friends next time, but it sure made things feel a little final. It felt more like summer was coming to a close than anything else. It felt like we should be going back to school on Monday, instead of me flying away tomorrow.

I sat alone and watched until darkness fell. I wanted to remember this moment for as long as I could. I was still staring out at the water when I felt Brad come up behind me and sit down. I scooted between his legs and went willingly into his open arms, relaxing my head against his chest. That's when I started to let the tears fall. I knew that the only reason I was feeling this way was because I was afraid of what would happen after tomorrow.

I wanted to stay in Michigan. I wanted to start my senior year with my friends. I wanted to watch the sunset over the lake a million more times that summer. Most of all, I wanted to stay wrapped in Brad's arms. I wanted to feel like I did when his fingers grazed my ring. I wanted to feel like it all had meaning, that I had meaning, that *we* had meaning.

As the night started to wind down and everyone started to pull out their sleeping bags, I made sure I placed mine next to

Brad's. We had barely spoken since this afternoon other than in passing. With the exception of the sunset, he kept his distance from me, and with only a few more hours to spend together, I was going to make sure that we actually spend it *together*, not tiptoeing around each other.

This was my last chance to explain to Brad how I felt. I was a nervous wreck, and the possibilities of how the conversation could go were endless. I wanted once again to tell him the truth about my feelings for him, but I knew that it would only make my decision harder on him and on me. After everything was said and done, he might never want to speak with me again, and just the thought of that scared the hell out of me. I was not willing to lose my best friend.

Everyone started to settle in for the night, except Brad. I sat up and looked around, but I didn't see him anywhere. I grabbed the closest sweatshirt, his, and tugged it over my head before I started my trek down the beach. I let the cooling sand slip between my toes, but I made sure to stay away from the water.

I found him about fifty yards away, lying in the sand, staring up at the stars. As I approached him, I expected him to acknowledge my presence, but he never even stirred. I sat down in the sand and laid my head on his stomach, our bodies forming a *T* in the sand. I stared up at the stars and started to wonder where it all went wrong. Our relationship was never complicated before I left. It was perfect. It was the kind of friendship everyone dreamed about. We truly made each other happy just by being there for one another. Things were unconditional.

As I thought more and more about our life before the move, I realized that we were never just friends. Maybe we had started out as just friends but things had definitely changed between us before I moved. We had become a couple. We were in love with each other long before I moved, and neither of us was willing to admit it, so we danced the dance and became everything to one another—everything but the one thing that both of us wanted and were too afraid to take, knowing that we may lose each other if we jumped.

I finally understood what Claire had been saying the day she called me. I finally understood why she blamed me for taking Brad away from her. I finally understood why she thought that he had broken up with her for me. She was right. I knew it then, but I denied it. Now I know that I was a fool. I had not truly stolen him from her. She never had him completely in the first place. I fell asleep with those as my last thoughts.

My flight was leaving in three hours. I was literally throwing clothes in my suitcases, and I was pretty sure that some my winter clothes had made it in with my bathing suit. I didn't really care at the moment. All I cared about was making it to the airport on time so I could get out of this place, so I could get back home to Ethan.

I had been driving myself crazy the last twelve hours. The only thing I could think about was how I tore apart Claire and Brad's relationship. Of course, I didn't do it on purpose. I didn't even know that I was doing it at the time. Okay, so the kissing before I left was not the brightest thing to do, but if I remember correctly, he started it. Wow! That was incredibly juvenile. This place really was making me crazy.

I zipped up my suitcase, hoping that I had everything I need, or at least most of it. I know that my tennis bag was waiting by the front door, and that was all that really matters. As I dragged my suitcase down the stairs, I could feel his presence in the house. I knew that he would be here to see me off; he told me that when we woke up this morning tangled up in each others arms. Remembering the warmth of his breath on my neck and the sound of his heart beating against my ear sent a shiver down my spine.

I rounded the corner and almost ran him over. I bumped into the back of him as I came to a stop, and I could see the tension in his body even before he turned to look at me. His eyes told the whole story. He knew that once I left, he would lose me. He would lose the chance of a relationship more than a friendship, which he so desperately wanted.

"Hey, you're here already."

"I wanted to make sure that you got packed. I see that you did. Want me to take that to the car for you?" He was rambling and speaking faster than normal. Nervousness was not something that easily consumed his body.

"Sure. Thanks." I didn't really know what else to say to him. I wasn't ready to say good-bye yet, and that was really all I had left to do.

He grabbed the handle of my suitcase and lifted it off the ground. I had been dragging it behind me, and he was carrying it like it weighed as much as a piece of paper. I followed him to the door and snatched my tennis bag before heading outside. I turned around and scanned the living room one last time. I wasn't so much looking for anything as I was memorizing what it looked like.

He had already put my bag in the trunk, and I could see that my sister was strapped in and ready to go. My dad was standing by the trunk, waiting for me to put my bag in, when he saw the look on my face and decided that it was best to get in the car as well. Bless him for letting me do this with a little bit of privacy.

I slowly made my way to the back of the car and tossed my tennis bag in, but I made no move to shut the trunk. Brad inched closer to me and pulled me into a hug. With the trunk shielding us from my dad and sisters view, he held me for what felt like forever but not long enough at the same time.

When he finally pulled away, he kissed the top of my head and started to walk away. I couldn't let things end like this. It didn't feel right. I had a similar feeling when I took him to the airport after he visited, but this was multiplied by ten, at least. It actually felt like we were saying our final good-byes to each other, but neither of us had actually spoken the words.

I put my hand over my heart and spoke with true conviction in my voice. My words stopped him in his tracks. "You live here. You will always live here."

He slowly turned, and when his eyes met mine, I could see the fires blazing. The ten steps he had taken away from me only took him five to get back before I knew what was happening, I was off the ground and his body was molded to mine. As he swung me around, the hug that he was giving me felt final. He was squeezing me so tight I wasn't sure I was able to breathe.

As he set me back down, he leaned in and kissed me softly on my lips. "You cannot use my words against me like that. It's not fair."

"Well, fair or not, I meant them. You will always have a place in my heart, a piece of my heart."

"I sure hope he takes care of you because if he slips, I will be there to catch you and I'll never let you go."

"I know." With that I kissed him just as softly as he had kissed me, and I got in the car. He was still standing on the sidewalk, staring at me as we drove away.

CHAPTER 18

The air smelled different. The woodsy smell of Michigan was long gone and had been replaced with the warm smells of the desert. It was also about twenty degrees warmer here, if not more. It was hard to tell how warm it was because it was so dry. It was so sticky and humid in Michigan compared to here. They say that it rains a lot at the end of July, beginning of August. I guess I'll find out here in about a month.

I probably should have planned better for the change in weather. I was only wearing jeans and a t-shirt, but it felt like too much, and I knew that I would be sweating the second we left the air-conditioned airport. Maybe I'd get lucky, and it won't be *that* hot outside today. With my luck, probably not.

That first step I took off the plane was the hardest. I was excited to be back, excited to see Ethan, and yet very nervous about seeing him at the same time. The things that had happened over the past few weeks had led to me think and rethink just about every decision I had made. The biggest decision was leaving Brad behind. The fact was that I kept telling myself that I was leaving him behind, but in actuality, he was still right here with me in my heart. He'd always be, and I don't think I would be able to change that. Ever. I could still smell him on my shirt from our hug hours ago. His scent was lingering, toying with my emotions. It was almost like he sprayed my shirt with whatever scent he wore before I put it on that morning. I knew it wasn't true, but his smell was intoxicating, and with every deep inhale I took, it was all I could smell. My head was filled with so many thoughts of him that I could almost feel his arms around me.

Rounding the corner to head past the security checkpoint and to the baggage claim, I could see his familiar face come into view. With one last deep breath, I tugged on my sister's hand and weaved through the mass of people that were headed in the same direction, only slower than I want to go. My tennis bag was slapping against my hip as I rounded the glass security wall and slammed my body into his.

He pulled me in as close as possible and held me tight. I could feel his warmth seeping into me through his clothes. I closed my eyes, let my hands roam, and took in all of the wonderful things that are pure Ethan. I loved the way he smells, the feel of his muscles as they move under my roaming fingertips, and finally, his nipple piercing. Once I found it, I gave it a little tug and felt him flex under my hands.

Pulling out of our embrace before things go beyond a little PDA, Ethan gave me a quick kiss to the lips, and we headed to baggage claim hand in hand. The unspoken hellos were given as he squeezed my hand and I squeezed back. I could feel my sister eyeing me from behind and wondered exactly what was going through her mind.

"Glad to be home, Amy?" Ethan asked sounding overly excited. The sound of his voice radiated through me. It had only been hours since I had spoken with him, but it felt like there was a filter on my phone compared to being next to him. I'm pretty sure I gave a little sigh at that moment.

"Yep. Can't wait to sleep in my own bed for a change. When's Mom going to be home?" Amy asked sounding annoyed.

"She's there right now." I said. This means that my sister would move a little faster. "She worked last night so she should be up by the time we get there, but she has to go back in tonight, so she needed to sleep. Ethan was nice enough to pick us up."

"Cool. I need to use the bathroom. Can you grab my bag for me?" Amy replied still sounding annoyed. Without waiting for an answer, she headed off in the direction I assumed the bathroom was in. I didn't care. This gave me a moment alone with my boyfriend, and I hadn't had one of those in weeks.

"So did you miss me?" I asked. It was supposed to be a rhetorical question, and I was hoping that the playful tone in my voice gave that away.

"Did you go somewhere?" Ethan asked, trying to sound confused. He was grinning from ear to ear when I looked up at him with my most offended expression. His eyes were sparkling against the horrible lighting, and as I started to speak, my mouth went dry. He has stolen my breath away with his beauty. "I missed you."

That time, his tone was light, and although I heard him perfectly, no one else heard him at all. Those words were just for me. The hint of desire in his voice was just for me. The story his eyes were telling was just for me. No one else existed in that moment except for me and Ethan.

I reached up and put a hand on either of his cheeks. I caught a glimpse of my ring, and with it so close to his eyes, I could see no difference in the color of the two. "I missed you too."

That was all I was able to say before I cover his lips with mine. The kiss might have looked innocent, but it felt incredibly different. It was passionate and intense, and when we finally pulled apart, you could see the lust in our eyes. It was everything we had kept bottled up for the past three weeks. I felt like I was going to burst. It was good to be home.

The next few weeks went by quickly. I knew that time was going to fly by because more than anything, I wanted it to go slow. Ethan was leaving for college at the end of August, and I wanted to savor every moment with him.

He had made his decision but was not sharing with me. It bothered me a little at first, but I figured he would tell me when he was ready. Plus, the last thing I wanted was to fight with him when we only had a limited amount of time to spend together. If I knew how far away he would be in a couple of month, it would consume all my thoughts, and I would probably pout the entire summer. I wanted to enjoy the next few weeks, not dread them ending.

Toward the end of July, as we were playing on the courts at the high school, I noticed that someone was watching us. The man stood off in the distance for a while, but as he came closer, I got butterflies in my stomach and started to feel like I was going to vomit. I knew who he was. I had seen him around since the start of my tennis season. He had come to watch a few of the home matches, and I had always wondered who he was keeping his eye on.

I was so distracted at that very moment that I missed the ball and sliced the air with my racket. The look on my face must have told Ethan the whole story because he turned to see that the man was now standing just outside the fencing of the courts. He was definitely watching us.

As Ethan turned back around, a small smile started to spread across his lips. "You know that I'm spoken for, so he must be here to see you. That was a hell of a way to impress a scout." He was referring to my complete miss moments earlier. I smiled at his comment as I felt the pink flush my cheeks.

I walked over to the gate and let myself out. Ethan was right behind me as I approached the man with as much confidence as I could muster at the moment. As he turned toward me, I could see the schools emblem stitched over the breast pocket of his crisp white polo shirt.

"Rebecca Blake," I said with my hand held out to him. He shook it and nodded his head in acknowledgement.

"I know who you are, Miss Blake. I watched you destroy a young lady the first match you played here. I was impressed then, and I'm impressed now." He was smiling at me. He really came here to watch me? That's *unfreakingbelievable*! "I'm Scott Jones. I'm the assistant coach for the men's and women's tennis teams at the U."

"It's nice to meet you. Mr. Jones, this is my boyfriend, Ethan Green." I motioned to where Ethan stood behind me.

"Nice to see you again, Mr. Green."

Again? Had Ethan been looking at the U as a possibility? Had they offered him a scholarship? I turned to Ethan to ask him all these things when I was cut off.

"Well, Miss Blake, the reason I'm here is because we have a program that I thought you might be interested in that starts here in a couple of weeks. We are starting a small women's tennis competition within the state of Arizona for high-school senior tennis players. Only high-school senior girls with potential to play in college are being invited to join."

"I don't understand. I would be playing for the university?"

"Yes and no. You would not be a part of the U's team, but you would be representing the U in a way. The program is designed to bring together all the top-performing senior tennis players in the state for scouting purposes. All the scouts would be able to watch you girls play each other twice a month, and you would have the opportunity to showcase your talent with the possibility to snag an available scholarship."

"Wow! It sounds like a great opportunity. What do I need to do?"

"Well, I need your parents to sign these." He pulled a stack of papers out of his bag. The stack was about as thick as a DVD. Obviously, I would be reading this tonight. "Then if they agree to everything, you would need to enroll in one class at the U. You will get dual credit for this class with the high school and the U, and because it will be classified as dual enrollment, it won't cost you a thing."

I took the stack of papers and stared at them. I could feel Ethan behind me; he had moved a little closer. He reached around me and took the stack of papers. I could hear him flipping through them, probably skimming the "fine print."

"When do you need an answer?" I asked.

"As soon as you make a decision would be great. Each team only has seven spots. We showcase three singles players and two doubles teams. I have filled five spots so far. I would like for you to play one singles for us and see what possibilities are out there for you."

One singles? Did he really just ask me to play one singles for the U? I felt my heart beginning to race, my legs starting to tremble, and before I even realized that they were going to give out, Ethan's arms were around my waist, holding me up.

"She'll get back with you tomorrow." Ethan stated firmly from behind me.

I was going to say the same thing, but the words were not coming out. Thank God Ethan was there to catch me.

I watched Mr. Jones nod his head in understanding and then walk toward the parking lot. As soon as he was out of sight, Ethan turned me toward him, I stood on my tiptoes and hugged him tightly. I couldn't believe what just happened. Did I just get offered to represent one of the best tennis programs in the state? Holy crap!

"You are going to be amazing. This is such a great opportunity." Ethan praised.

"It's..." I stuttered but could not find my voice. I couldn't think of words to describe how I felt right now. My body was trembling still, and I felt like I might faint. I wanted to scream or cry or something. I was completely overwhelmed.

"Let's pack up and go talk to your mom. If you want to do this, you are going to need to read these papers. There's a lot of information here, and you need to know what you're really getting into before you sign on the dotted line."

"Right. Read...talk...sign." That was all I could manage at that moment.

He pulled me to his side, and we walked back inside the courts. With his arm wrapped protectively around me, I felt safe. I felt like I could do almost anything at that moment, even play for the U. The only thing I was concentrating on though was standing upright.

Coming back from an injury was hard. Staying strong after an injury was even harder. All my insecurities about my game were centered around getting hurt again. If I hurt my shoulder, I could be done with the game forever. Did I want to risk that by playing this fall? If I got hurt, would I be able to recover in time to play for the high school in the spring? Would I be able to recover at all?

We packed up and headed back to my house in silence. There really wasn't much I could say that was going to change how scared I was about getting hurt again. I needed to stay healthy, I needed to stay strong, and I needed to make sure that, above everything else, I didn't push myself beyond what my body was capable of. At least not until I know that I am completely healed. I was very lucky to make it through the spring season.

My mom thought that it was a fantastic opportunity. We go through the contract line by line after dinner, with Ethan there to help interpret some of the jargon for us. He seemed to know a little more about the program than he let on in the beginning. By the end of the night, my mom had agreed to let me do this if I wanted to. I agreed to at least let myself try. It was the only way that I could prove to myself that I might still be good enough to get a scholarship. It was the only way that I would be able to prove to myself that I was good enough to compete on a higher level.

I signed the documents the next morning, and so did my mom. Ethan agreed to drive me to the U to bring them to Mr. Jones. As I handed them over, fear swept through my body. I knew that I was making the right decision, but I couldn't help but admit to myself that I was scared.

The only thing left to do was to enroll in at least one class to make it official. Ethan walked me over to the admissions office and gave me a small tour of the campus in the process. I decided to take a journalism class and a graphic-design class. If I was going to make the trek downtown to campus twice a week, I was going to make it worth my while.

After a pit stop at the high school to sort out my regular class schedule, we went to lunch to celebrate. I was not sure if there was really anything to celebrate yet, but at the moment, I really didn't care. Today had been a big day for me. I had enrolled in my first college class, and I was officially playing tennis for a major university, sort of.

"So are you excited?" Ethan asked.

"*Nervous* is how I would describe it. We start practice the week after next, and I have no idea what I'm doing. Thankfully you'll be able to be there the first week. When do you leave again?" I rambled.

"I have to move into the dorms the last Friday of the month."

"So basically, you'll get to see me practice the first four days, and then off you'll go. That sucks! I wanted to do something special for your last week here. Now I have practice all day."

"You'll be fine. We'll find time to hang out. It's not like your practice last from sun up to sun down. You're done by lunch every day, and I will make sure you get to bed early enough to get a solid eight hours of sleep. Promise."

"I'm not worried about being well rested. I'm worried about you leaving me. With all the time I've committed to this program, how am I going to be able to see you now?"

"We will make time. You'll see. We'll see each other so much that it'll feel like I'm suffocating you." He was teasing me, and when my eyes locked on his, I could see the promise he was making me. I could see something else in his eyes, something I've never seen there before. Love?

No. There's no way that this man loves me. He's never once said it, but I can feel it. I can feel how much he cares for me. Can't I? Are those the feelings he has for me, or are those the feelings I have for him?

"Well, I would hate to feel suffocated." My voice cracked as I forced the words out of my mouth. I was trying to lighten the mood, but since our eyes were still locked on each other's, it felt like I was suffocating at that very moment. I was drowning in every emotion that I felt. I was scared. I was worried. I was in love.

CHAPTER 19

*I*nseparable. It was the only word to describe how Ethan and I have been over the last two weeks. Since I signed my contract with the U, he and I had been prepping each other for our upcoming seasons. Every morning, we go out early and play. Every evening, after it starts to cool off, we would go for a run. It's the same routine every day, and just as my body was starting to adjust, it was time to start practice with the U's "Super Seniors" team. Thank you, Ethan, for that ridiculous nickname.

On the first few days of practice, Ethan drove me there. He didn't stay and watch, knowing that I would be even more nervous if he did. Instead, he went back to his house and packed while I practice. The thought made me sad and a little bit nauseated. I knew that he was leaving on Friday, but I had to keep my head on straight, or else the coach would take it off for me.

The other girls that were selected to play were good. I was the only one from my high school, which surprised me. I could see that some of the other girls already knew each other. I wondered if I was going to be able to make friends or if they were going to make this a competition between us. It really was a competition between us in a way.

I kept my focus on the ball. I was hitting with the two singles player, Kennedy, and practicing my backhand when I see Ethan outside the fence. I was comfortable in his presence, but Kennedy was obviously not and completely missed an easy shot. I knew that she was staring at him. I used to have the same look on my face the first few times I saw him. His raw beauty would stop you in your tracks.

"That's about it for today, ladies." The coach's voice sliced through the air, and I turned to see that he was standing just inside the court with a stack of papers in his hand. "I have your schedules for practice and tournaments. They may change a little, but this will give you the big picture. Most of your tournaments are set in stone, so if you have a conflict, I need to know in the next couple of days."

We all packed up our stuff, walked toward the coach, and, one by one, grabbed our schedules. The first thing I noticed was that the last tournament was on my birthday. *Ugh!* Who plays tennis in December? People without snow, I guess.

Scanning the area for Ethan, I was almost to the gate when I noticed that he was talking to my coach. When did he come onto the court? I turned around, dropped my bag, and headed back in their direction, but as I approached, they stopped talking. That's odd. What information was I not privy to these days?

"Hey, gorgeous. Ready to go get lunch?" Ethan asked a little too eagerly.

"Sure." You could hear the hesitation in my voice as I dragged the word out a little longer than necessary.

As if he hadn't heard the difference in my voice, he grabbed my hand, and we started to walk over to the gate to pick up my bag. "Where would you like to go today? There's this really good Indian place just off campus if you wanna try some place new."

"That sounds fine." I hesitated only a second before continuing. "What were you talking to coach Miles about?"

"Nothing really. I've know him for a few years. I was just saying hi."

"Oh, okay." There I was, dragging out the syllables again, hoping he would continue. He did not, so I asked the question I knew he didn't want me to. "How do you know him?"

"He's been around for a while. He used to scout for the U, and I've talked to him a couple of times."

"Does that mean that he tried to get you to play here?"

"Yeah. We talked a while back."

"And…?" This time I was sure that I was getting the message across. Just to make sure, I stopped walking and looked him straight in the eye, giving him my best "Tell me more" look.

"I told you. I made my decision before you came home. Other than that, there's nothing else to talk about. A lot of places scouted me." Ethan stated firmly.

I guess that was the end of that conversation. He tugged lightly on my hand, and I fell in step with him. This was such a touchy topic for him that I let it go. He was planning on telling me on Friday before he left, right?

Our conversation over lunch was kept light. No talk of college, tennis, or anything that was going to make either of us think on a deeper level. I was relieved that we were able to keep from talking about tennis. We had done nothing but practice and play over the last few weeks, and a mental break from it was what I needed. We hadn't played each other since I started to practice with the U team, but we still kept to our nightly runs.

I couldn't help but allow my mind to drift back to the courts a little though. Playing with Ethan was special. He challenged me in ways that no coach or opponent ever would be able to. I remember the day the scout showed up. *Wait. He knew the scout. He knows my coach. What am I missing?* Did he visit the U while I was in Michigan? Should I ask? He obviously didn't want to talk about it, but I had to know.

I was about to ask him as we pulled up to his house. As he opened the garage, I noticed that his dad's car wasn't there. We were alone for the time being. His dad would be at work for another two hours or so. I couldn't think of anything better than cuddling up to Ethan and watching a movie right now. As he hustled me out of the car and into the house, I realized that he had other plans.

He pulled me across the threshold of his room and closed his door as I realized what his plans were. There were candles and rose petals scattered around his room and a red rose on his pillow. I know that different-colored roses mean different things, but I wasn't sure what red meant. I would have to look that up when I get home.

Before I realize what's going on, Ethan had lit every single candle and closed the curtains. The room was dark except for the light coming from the fifteen or so candles that were burning. I could feel him approach me, and when he wrapped his arms around my waist, I melted into him.

I felt the heat from his body as his hands reached for the hem of my shirt. I didn't hesitate, knowing what he wanted, and lifted my hands above my head, giving him permission. It took all of two second before it hit the floor, and Ethan's lips were on my neck. I turned in his arms and stripped him of his shirt as well, while he reached behind me and flicked the clasp of my bra open.

I had never felt so alive in my entire life, standing half naked in front of another person. I knew that I could say one word and this would be over, we wouldn't go any further, but I didn't want to. I wanted to be with Ethan. In that moment, I felt like I needed to be with him as much as I needed air to breathe.

I knew in my heart of hearts that that was the moment I had been waiting for and that Ethan was the person I had been waiting for. Every girl wants their first time to be special. Nothing was going to be able to compete with that moment for me and that's how I knew that it was special, that it was right. I would remember that moment for the rest of my life and never regret a single second.

I sat down on the edge of the bed and motioned him forward with my finger. He gave me the sexiest grin I had even seen cross his lips and complied with my small request. As he kissed his way up my body, starting at my navel, I started to feel my body unravel beneath him. By the time he reached my neck, I was breathing heavily, and so was he.

As our eyes met, he silently asked me if I really wanted this. I nodded my head once. As I waited for him to touch me again, my body calmed, but I could feel him watching me, staring at my naked body. I found his eyes as they swept over my body and came to meet mine. I nodded once more, letting him know that I hadn't changed my mind. He leaned over and pressed a light kiss to my lips. I knew what's coming next, and I was ready for it.

As I woke up, I wondered if it was all a dream. The fact that I could feel Ethan's naked body pressed up against me made it all too real. My body was sore, and I had to use the bathroom. I quietly pulled away from him and searched the floor for my underwear. After finding them and tugging on Ethan's t-shirt, I slipped out of his room. Of course, his mother would begin remodeling his bathroom before he left for college. How inconvenient for me at this very moment.

Down the hall, I could see a light under his parents' door. I hoped they weren't home. I couldn't hear any sounds coming from their room. I headed into the bathroom and cleaned myself up. Looking in the mirror, I barely recognized my own face. I had a wicked grin from ear to ear, and it didn't even begin to describe how I felt at that moment. I quickly ran my fingers through my hair and pulled it back up into a ponytail.

I slipped back into Ethan's room and checked the time. It was only a little after five. My mom wasn't expecting us for dinner until six, so we had plenty of time to get around. I sat on the edge of the bed and stared at the man before me. He looked peaceful in his sleep. His naked torso was begging to be touched, and just as I was about to reach for him, his eyes opened.

"Hey, gorgeous. You look beautiful." Ethan said sleepily.

His words made my heart flutter, and I couldn't keep a smile from spreading across my face.

"You look pretty good yourself. We have to get dressed. My mom is expecting us for dinner in less than an hour." I moved to stand up when I felt his arms wrap around my waist and pulled me down to him.

Instead of resisting him, I snuggled up against him and rested my head on his chest. I could spend the rest of the day like this. I wanted to spend the rest of the day like this. If we didn't have to be at my house for dinner, I would spend the rest of the day like this.

"Are you okay?" Ethan asked concerned.

He was asking because he cared. He did everything possible to make sure that my first time was perfect, to make sure that I was comfortable. I nodded to let him know that I was. I stretched up and gave him a quick kiss on the lips, and he released me. He knew we had to get moving before we got caught. His parents usually get home by six, and if they catch us in here alone, they would have a major issue with it.

After we were dressed and ready to leave, he pulled me back down on the bed and started to kiss me again. Before I could stop myself, I was kissing him too. His hands were moving slowly under my shirt. I could feel my desires beginning to stir again, and then, as if the heavens knew that we needed to stop, we heard the garage door open.

We pulled apart and both stood quickly. I smoothed my top back down to cover my stomach, and we quickly exited his room. All the rose petals and candles were picked up, but there was still a moment when I thought that our actions would be obvious to everyone around us. If I could feel a change, could they?

We said a quick hello and good-bye to his mother before darting out to his car. We were officially running late now due to our last moments of weakness. We needed to hurry and get to my house before my mom started to wonder where we were.

Only five minutes late, my mom was setting the table when we walked in. I excused myself to go take a quick shower, knowing that the sweet smell of sweat and Ethan was all over my body. I was back in less than ten, and dinner was just being served.

CHAPTER 20

The rest of the night went by quickly. I knew that with only one more day before Ethan leaves, the hours would just fly, unlike this weekend. This first weekend apart from him was going to drag. My first college class was Monday morning, but I didn't start school until the following Tuesday. I planned on filling the long hours with clothes shopping, and I had to make a pit stop at the bookstore on campus.

I talked to my coach about missing practice on Thursday, but he was less than enthusiastic. Ethan forced me to go anyway. He didn't want me to miss on account of him, and he knew that we would have the whole day to spend together after it was over. I appeased him and went, but my mood was a little sour.

I raced over to his house after practice ended to find that he wasn't home. I sat in his driveway for a few minutes before I sent him a text.

WHERE ARE U?

HAD AN ERRAND TO RUN. B THERE IN TEN.

I'M AT UR HOUSE.

K. BE THERE IN TWENTY THEN.

My mind started to wander as I waited for him to arrive. I started to think about what my life would be like without him here every day. I started to wonder if I would be able to focus on tennis, knowing that he won't be there to watch me play, to cheer for me like he had so many times in the past.

My phone alerted me to a new text, and I looked at the time. It had been almost a half hour, and he was not here yet. Where was he?

How's TENNIS GOING?

Brad. I've only spoken to him maybe twice a week since our "moment" in my dad's driveway. I know that he was giving me space. He was letting me figure it all out. Didn't he realize that I figured it out before I left? I came home to Ethan. Even thinking that made me feel bad, but I had to choose, and I did.

GOOD SO FAR. JUST GOT OUT OF PRACTICE. I START MY FIRST CLASS ON MONDAY. KIND OF NERVOUS.

He didn't text back right away. Ethan's car was pulling in the driveway when I heard my phone beep, but I ignored it. I only had a few hours left with him, and I wanted to enjoy them. I didn't want to spend them thinking about anyone else.

"Finally. Sorry it took me so long. You wouldn't believe the line I had to stand in. You better get your books soon." Ethan stated.

Books? Why was he at the bookstore?

I could see the emblem on the front of the bag as he pulled it out of the car. I was confused for only a moment before I realize what he had. He handed the bag over, and I practically ripped my gift from his hand from excitement.

It was perfect. He was perfect. I was now the proud owner of a new tennis bag with the U's emblem stitched across the outside. I could not believe he got this for me. How did he always know what I needed?

"Thank you so much." I wrapped my arms tightly around his neck, and he pulled me into a hug, lifting me off the ground a few inches. He kissed my forehead before setting me back down and taking my hand in his.

"I thought it would be nice if you showed up to your first tournament in style." *Yes, it would.*

"Plus, you've worked really hard to earn your place with the team. Hopefully, you'll be able to use it next year as well." Ethan said excitedly.

I knew what he was referring to. Play well now, and land a spot on the "real" team with a scholarship in tow. That would be ideal, but there were six other girls that were hoping for the same thing.

"You are awesome. I can't wait to put my rackets in here." I exclaimed.

"Well, I thought you may need a new one of those too." As he said this, he reached back into his car and pulled out a brand-new still-unstrung Prince.

My breath caught in my throat, causing me to cough. It was the same kind that I was currently using, only new and without the battle scars. "It's beautiful." I whispered. I was holding the most beautiful gift anyone had ever given me. It wasn't the gift itself; it was the thought behind it. It was the person who gave it to me. I was truly touched.

"Well, it still needs to be strung, but I made you an appointment to do that tomorrow. The pro shop across from campus will take care of it for you."

"Thank you. You are too good to me."

"Yeah, well, I couldn't leave you with just one good racket if you plan on kicking serious ass this fall, could I?"

I had planned on buying another racket this weekend when I went shopping, but I hadn't shared that with him. I had been completely focused on savoring every moment with him, and not too many of those moments included talking.

I put my gifts in my car, and we went inside. Not knowing what he had planned for the rest of the day was turning my stomach in knots. I knew what I had planned for tonight, and his gift was waiting for him in my room, hidden under my bed. We would have to head over there eventually.

Ethan popped in a movie and headed into the kitchen to make us some lunch. He returned with two sandwiches and two bottles of water just as it started. We ate in silence, and when we were both done, we put our plates on the table and lay down next to each other on the couch.

Ethan was making small circles on my hip, barely touching my skin with the tip of his index finger, when I finally broke the silence. "Is this really what you want to do all day? Lie around and watch movies?"

"No. What I really want to do is take you to bed, but I figure I should at least wait until dark." Ethan said with a hint of mischief in his voice.

I chuckled at his blatant honesty, but I was also a little turned on. I wanted nothing more than to do the same, but he would have to wait and so would I. I wanted our last night together to be perfect.

"Well, at least your gentleman enough to wait until dark." I ground my behind into him as I said this, knowing that he'd react as anything but a gentleman if I tried hard enough.

"Keep doing that, and we won't even make it to my room." His voice was not begging me to stop but pleading with me to continue. "Should we pause the movie?"

I stopped grinding on him, and I heard a small moan escape his lips. I had to close my eyes and take a deep breath to calm myself before I spoke. "No. Let's head over to my house, though. My mom wants to say good-bye to you, and then I was thinking that you could stay with me tonight?"

It wasn't meant as a question, but it came out that way. Would he want to stay with me tonight? I was sure that he would, but I had a feeling that it would be harder in the morning to say good-bye to him.

I instantly flashed back to my last night in Michigan. Brad and I were cuddling on the couch in my living room, holding on for dear life, knowing what the morning would bring. Waking up the next morning was surreal, and saying good-bye was painful. Then I did it again over the summer. I woke up in his arms on the beach. I had to say good-bye all over again. The only difference was that last time I was trying to hold onto him as I was finally letting him go.

"I can't stay with you tonight. I have to pack up my car, and my parents wanted to have a late dinner together."

I could hear the reluctance in his voice. He wanted to stay, but he knew that he shouldn't.

"Do you want to head to your house now then?" He asked.

"Okay." I said, my disappointment apparent from just the single word I spoke. I was not interested in reliving the feeling of loss. I wanted to hold on to Ethan as long as possible. I wanted to wake up next to him in the morning and not have to let him go. I wanted a miracle to happen so that I don't have to relive history and deal with all the pain that I knew was in store for me.

We made it to my house just as my mom was waking up. She had to leave for work in a couple of hours, but she didn't rush Ethan out the door like I expected her to. She actually left before he did, which surprised me more than anything. Alone with a boy in the house was not usually okay with either of my parents, but apparently, they were learning to trust me.

Standing outside, saying good-bye to my boyfriend was the hardest thing that I had to do. I let him hold me, knowing that it would be the last time for a while that I got the chance to feel his arms around me. I felt the tears building up, so I pulled back before they could fall.

"See you soon, Becca."

As he whispered this in my ear, I could feel the tears running down my cheeks. So much for holding them back. The back of his hand came up to softly wipe them away, just to be replaced by more seconds later.

He kissed my forehead, moving his way south. My eyes were next, each of them already closed to try and fight the tears that wouldn't stop, followed by each cheek, my nose, and then finally my lips. He didn't linger or try to deepen the kiss, like I assumed he would, but the intensity was there without trying. The sobs started coming now, and he pulled me tightly to him, resting his chin on my head.

"We will see each other before you know it. Trust me."

Something in the way he said "Trust me" made me believe him unconditionally. *We would see each other soon. We would see each other soon.* I keep that chant going in my head as I watched him pull away and disappear in the distance.

I headed back inside and up to my room. My phone alerted me to a new text as soon as I walked through the door. I had two waiting for me. I read Brad's first, knowing that his won't make me cry.

GLAD THINGS R GOOD. TELL ETHAN I SAID GOOD LUCK AND CALL ME AFTER HE LEAVES IF YOU NEED TO TALK.

Well, I did need to talk, but I didn't really feel like I could form a coherent sentence right now. I'd call him later or tomorrow— whenever I start to feel like I can breathe again.

STOP CRYING AND REMEMBER WHAT I SAID. I WILL SEE YOU SOON. TRUST ME.

I was still crying when my sister came home. She knew why and left me to myself. Hours later, when I finally dragged myself out of bed, I heard the front door open and close again. It was almost midnight, and Amy was sleeping.

I grabbed the first large object I saw, an umbrella, and headed toward the living room. I rounded the corner and bumped into a firm chest, letting out a shriek. He covered my mouth to stop the scream, and immediately, I recognized those hands—Ethan's.

"What are you doing here?" I mumbled through his hand.

"I had to see you. I missed you."

I didn't give myself time to think or contemplate what I wanted. I knew exactly how I wanted to spend the next few hours with him before he leaves. I dropped the umbrella, grabbed his hand, and dragged him down the hall to my room, closing and locking the door behind us.

CHAPTER 21

THE PRESENT

When I woke up the morning after Ethan left, I felt completely empty. I stayed in bed for most of the day crying on and off. About the time my mom woke up, I was finally dragging myself into the kitchen to get some food.

"So I take it he left this morning?" My Mom said.

I nodded. I couldn't bring myself to speak for fear that I would start crying again, and I was not sure if I had any tears left in me. I was probably dehydrated at this point.

"Has he called yet?"

I shook my head.

"He will probably call tonight after he's settled."

I nodded once and excused myself.

I needed a shower, and I needed to go back to bed. My body was drained from lack of sleep and crying. My chest hurt inside and out. The muscles were numb at this point from all my sobbing. I don't remember it hurting this much last time. I don't remember feeling completely alone, completely empty and void of everything.

I headed to the bathroom and undressed slowly. I took my ring off and dropped it in the jewelry cleaner on the counter, running my fingers over the smooth surface of the emerald, remembering the resemblance to Ethan's eyes. I needed to call Brad. He was my rock, and I needed him right now. Maybe after a hot shower, I would feel up to it.

As I got out of the shower, the smells from the kitchen surrounded me. Crap! My mom was making enchiladas. Why would she do this to me? She couldn't possibly have any bad news, so I guess we were "celebrating" Ethan's departure.

I pushed back the tears, wrapped a towel around myself, and rushed into the kitchen. My mom was browning the meat, and my sister was busy shredding cheese. They were both singing and dancing to the stereo, smiling at each other. This did not look like bad news. This looked like a family dinner.

"Hey. What's going on in here?" I asked. I tried to sound casual, but I knew they could both hear the hesitance in my voice.

"Mom thought it would be nice to have dinner as a family tonight." Amy replied with a smile plastered to her face.

"Enchiladas?"

"Yes," my mom said proudly, "this was a big week for you, and come Monday you are starting college. I feel like we need to celebrate."

"But any other time we have these, we're not 'celebrating' anything good. Today's not really been the best day for me, and I would rather…"

I wanted to finish my sentence, but I was cut off with a stern look from my mother. "We are starting a new tradition. We are only eating enchiladas when we are celebrating, starting today," my mom stated in her no-nonsense kind of way.

That conversation was over. I knew the tone she was taking with me. I didn't want to upset her. She was trying to make a nice dinner to celebrate all my accomplishments. Bad timing on her part with Ethan leaving today, but maybe that was on purpose. She probably didn't want me to sulk all day. Well, the rest of the day anyway.

"All right. I have to run downtown to the pro shop and get my new racket strung. I shouldn't be gone long, maybe an hour. I should be back in time for dinner."

"You *will* be back in time for dinner," my mom said. The emphasis on *will* was hard to miss. She was not taking no for an answer. I nod in agreement before I headed to my room and got dressed.

Walking into the pro shop, a calm descended upon my body. I felt at home around anything related to tennis. I allowed my eyes to glance around and take in the store. Rackets lined one wall, shoes on the other. I saw at least a dozen racks of clothes that I knew I wouldn't be able to pass by without looking at. As I was taking in my surroundings, I could feel a pair of eyes on me. I spotted the service counter. With my racket frame in hand, I approached the pretty young girl.

"Can I help you?" She asked sounding irritated by my presence. Her tone was cold and uninviting, the opposite of the feeling this place gave me. A glance at her nametag told me her name was Jennifer.

"Yes. I have an appointment to get this strung today," I replied firmly. *I can be cold too.*

"Name."

"Becca Blake."

"Oh, Miss Blake, glad you could make it! Do you know how much tension you would like in your strings?"

Wow! Her tone had sure changed. It went from frosty bitch to "Let me see how well I can kiss your ass" in two seconds flat. What had Ethan paid these people?

Twenty minutes later, I wrapped up with Jennifer and arranged to pick up my racket on Monday after my second class. I had practice that night, so I should be able to spend a few hours breaking it in before then.

My cell rang just as I was pulling out of the parking lot of the pro shop. It was Brad. Wondering if I had enough strength to have the conversation I knew was coming, I answer the phone anyway.

"Hey." I said in the way of a greeting as soon as I picked up the phone. I tried to sound excited to talk to him, but I was pretty sure it didn't come across that way.

"Hey yourself. How are you doing this afternoon?" He asked hesitantly.

I let out a little sigh. That about covered how I was feeling right now. "Not really sure how to put it into words, I guess."

"Hang in there. It will get easier, I promise."

There was something in his voice that made me think he knew something I didn't. I wanted to ask, but my phone beeped, and I saw that my mom was calling on the other line.

"Hey, Mom's calling me. Can I call you back later tonight?"

"Why don't you call me Monday when you get home from practice? I sent you something today, and I want to be on the phone with you when you get it."

It had been like this for almost a month. We'd talk for five minutes, then "Call you tomorrow" or "Call you next week." I could feel the ground crumbling under our friendship, and there was nothing I could do to stop it. I really did want to talk to him, to know how he was doing. I still cared about him—I always will. I just couldn't do it right now.

"Sounds good. Talk to you then." I flipped over to my mom's call without waiting for him to reply. "What's up, Mom?"

"Are you on your way home yet?" Mom asked sounding irritated that I was not home already.

"I should be there in about ten minutes. Why?"

"Just wondering. Dinner should be done by then."

"Great." I tried to put a little enthusiasm in my voice, but I knew that I failed miserably. "See you in a minute then."

I needed to think about something else right now. Ethan, no. That would be depressing. I could call Brad back, but I still didn't want to talk about Ethan and he would want to. Wait. Did he say that he was sending me something? I'd have to ask him when I call him later. I was dreaming about what he could have possibly sent me as I pulled in the driveway and hustled through the front door. The smell of enchiladas brought me back to reality.

What was I really celebrating? I made another elite tennis team? I had done this before. I was starting college? Not really, it was only two classes. There wasn't much to celebrate, and I wasn't in the mood to celebrate.

I rounded the corner, fully intent on telling my mom how I felt, when I stopped in my tracks and my breath caught in my throat. What was he doing here?

"You're mom invited me over for dinner. I hope you don't mind." Ethan said, his voice dropping a few octaves as he looked me up and down like I was on the menu tonight.

Mind? Why would I mind?

"Um…no. How? Here? What?" I stuttered. I was making no sense. I didn't know what I wanted to ask, but I knew that I had a shit load of questions.

"How? That's easy. I drove. Here? It looks like I'm here. What? I'm not sure how to answer that one."

The grin on his face caused me to smile. He was teasing me. I rushed into his arms, and it felt like his body swallowed me whole. How was it possible that just over twelve hours ago I was wallowing, and now here he was standing in front of me?

"What are you doing here?" I finally got a full sentence out before his mouth captures mine in the most intense kiss we've ever shared. It was the most intense kiss I've ever had.

"Well, going to school at the U has its privileges. One of them is that I can see you whenever I want." He leaned forward and pressed a kiss to my neck before whispering in my ear. "I told you to trust me. I promised we would see each other soon, and I always keep my promises."

As I pulled away from his embrace I realized that he's wearing a U t-shirt. I was so caught up in showing him how I felt last night that I forgot to make him tell me what college he finally chose. He had been avoiding talking about it all week, and I hadn't pushed for an answer.

"You're going to the U? Why? What made you chose them?"

"Well, their team is great. All the teams were great, though. It came down to the one thing that I didn't want to live without." He was staring straight at me, and when our eyes met, I knew I was that one thing. "When you were at your dad's, you were the only thing I could think of. I went to all those camps, and you were the one thing that was missing. I didn't choose the U, Becca—I chose you."

I took a deep breath and took in every word he just said. *He chose me.* "What about your scholarship?" I closed my eyes, fearing that he gave up a scholarship for me.

"They were one of the three I had to choose from. It's a full ride."

I could feel his breath on my neck. I knew that he was going to kiss me before it happened, and I couldn't suppress the smile that was going to become permanently plastered on my face. I reached out and found his nipple ring and gave it a little tug, knowing that I could get him to moan. It was so soft that I was the only one that could hear it.

I needed to say something before I lost the nerve. I could feel the air rush from my chest as the words slipped past my tongue. "I love you."

"I love you too, gorgeous."

I wasn't sure if my mom and sister could hear, but at that moment, I really didn't care. The only thing I cared about was kissing him, so I did.

Our perfect moment was interrupted by the loud ringing coming from my pocket. I pulled back and rested my forehead on his, but I kept my eyes closed. I didn't need to look at him to know what he was feeling right now—I felt it too.

As soon as my phone stopped, I could hear my mom's cell start ringing in the other room. My body became immediately alert that something was wrong, and I was looking at my screen as I heard her answer.

Brad's mom? Oh my god. What's going on? I immediately grabbed for my ring, remembering that I took it off to shower this morning and never put it back on.

I looked up to see that my mom had tears in her eyes, and my legs gave out. My senses were overwhelmed, the smell of enchiladas filling the room as my sister walked in with them in her hand. The last thing I saw was Ethan's face before the world around me went black.

CHAPTER 22

The hours following that horrific phone call were a blur. I remember talking to Brad's mom. I remember packing a bag and getting on a plane. I don't remember my flight or my dad picking me up at the airport. By the time I was wrapped up in the arms of Brad's parents, I was exhausted physically and mentally. I hadn't slept in over thirty hours, and my body was beginning to shut down. I had cried for almost an hour straight before Ethan was finally able to calm me down. He held me in his arms on the floor of my dining room while my entire body shook.

I could hear someone calling my name. It sounded distant, but I made myself push through the fog and opened my eyes. I didn't see anyone, but I heard my name again. As I started to lift my head, I realize where I was. I could almost smell the hospital before it registered.

Again, I heard my name, but when I looked up, I was alone in the room, except Brad. He was laying there, perfectly still. They took him off life support, but we still needed him to wake up. With most of the tubes and wires gone, he almost looked like my best friend again, but not exactly. I kept talking to him, telling him to hold on, squeezing his hand to let him know that I was here, waiting for him to wake up. The doctors said that it was good to talk to him. I felt stupid sometimes when the nurses would walk in and I was in the middle of a one-sided conversation, but I was past the point of caring. I was barely holding it together at this point.

It had been four days. It had been the longest four days of my entire life. I was pretty sure that I smelled bad, and I knew for a fact that I look bad. The only thing I had managed to do in the last four days was brush my hair and teeth. I tried to give myself a washcloth bath in the restroom but found that it was harder than it sounded. I basically ended up with damp clothes that smelled of me. I settled for spraying myself with body spray every morning and night. It was Brad's favorite.

I got up and stretched, knowing that it had been at least three or four hours since I fell asleep next to him. The nurses and doctors had been great, letting me stay overnight and pretty much never making me leave his side. They rolled a cot into the room for me two days ago, but I have yet to use it. Once they took out the major "equipment" that saved his life those first few days, I had managed to get away with sleeping in the bed with him.

I heard my name once more, and it was so faint that I almost wondered if I was dreaming. I looked over at my best friend, and as I brushed my hand across his cheek, I could feel his quick intake of breath. I pulled my hand away and stood there shocked. That was the first time he had had any kind of reaction to anything we've tried. I reached forward again and ran my hand down the other side of his face. This time, the quick intake of my own breath matched his.

I needed to get a nurse. I rushed toward the door, but before I could even reach the handle, I heard my name again, and I turned around. That was perfectly clear. I was certain that I heard my name, and I was certain that I was not dreaming. I pinched my arm anyway to make sure I was awake. I was. I reached for the doorknob once more when I heard it.

"Stay."

Oh my god. His voice brought tears to my eyes, and I didn't know if I was ready to turn around yet. It had been the most excruciating four days of my life. Hearing his voice again brought back the reality of the situation, and when I closed my eyes, I saw the look on my mother's face again. I could feel the tears falling, but I kept my eyes closed.

When I turned around and finally opened them, my eyes met his and I practically fell apart on the spot. As I slowly made my way back to his bed, I never took my eyes off of him. He was alive, and that was the only thing I needed to know right now.

As I sat down on the side of his bed, he reached up and touched my cheek, wiping away a few fallen tears. I could feel how shaky his hand was, and it must have been hard for him to lift it. I was at a loss for words right now, so I held his hand to my cheek, trying to take some of the weight from him. I thought I had lost him, and now he was awake, smiling, and his voice was trying to soothe me.

Before I realized what's happening, I was curled up in his arms, and he was rubbing small circular patterns down my back. I hugged him as tightly as I thought I should, not very tight at all, and began to shake.

"We need to call the doctor. I promised I would if you woke up." I barely choke the words out above a whisper.

"Just give me one more minute with you. I need to know that you're really here, that I'm really here," Brad replied, pulling me tighter into his side.

"Trust me, I'm here, and you can probably smell that." I let out a small laugh to lighten the mood, and I tried to pull back just a little, but he held me firmly in place. As bad as his accident was, he was still stronger than me. "Do you want to tell me what the hell happened?"

"I don't really know what happened. I remember being in my car talking on the phone to you, and then my mind goes blank."

I pulled back just a little, and he was staring straight into my eyes.

I can see the wheels turning. I can see that he's trying hard to remember what happened. He breaks eye contact with me before continuing. "The next thing I remember was smelling peaches and apples, hearing your voice telling me to keep holding on and then calling your name but not being able to get to you. When I opened my eyes, and you were here, I thought I was dreaming."

"You are not dreaming—I'm here. I've been here since about eight hours after the accident, and I haven't left your side since they put you in this room."

"Tell me, Becca. Tell me what I don't remember, please."

I could hear the pleading in his voice. He wanted the details. I had them, but I wasn't sure I was ready to talk about it yet.

"Let's have the doctor check you out first, and then I will tell you. Deal?"

He gave me his "knowing" look. I was stalling, and he was right.

"I'm gonna grab the doctor and I'll be right back." I said breaking eye contact.

I slipped out of the bed, and when I reached the door, it opened for me. Stepping back to let them in, I inhaled sharply when his scent reached me. I pulled hard on the door and found Ethan standing on the other side. What was he doing here?

I jumped into his arms and wrapped my legs around his waist. I was so excited to see him in that moment that I almost forgot what I was doing. As he set me down on the ground and kissed my forehead, I was finally able to catch my breath.

"He's awake," I choked out. "He just woke up, and I…I have to get the doctor." When our eyes met, he knew what I was saying. He reached for my hand and intertwined our fingers, holding me tightly and pulling me toward the nurses' station. His presence calmed me in a way that no one else's could. It gave me strength, and from that strength, I knew that I was going to make it through this, Brad was going to make it through this, and everything was going to be all right.

We informed the nurses that he was awake, and a mixture of shock and excitement flooded their faces. We were asked to wait in the waiting room so that he could be checked out. I popped my head back in the room to let Brad know what was going on and told him I would be back as soon as the doctor said I could.

I made my way to the waiting room and called Brad's parents. They had been at the hospital longer than I had when I sent them home last night. I told them to get some sleep and promised to call if anything changed. The panic in his mom's voice when she answered told me just how scared she still was.

Two little words set her into a downward spiral like no other. When Mike, Brad father, grabbed the phone in a state of panic, I told him the same thing. "He's awake." I heard a lot of crying in the background, and I think I heard Brad's mom start to pray.

"When?" Mike was on the line again, more composed this time.

I took a deep breath and held it for a second before I started to speak. "He woke up about fifteen minutes ago. The doctors are with him right now." I paused because I knew that I had to tell him he was asking questions. "He wants to know what happened. The last thing he remembers is talking to me on the phone in his car. That was about ten minutes before the crash."

"He needs to talk to the police first. If he doesn't remember by the time he talks to them, then I will tell him what we know." Mike said. His voice was firm. He knew that this was how things had to be. He said that they would head right to the hospital and that Mike would call the detective on the way in.

I was sitting on Ethan's lap, cuddled up to his chest, when the doctor came to get me.

"Well, young lady, I'm not sure what kind of miracle you performed, but that boy is very lucky. We were not expecting him to wake up anytime soon, let alone be doing this well," the doctor said with a smile on his face.

I drew in a deep breath, being reminded of how severe the situation had been. If the doctor was impressed with his condition, then his body must be recovering better than most.

"You can go back and see him now if you like. Are his parents on their way?

"They should be here soon."

I turned to Ethan as the doctor walked away. I knew that he would want to come in with me, but I didn't think that I could handle that right now. As if reading my mind, he nodded his head in agreement and motioned with his eyes for me to go.

"I'll be back in a minute. I want to go get a real shower and lie on a real bed now that I know he's going to be fine." I said reassuringly.

"Okay. When his parents get here, why don't I take you to your dad's so you can clean up." Ethan suggested.

"That sounds perfect." I started to walk away when the reality of the situation hit me. I turned around and found his eyes watching me. When they finally met mine, they were filled with nothing but love. "Thank you. I don't know why you would want to be here for this, but thank you. It means a lot to me."

"I will always be here for you, Becca. You're my world."

"And you're mine. I'll be right back."

I walked into Brad's room to find him standing beside his bed holding on for dear life. I rushed over and took a hold of him at the hips. I knew that if he fell I would probably go down with him, but I didn't really know what else to do in that moment.

"What the hell are you doing out of bed?" I screamed, surprised to find him up and moving around.

"They took the catheter out, and I really need to go to the bathroom all of the sudden." Brad replied wincing in pain each time he moved. He looked sad because he knew he couldn't do it alone. "Will you help me to the bathroom?"

"Of course. Hold onto me, and we'll take it slow, okay?"

Five minutes later, I was sitting him down in the tiny little bathroom and letting myself out. I waited for him to call for me so that I could help him back up. When I faintly heard my name, I was reminded of an hour earlier when I was pulled from sleep by that very sound. I pushed back the tears as I opened the door and helped him up.

Once we made it back to the bed, I told him that his parents were on their way. I also told him that Ethan was in the waiting room. I expected his face to show some sort of discomfort, but it didn't. His smile widened, and he wrapped his hands around mine.

"I'm so happy for you. I knew that I was leaving you in good hands." Brad said.

His words brought tears to my eyes again, and I was surprised that I still had any left after how many I had shed the last few days.

"I am in good hands." I replied firmly. I was smiling now too as the tears made their way to my chin, and one dropped on our hands that were still locked together, holding on as if we feared something would tear us apart again. "We're going to head to my dad's so that I can change and shower, but then we'll be back."

"You sound like you need a nap too. Why don't you rest and eat something—I know you haven't—then come back if you want. I'm probably not going to be released for at least another couple of days depending on how I feel. The doctor wants to observe me."

"I can go without a nap. Do you want me to bring you something to eat?"

He stared at me with his "I know you better than that" look and waited for me to tell him the truth. I was not going to back down this time.

"The nurses told me that you've been here almost as long as I have and that you refused to leave my side. I want *you* to get something to eat and don't come back until you do." His voice was stern, but you could hear the concern as well. He sounded like his father had on the phone when we were talking about keeping the details of the accident from him. "If you think you can stay awake, fine, but I still think you should take a nap too."

"Fine." I was grumbling, but I was smiling at the same time. He was still trying to take care of me when he was the one who needed it right now.

"Go. My parents will be here soon, and you need to get out of here. I'll still be here when you get back. Promise."

We said our good-byes. I tried not to get emotional but failed miserably. I was sobbing like a baby by the time I reached Ethan in the waiting room. He stood and brought me to his chest in a big hug. We must have stood there for a few minutes because when I heard Mike's voice behind me, I realized that I was being held up by Ethan. Had I fallen asleep in his arms?

I introduced Ethan to Brad's parents, and we excused ourselves to leave. Before we could go, Brad's mom pulled me aside into a tight hug. I thought she was never going to let go until I heard her mumble her thanks in my ear and pulled back with tears in her eyes. I watched them walk toward Brad's room hand in hand and realized what a sense of relief they must feel right now. What I was feeling was nothing compared to what they must be feeling, knowing that they had not lost their child after all.

I helped Ethan navigate to my dad's house. Giving him directions was about the only thing keeping me awake at that point. We passed the road to Brad's, and I shed a tear. We passed the high school, and I shed another. When we drove right past my dad's house, I regained my composure and turned us around.

One hot shower later and I was ready for a nap. When I walked downstairs, I found my dad and Ethan in the kitchen cooking me breakfast, even though it was well past lunch time. They forced me to eat everything on my plate, and then Ethan carried me up to my room, dropped me on my bed, and tucked me in. He promised to wake me up in a few hours so that we could go back up to the hospital. I closed my eyes and was asleep before I heard the door close.

CHAPTER 23

I awoke with a start. Visions of Brad's totaled car running through my mind. The television had shown the aftermath of the accident. I couldn't seem to get rid of that visual. I was extremely grateful that he was alive and healing, but I was still scared that I was going to lose him.

I heard the door open, and Ethan walked in. It was dark outside, and I had slept longer than I had intended to. He had promised to wake me up. Why hadn't he?

"Are you okay?" Ethan asked. His voice was barely above a whisper as he sat down on the bed next to me.

"Yeah. Fine. Let me change, and we can go back up to the hospital," I said. I was talking faster than normal and I could still feel the rapids beat of my heart.

"Becca, it's two in the morning. Why don't you go back to sleep, and we'll head up there first thing tomorrow?"

"What?" I was wide awake now and screaming. "Why did you let me sleep that long? You promised to wake me up!"

"I tried, gorgeous." He was still whispering and being that it was 2:00 a.m. I realized why now. "I had to check for a pulse to make sure you were still alive. You wouldn't wake up, so we decided to let you sleep and face the consequences later." He was giving me the look that says he was facing those consequences right now.

I pulled back the covers and scooted over. The look he was giving me said that he was uncomfortable with this, but he crawled in anyway. I cuddled up to his chest and felt his hand rubbing up and down my back, staying as far away from the bottom hem of my shirt as possible. One touch of bare skin and we were both goners.

I woke up in Ethan's arms, and a small smile crept across my face. He was already awake and was staring deep into my eyes. I felt completely refreshed, and I was ready to go back to the hospital until Ethan leaned down and kissed me. Now all I wanted to do was rip his clothes off and stay in bed all day.

Before things could even begin to progress, I heard my dad clear his throat and looked up to see him standing in the doorway, watching us. I could feel the heat creeping up my cheeks and had to look away. Ethan quickly kissed my forehead and pulled the covers back to show my dad that we were both fully dressed.

After another amazing shower and a quick breakfast, Ethan and I headed back up to the hospital. I had spoken with my mom that morning to let her know he was awake. She was thrilled but wanted to know when she should book my ticket home. I hadn't even thought about it. I knew that I had missed my first few days of college classes and that I missed practice. I would start school on Tuesday, so I needed to head back before then. What about Ethan? He was missing class right now.

After hanging up with my mom, deciding that I would catch a flight home on Sunday, I turned to Ethan and asked him about school. The last thing I wanted to do was put his scholarship in jeopardy.

"I talked to all my professors Monday and explained the situation. I talked to yours too and our coaches. We are excused for this week. Everyone expects us to be back on Tuesday. My flight leaves Sunday morning. Your mom will probably try to get you on my flight. She knows which one it is."

I was taking in everything he was saying. He took care of it. Without being asked, he took care of everything for me. Then he flew out here to be with me. I didn't even know that I needed him until he was here, but he knew that I would need him.

"Thank you" just didn't seem like enough. "I love you so much. You know that, right?"

"Of course. I love you too, gorgeous."

We drove the rest of the way to the hospital in silence, aside from me giving him directions when he needed them. Walking out of the elevator, I could see that some of our friends had gathered in the waiting room to see Brad. I was not planning on waiting, though.

I gave them a smile and a wave and headed straight down the hall, past the nurses' station, and into his room. Emma and Ella were inside when we got there, and both their mouths dropped open when they saw Ethan standing beside me. I had talked about him to Ella, but I had never really explained how incredibly sexy he was. Gorgeous, yes, but I never really mentioned his sex appeal. That was something I wanted to keep to myself.

He was eye candy, and he knew it. The looks he got on a regular basis never seemed to shock him. I wasn't usually a possessive person, but when I felt the need to remind people he was with someone, I would always find a way to touch him. I didn't feel that need now as two of my best friends ogled him for a brief moment before collecting themselves.

I gave Brad a big hug and then introduced Ethan to Emma and Ella. They managed to shake his hand and say hello without drooling on him. I knew they were embarrassed when they wouldn't look at me and said good-bye before quickly exiting the room, leaving just me, Ethan, and Brad in awkward silence.

Ethan said hello and pulled Brad into a man hug, breaking the lingering silence between the three of us. I sat down on the bed next to him, and Ethan pulled a chair up beside me, resting his hand on my thigh. Who was being possessive now?

"I missed you last night." He turned his attention from me to Ethan and asked, "Couldn't wake her up, could you?"

They both laughed, and I smacked them each in the chest, Brad lighter than Ethan. "She was dead to the world. I even checked for a pulse." As soon as he stopped speaking, he knew the words he had chosen were wrong. "Sorry, man, I didn't mean it like that. I just—"

"Its fine," Brad interrupted. "She has always slept like the dead when she's overdoing it. I know you didn't mean anything by it."

"I really didn't, man." He paused for a second before he whispered, "I'm glad your okay."

"Me too. Who else is going to make sure you take care of her? If I didn't threaten to kick your ass every now and then, I would feel like I was failing as her best friend."

I knew his words were coming from his heart, but he was trying to play it off in a joking manner. He was trying to make sure that Ethan knew where he stood. He was also trying to make sure that I knew we were going to be okay. He must have felt the ground crumbling as well.

"Well, bestie, you need to get the heck out of here before I have to go back home. We leave on Sunday."

"That shouldn't be a problem. This morning the doctor said that I would probably be able to go home on orders of strict bed rest tomorrow afternoon." He paused for a minute, and I didn't think he was going to continue at first. The look in his eyes told me that he had more to say. "After you left last night, a detective came in and asked me about the accident. When I told him what I remembered, he said that my parents could fill me in on the rest of the story. They won't tell me anything yet. Will you?"

I didn't want to be the one to tell him. I squeezed Ethan's hand, and he knew what I needed. As he got up from his chair, he pulled our hands to his lips and kissed my knuckles once. He quietly left the room, and once the door shut, I hopped off the bed.

I couldn't turn to look at Brad. I knew most of the story, but not all of it. I would tell him what I knew, and maybe that would jog his memory a little. With my back still to him, I started telling him about his accident.

"You were leaving the post office. Apparently, you got off the phone with me and went inside to mail me something. I remember you saying something about it on the phone, but it didn't really register with me until after the accident. When you came back out and put your car in reverse, they think you dropped your phone. You went to reach for something as you pulled out of the parking lot and must have hit the gas instead of the brake when you reached for it. You got hit on the passenger side."

I had to pause because I could feel the tears streaming down my face. My breathing was shallow, and I knew that if I didn't sit down I would pass out. I slid on the bed next to Brad and cuddled up against his chest. He stroked my back while I continued.

"You were hit by a semi truck that was going probably fifty miles an hour. Your car was completely smashed in, and they had to use the Jaws of Life to get you out." *Okay, here comes the hard part. I can do this.* "When they finally got you out, they lost you."

I could hear his breath catch in his throat. His hand stopped moving along my back, and his other went to his chest. I knew he had to have marks from where they shocked him. He was gone for almost two minutes before they got him back according to the paramedics.

"They got you back just as the ambulance was pulling up to the hospital. They rushed you in for scans but found no internal bleeding. By the time I got here, you were in here, hooked up to all kinds of machine that were monitoring your body, keeping you alive at that point, according to the doctors. They put a tube in your throat to make sure you could breathe."

His hand moved from his chest to grasp his throat.

"They put you in a medically induced coma to make sure that your body had time to heal before you woke up. Once they were sure they hadn't missed anything, they took the tube out of your throat. You woke up two days later."

I was sobbing by the time I finished telling him what had happened. I could feel his chest rising and falling, and his heartbeat was erratic. I didn't know what he was thinking right now, but I knew that he was trying to figure it all out. I felt his tears on my forehead and pulled back to look at him. His eyes were bloodshot, like he had been crying for a while. The look on his face told me that he remembered everything, and that pained me in a way that I'd never be able to describe.

"I was reaching for my phone and felt my foot slip." Brad said, his voice shaking as he spoke. He was about to confirm my worst fears. He lived through it, but now that he remembered it, he would have to live through it again and again for the rest of his life. "I wanted to call you back. I could tell something was wrong and wanted to talk to you."

Oh my god. It was my fault! I tried to pull away from him, but he wouldn't let me. He was even stronger today than he had been yesterday. I should have expected his body to heal this fast. He always was trying to prove everyone else wrong, trying to defy the odds.

"It's not your fault, Becca. I didn't tell you that to hurt you. I told you that because I wanted you to know that the last thoughts I had before I was hit were of you. In that moment, I was happy."

"That does not make me feel better." I said firmly. I gave him a stern look, and when he grabbed my hand, I knew what he was going for. I was twirling my ring, and he reached over to stop me.

"I was hoping you would still wear it."

"Of course. My best friend in the entire world gave it to me. I will always wear it." I would, and I meant it. Ethan understood why I wore it, and that was all that mattered. I would never take that ring off for the rest of my life. The one time I did, something bad happened. I was not about to tell him that, though.

"Well, I'm glad to hear that."

It suddenly felt like the room was getting smaller and the uncomfortable silence that fell between us was deafening.

"I am getting a little tired. Mind if I take a nap for a while?" Brad asked.

"Sure." I hopped off the bed and gave him a quick kiss on the cheek. "I'll be back later this afternoon—with food."

That earned me a smile. I was sure hospital food was nasty.

"I wouldn't complain if you happen to bring me a burger and fries, but you may not want to share your plan with the nurses."

I went to leave, but my curiosity got the best of me. I couldn't wait until I got home to know what he had sent. I hadn't thought about it until now, but I knew it was something special. He was still looking at me when I turned around. Our eyes met, and it's like he read my mind.

"You wanna know what I sent, don't you?" He asked, a big smirk on his face.

"Smartass. Of course, I do. Are you going to make me call my mom and find out, or are you going to tell me?"

"I guess I could tell you but—"

"Just tell me!" I screamed.

The anticipation was killing me. He knew that I was impatient and was trying to drag this out.

"Okay, okay. Calm down. I just sent you your yearbook. Ella brought it over and asked me to send it to you. You guys won some award or something. You'll have to ask her."

So that was why Ella looked so awful when I walked in. She was probably blaming herself just like I was. I knew exactly how she felt. I wanted to make that feeling go away. I wanted to rewind time and find a way for him to avoid the accident. I wanted my guilt to go away. No chance that was going to be happening any time soon.

"Thanks. I can't wait to see it. Did you at least sign it before you sent it to me?" I asked, already knowing the answer to my own question.

"You know I did. Same place as always." He replied. His smirk told me that his message would be worth reading. He was the only guy I knew that took the time to write something meaningful, and it was always the perfect thing to write, especially since he wrote over the cheer team's page in Sharpie every year. He has always harbored hatred for that sport.

With a wink and a little wave, I left Brad to take his nap. I found Ethan in the waiting room with the rest of my friends. He was in the middle of talking to Ella when I walked up, and he barely stopped his conversation as he pulled me onto his lap and kissed me on the cheek. Ella, on the other hand, about fell out of her seat at the sight of it all.

I could feel the blush creeping up my neck and into my cheeks. I had talked about Ethan the entire time I was here over the summer, but it never occurred to me that my friends would meet him someday. These were not the conditions that I wanted him to meet them under, but he was here now. They had only seen crappy cell-phone pictures of him that barely did him any justice. I hadn't thought to bring pictures with me. Ella had a reason to ogle him, and I knew it.

As I glanced around the room at the friends I had known most of my life, the ones that I had been closest to nine months ago, I realized that time does change things. Sometimes it's the little things, sometimes it's the bigger things. Mostly it's just the distance that makes you find a way to bridge the gap in any relationship. My friends and I had each found a way to bridge the gap, and our relationships were still strong.

Brad and I were a shinning example of coming full circle. We had always wanted to be best friends, tried, and succeeded at times. Mostly, we were always fighting our feelings for each other behind something or someone. I used tennis and school as my barricade; he used girlfriends. Now we were both honest with each other, accepting of each other, and, after the scare of a lifetime, closer than we ever thought we could be. We were truly best friends, with no hidden intentions this time around.

Becca,

This year has been one of the hardest of my life. I thought I would lose you and in the end I did, but not how I thought. I am so happy for you. I am glad that you found your place in this world, that you are happy and that I can still be a part of your life. Hopefully an important part. Have a great senior year. It will suck without you here but I know that we will see each other again soon.

Love,
Brad

PS: Make sure you let me know if I need to kick Ethan's ass. I will always have your back.

EPILOGUE

ONE YEAR LATER

Holy crap! I'm gonna be late. I can't be late. I did not want to be that person who walks in late on the very first day. I could see it now: the door slamming behind me and echoing around the room, everyone turning to stare in my direction. I would probably top that off with tripping down the stairs or something from mortification. *I cannot be late.*

I grabbed all my bags and rushed outside. I hit the sign on the crosswalk and prayed that it would change soon. I had ten minutes to do a five-minute walk, but I knew that if the crosswalk didn't cooperate, I would have only about five.

It changed, and I rushed across the street without looking. It was just after morning rush hour, but I should have looked. Living so close to campus was a blessing and a curse. I could take advantage and sleep in, but then I'd feel like a maniac and rush around. If I get caught by traffic or if the light refuses to change, then I could be late. I needed to get myself motivated, get up a little earlier, and not feel so rushed in the mornings.

It's only been two weeks since we all moved in, but it has been the best two weeks of my life so far. I was shocked when my mom and dad agreed to let me live off campus in to a two-bedroom house with one other girl and two guys. I thought they would have freaked out, especially when they found out the sleeping arrangements. I truly believe that they love Ethan more than I do.

I rush inside my classroom, and when the door slams shut behind me, I close my eyes and secretly pray that it wasn't as loud as it sounded. When I opened them again, I notice that not a single person was looking at me, and when I heard the door open behind me, I headed to find my seat. I was smiling wide, thinking to myself. This was my first college class as an *actual* college student. Last year, I felt like an imposter. I kept mostly to myself for the first few weeks after Ethan and I came home, but then it was impossible to remain invisible.

Once the tennis season got in full swing, Ethan was in the spotlight. I was right there next to him most days, and that meant I was in the spotlight too. Toward the end of my season, now that everyone knew who I was, I created a spotlight around us as well. Not only was I playing at the top of my game and getting attention for that, but my relationship was also garnering attention, no matter if I wanted it to or not.

I received two offers for scholarships throughout the season, neither of which were at the U. I knew that if I had to, I would go to college without a scholarship. I planned on staying there and staying with Ethan. Unlike him, I was able to make that decision quickly and before it was necessary. I was rewarded for my patience when the coach offered me one of the two scholarships available at the end of the season. I said yes on the spot, and the rest is history. Well, sort of.

That history was about to begin at three o'clock this afternoon. I'd be having my first match, and although I was not playing at one singles today, that would be unheard of as a freshman—I was playing my arch rival. I knew that she had been preparing for me since I beat her that first time a year and a half ago. Although we played each other a few times during my run last fall with the U and again in the spring against her high school team, she had yet to beat me, and I was pretty sure she was getting annoyed with that little fact.

Not only had she never beaten me, but she made calculated mistakes. They were easy to spot, and I knew how to push her buttons enough to get her to make them. That might sound mean or conniving, but that's the game. If you want to win, you have to outplay your opponent and that means taking advantage of their weaknesses. I planned on taking advantage of all her weaknesses this afternoon and starting out my collegiate career with a win.

I turned my focus to the professor as she walked in. This class should be a breeze, Photography 210, but the smile that engulfed her face as she said what I was thinking told me otherwise. She looked like a kid with her hand in the cookie jar. She introduced herself and started explaining what the class was all about. A couple students that were handpicked from the front row were now passing out our syllabus.

I cringed slightly when I saw that this class was going to be harder than I thought. I looked around to gauge the reaction of the other students and realized that they were thinking the same thing I was. I skimmed the first page, then the second. On the third page was a list of office hours, phone numbers, and teacher assistants. When I reach the bottom of the page, I smiled and focused back on my professor. I would do just fine in this class. I had the advantage of a live-in tutor if I start to struggle.

Once the class was over, I made my way to the campus bookstore. I bought all my books last week, but I had a lunch date. He got a job the day he moved into the house, and now I felt like I was seeing him even less than before. That was not really possible, but I was starting to explore the more dramatic parts of my personality these days. I was told it was the influence of living with guys. Apparently, you need to make a big deal out of *everything* in order to get them to make a big deal out of *anything*. I had yet to really test this theory.

I walked in and looked around until I spotted him through the thick sea of students. His shift ended ten minutes ago, but he was still behind the counter ringing up books. I could tell he was ready to go just by the look on his face. As I began to approach, he looked up, and our eyes met. A slow, lazy smile started to creep across his face, and his eyes lit up.

"Joe, I was supposed to be done"—he paused to take a look at his watch before continuing to scream across the room at his boss—"ten minutes ago, and my lunch date is here to get me." He wiggled his eyes at me, and I rolled mine high so that I was sure he saw me.

A handful of eyes followed his gaze. There were a few who looked a moment too long, probably trying to place me outside the tennis courts. Those few people gave me a wave like we were old friends and not just passing acquaintances. I didn't care either way and waved back with a smile.

My smile disappeared when I felt Joe walk up behind me. He was creepy and weird but very nice. I hated it when he would touch me, but if he kept his distance, I could be comfortable. Today, that was not possible as he pushed his way through the crowd and bumped into me from behind. My body automatically shivered in response to him being so close to me, but I realized that he probably didn't do it on purpose.

"Brad's a bit cranky today. You better keep an eye on him," he said but never stopped walking, thankfully. I saw him take Brad's place behind one of the registers, and Brad disappeared into the back room. He emerged with his backpack in hand, and I motioned that I would meet him outside.

I was only about twenty seconds ahead of him, but getting out of the chaos was refreshing. It felt like a mosh pit in there. Too many bodies, not enough room, and the temperature was about 102° today, so the mingling of scents was becoming overpowering. I pushed past the last few people and felt immediate relief as I stepped out into the scorching heat of the city.

"Hey, right on time. How was your first class?" Brad asked excitedly.

As we took our first steps toward the cafeteria where we were meeting Ethan and Ella, I realized that Brad and I had not been alone together since he was in the hospital last year. Ella or Ethan were always with us, no matter what we were doing. I don't think it was on purpose or a safety measure for them; it just happened to be that way most of the time. I was excited to be able to spend time with my friend, my roommate.

When Brad told me that he applied to the U and was accepted, I about fainted on sight. We were in Cancun with a bunch of our friends, and Ethan was standing behind me to catch me. He was incredibly supportive of our friendship, especially after I almost lost Brad. I don't think he really understood what he meant to me until that moment in the hospital when Brad first woke up.

I was excited for him, and we were hugging each other when Ella walked up and told me the same thing. She and Brad had started dating shortly after he recovered. He had called me first to tell me. She called me as soon as I hung up with him and asked me for my permission. I thought it was funny at the time but gave her my blessing. I now realized that our love for each other must have been apparent to others before it was apparent to us. She didn't need my permission, but I was happy that he was dating someone that I thought would finally make him happy. My shock had finally worn off when I saw them at Christmas, but it still felt weird.

I gave her a big hug and congratulated her. When I realized that I would be going to college with two of my best friends in the world and the love of my life too, I started to cry, which prompted Ella to cry. Brad and Ethan stood by our sides, rubbing our backs. I started to think how great this was going to be and how wonderful they were when I looked up and realized that they were silently laughing at us. I composed myself and smacked them both on their very defined chests, and so did Ella.

My joy was compounded when Ethan suggested that we all get a house together, instead of living in the dorms. I was shocked that he would want to live with Brad, but after observing them on our vacation, I saw why. They were becoming friends. I was their common thread at first, but now they were finding things to talk about besides me (thank God). At the end of spring break, when we parted ways at the airport, I noticed them do the man-hug thing again, and this time, it looked comfortable to them. I was excited for high school to end, college to start, and the next chapter of my life to begin.

As we approached the cafeteria, I saw Ella and Ethan waiting for us on a bench outside. Ella ran up and jumped in Brad's arms, wrapping her legs around his waist and kissing him fiercely. It reminded me of how affectionate Ethan and I used to be. Now we saved all that extra affection for our moments alone. It was *so* much better that way.

I grabbed Ethan's hand as he approached, and he twirled me into his arms. With my back pressed against his chest, he kissed my neck. I had never been so happy I was running late and pulled my hair up that morning! He loved when he had full access to my neck, and truthfully, so did I. If I never wore my hair down again, I would die a happy woman. Plus, I knew that he liked it when I showed off the emerald earrings that he had given me for graduation.

They matched my ring perfectly. He knew that I would never take that ring off until I had something to wear in its place, not that I was rushing for a replacement. It was no longer a symbol of love between me and Brad, although we still very much cared for each other. It was a symbol of friendship. To me, it was a reminder of how I found the love of my life, how I found myself. It represented the fact that no matter what happens in life, the only thing that matters are the people that you choose to surround yourself with and how you choose to live. Had I not moved here, I would never be the person I have become right now, and I would be forever changed because of it.

When his lips started to move north, I thought I feel my knees go weak. We were standing in the middle of a courtyard, people were walking past us, like nothing was going on, and all I could think about was taking him home to our bedroom. Too bad I had two more classes to go to today, and so did he. Finally, he reached my ear, and instead of nibbling like he normally would, he whispered my three favorite words.

I turned in his arms and planted a kiss smack on his lips. It was full of passion, heat, and mostly love. I knew he could feel what I was trying to say. The words never seemed enough, but when I pulled away, I said them anyway, just to make sure he got the message. His smile was mischievous, his eyes were dark with passion, and I knew at that moment that the words were not necessary.

"I love you, Ethan Green, so much."

"I love you too, gorgeous."

I wrapped my arms around his neck, closing my eyes and hugging him tightly. I opened my eyes to see Brad staring straight at me, Ella still wrapped around him. The look he was giving me was enough to make my stomach twist into a knot. His eyes were burning with passion, and even though we were not wrapped around each other, you would have thought we were the only two people in the world at that moment. Crap!